More to LILY

k. jaspersen

To request permissions, contact the author at katrionajaspersen@gmail.com

The story, all names, characters, and incidents portrayed in this production are fictitious. No identification with actual persons (living or deceased), places, buildings, and products is intended or should be inferred.

ISBN: 979-8-9987950-2-2 (Paperback)

Self-published in **May 2025**

Edited by K. Jaspersen and Avery Jensen (Ink & Insights Services)
Cover Art created by K. Jaspersen (K. Jaspersen Designs)

katrionajaspersen.com

To all the men too afraid to make the first move for fear of rejection, there's someone out there just waiting to approach you.

Content Warning

This book contains explicit language, graphic sexual content, and themes of cheating—stemming from a misunderstanding—that may be distressing to some readers. It also briefly addresses substance addiction and alcoholism, which could be triggering for individuals with personal experiences related to these issues. Please read with caution and discretion.

Please Note

I worked closely with someone from Italy for several aspects of the book including, but not limited to, the culture, customs and translations. Please note that while every effort was made to maintain accuracy, some cultural nuances may not fully capture the depth or meaning. There is a glossary in the back of the book with the English text and these translations.

Enjoy!

Lily

Six Years Ago

A night to remember. Little did I know that it truly would be, if you can even call it that.

I can count on one hand the number of times Paige has gone to a party with me—each time, unwillingly, until tonight. For the first time in the three years since we started college, I don't have to drag her out of the house or sweet talk her into going. Nope, this time, it's her idea.

As we take a step forward in line, her words reverberate in my head. *Fuck you.*

Not two hours before, I heard the anger resonating in her voice, a tone I rarely hear from my best friend. As she cursed him out, I could see the desperation reflected in his eyes. He knew he fucked up, but it was too late.

From the moment I met her boyfriend—now ex—I didn't like the guy. You could say it was instinct or the fact that he was like every other guy I'd met in college so far—

acting so sure of himself, like nothing bad could ever happen to him. Maybe to everyone else it was confidence, but to me, it was arrogance. But clear as day, I could tell their relationship was a time bomb. I could have predicted it from how often they fought, and thankfully, this would be their last.

I look back at her standing in line behind me and her expression is exactly as I imagine—a mix of sadness and self-reflection.

Every break up is hard, but breaking up because of cheating is even harder. I know that firsthand—I have been cheated on in the past, so I can only imagine how hard she's taking it. Finding out the person you love has been betraying you and lying to you. I wouldn't wish it on anyone, yet it's happened to my best friend, of all people.

As soon as he was out the door, I ran to comfort her. Her nose slightly running, the skin beneath her eyebrows bright red, yet the blue in her weary eyes was still as radiant as ever. I tried to give her an encouraging smile, hoping to bring brightness back to her face—anything to make her happy again.

I already had plans to go to this party, but seeing her like that, I knew I couldn't leave and I insisted on staying to keep her company, offering to watch a rom-com together— an idea she quickly dismissed. *I don't blame her.*

You can't believe everything you see in a romantic comedy. The exaggerated emotions, the lavish makeup, and the picture-perfect happily ever afters are entertaining, but they don't reflect real life.

Yet, despite that, I've always hoped for an over-the-top romance. One like the movies where the man swoons over you, begging on his knees for a chance to get you back. Or honestly, I'd even settle for a man who simply brings me flowers and cooks me dinner, especially with my subpar cooking skills. Unfortunately, that can't always be the case and I doubt a movie would have helped her at that moment.

"We both know that you're the one that likes the rom-coms," she scoffs, rolling her eyes.

Finally I get a glimpse of the old Paige again—the one that wasn't just hurt and broken by some dumb college boyfriend. She's already been through enough pain for one person in a lifetime.

"Hey, I'm trying!" I joke as I nudge her shoulder.

"I'm not really in the mood for a rom-com tonight," she mumbles, looking over at the television then back at me. "But thanks."

I'd do anything to make her happy, but just my presence appears to be helping. After a minute passes and we remain silent on the couch, she wipes the remaining tears from her cheeks. She glances at me through drooped brows and appears to be weighing her options.

"Actually, can I go to the party with you?" she hesitantly asks. "I think it'll help take my mind off things."

"What!" I practically shout as my mouth drops open. "The Paige Palmer actually wants to go to a party?"

My eyes widen and I swallow, trying to believe the words I'm hearing.

"Along with being an asshole, did he give you intense brain damage too?" I jest and it's nearly impossible to hide the growing smile on my face.

I hear her quietly scoff to herself as she reaches behind her head to rub her neck.

"I mean, it's better than sitting around and dwelling in my own sadness," she chuckles and I can tell she's trying to cheer herself up. "I definitely would have just cuddled myself on the couch all night."

I quickly stand up from the couch, pulling her up with me.

"Well then, no more couch time for you!" I insist. "We need to get you ready before you change your mind!"

Before we knew it, it was ten o'clock and we arrived at Another Night, 12 blocks from our upperclassmen dorms. Some people may think that is a long way, but if you grew up in the city, it feels like nothing.

While some parties tend to be on-campus and are pretty regulated, the fun ones are off-campus. I've been to my fair share of them and you never know what to expect.

Last year, I went to a party that was inside someone's massive apartment, but with 100 people dancing and mingling around me, it felt like a sauna. There was also the lack of alcohol, you'd get maybe one drink and you'd be lucky if it was cold. And, in less than an hour of being there, the party ended, which I could have predicted. The cops showed up due to a noise complaint and from what I heard, the guys that owned the place were evicted soon afterwards. Unfortunately, that's pretty typical for house parties, so I chose to stay clear of those moving forward.

While there's also plenty of rooftop parties or bars, for those who just turned 21—such as Paige and I—the club scene is the place to be. Groups of students will rent out entertainment or club venues, which offer endless hours of dancing and as a bonus—no room temperature beer.

We take another step forward and I can tell from the music coming out of the entrance that the club is most likely already packed.

I adjust my dress, which is almost too short for comfort but I chose to wear anyway, then look back up at Paige. Seeing her in something sheer, I'm reminded of how nice the weather is. Just last month, I was dreading standing outside freezing my ass off. Yet, surprisingly, it was tolerable out tonight and I'm thankful I didn't need a jacket. Not like I'll need one anyways once I'm indoors. I'll be warmed up immediately by the hundreds of bodies surrounding me.

"I know you have a knack for getting what you want, but I really dislike parties," Paige says over the sounds of the busy road.

"Maybe it's because you've only been to campus parties," I chuckle. "Those are boring anyways."

"Boring? I'd say overwhelming," she looks at me wide-eyed as she crosses her arms.

"Overwhelming?"

"Yeah, there was always too much going on around me."

I laugh as I imagine music playing in a room full of people, but they're all just sitting around and enjoying it. I roll my eyes and say, "That's because you were watching it all from the couch instead of getting up and dancing with me.

Under her breath, she jokes, "I prefer the couch."

"Well, lucky for me, there's no couches here!"

The line moves and I quickly pull us forward, still wary that she'll change her mind.

"I can definitely say this will be a new experience," Paige says, looking up at the building, then back to me.

"It's been a while since you've been to a party with me," I remind her, chuckling. "It's a good thing I've got a party replacement though!"

"Party replacement?"

"You didn't think I was going alone all this time, did you?"

Before she responds, a ping from my phone redirects my attention. I pull my clutch out from under my arm and grab my phone out, just as we take another step forward in line.

"Speak of the devil," I joke, noticing a text from Miles that says he's inside near the stairway.

Before I can reply, a light shines down from above me. As I look up at the light source, I'm met with the eyes of a large man, presumably the bouncer. He's tall, in his late-twenties with brown, mid-length swept back hair and dark eyes and he's wearing a plain gray t-shirt and blue jeans. Not much for club attire, but I ignore it. He's definitely handsome and my type, but by the look on his face, he's not looking to make small talk with me anytime soon. *What a shame.*

"ID's please."

He holds his hand out flat in front of him as it hovers over my phone. I lock my phone screen and immediately put it back into my clutch, before breaking eye contact with him to grab my ID. When I hand it to him, he pulls it close to his face, shines his flashlight directly on it while blinding me in the process. Behind the beam of light, I can see his eyes shoot back and forth between me and my ID.

Without saying a word, he gives a deep chuckle before raising an eyebrow in my direction.

"Yes?" I ask, knowing he's no doubt questioning whether this is a fake or if I'm actually of age.

"Nothing," he lies.

I roll my eyes at him as he hands my ID back to me before turning to Paige and giving her the same treatment.

"Enjoy," he says, stepping aside.

We walk past him into the club and the music immediately drowns out the bustling sounds of the street behind us. It's pitch black down the short walkway, but within a few moments, the room opens up and blue lights flash around us. The club is large, with a sunken down area in the middle of the room surrounded by several stairways that can't be more than ten steps each. On the raised sides of the room, there are rows of U-shaped booths with people drinking and mingling, and in the middle, it's packed with people dancing closely.

"Well, I certainly didn't expect this!" Paige shouts, trying to speak over the loud music.

I lean in closely to her and reply, "I told you! Much less boring than a campus party!"

As we walk further in, we reach a railing looking out over the entire club. I scan the room, searching the crowd and it's almost immediately that I see Miles standing near the closest stairway. As our eyes meet from across the room, he waves for me to come over.

"Come on!" I smile, pulling Paige along. "I want you to meet someone."

Paige follows me as I lead her around the railing and down the first stairway to Miles.

Ever since elementary school, people always pointed out how similar Paige and I look. 'Practically sisters' they'd say, but what they didn't know was that our birthdays were also in the same month. So, as soon as Paige and I turned 21, I hoped that this was the year she would finally start joining me at parties and I hoped that meant venturing into the club scene with me too. However, in true Paige fashion, she chose a date with the couch at home instead.

Last year when my choices were limited after the apartment party, I decided nothing was going to stop me from having fun. I was invited to a prestigious 18-years-and-up club early in the year, and I just had to go—even if it meant I had to go alone. As I walked into that party, I saw a group of students I recognized sitting in a booth. Prior to that, I had only exchanged a few words with them during class, but seeing as I am always the one to make new friends, I walked over.

There was only one person in that group I didn't recognize, and that turned out to be Miles. He immediately welcomed me to join their group and when everyone else slowly disappeared throughout the night, he stayed back. Maybe it was because he saw me as desperate or just thought I needed a friend, but from that point on, our friendship grew. When there was a club party happening, he would invite me to join and would stay with me the entire night until I finally danced myself out.

We had been going together for a couple of months and I enjoyed his company. He was fun, always had something to joke about and was always up to be my party replacement. I tried to get to know him better, but he always asked me more questions about myself and insisted that he was boring. I knew he went to the same college as us, he was studying for some business-type degree and by his assortment of suits, I assumed he had some sort of money. I didn't feel the need to press him for more information he didn't want to share.

For him, I think he used clubs to get away from everything, but I just found it nice having someone I could always rely on to be there with me.

Paige and I finally reach Miles on the stairway and he pulls me in for a hug before whispering, "Glad you could make it tonight."

As I pull back, I laugh, "When have I ever not been able to make it?"

"Very true!" he chuckles with a nod.

As always, Miles is dressed to the nines, wearing a full, three-piece black suit, while all the other men around us are wearing slacks with a button down. His dirty blonde hair is stylishly pushed back and he's already holding his signature bourbon drink—a name I can never remember.

Miles looks over at Paige standing next to me, raises an eyebrow, then looks back at me.

"Well Alcord, you must finally be sick of me, as I see you brought someone else this time."

I laugh, before pulling Paige next to me and wrapping my arm around her.

"This is Paige," I pause, waiting for him to realize who I've brought.

I look at her out of the corner of my eyes and then back at him.

"You know, the one that I've been trying to convince to come to more—"

Before I can finish, Miles chimes in and shouts, "Of course! That Paige!"

"The one and only!" I cheer, smiling widely. "And you may be shocked, but she actually chose to come this time." Miles' eyes widen and I add, "Willingly."

Miles leans over and hugs Paige, who appears to stiffen her body as she's hugged by the stranger. As he pulls back, the look on her face makes me realize my mistake.

I shake my head and yell, "Sorry! Totally forgot to introduce you!"

Stepping back, I rest my hand on her shoulder and with my other hand, gesture to him.

"This is Miles, your party replacement."

Paige laughs and I can tell that just being away from our dorm is helping her to keep her mind off everything.

"It's nice to meet you Miles," she says with a smile and I can see her body has now relaxed knowing he's not just some random man at the club.

"It's so nice to finally meet you! I've heard so much about you!"

"Hopefully good things?" she loudly questions, like I could ever say a mean thing about her.

"Only good," Miles reassures her with a wink and I see her immediately blush—something I haven't seen in a long time.

Miles tilts his head at Paige as a smile forms in the corner of his mouth and he turns back toward me.

"Damn, if I had known your friend was so beautiful —" He glances at Paige again out of the corner of his eye before continuing. "—I would have helped you convince her to join us a long time ago."

I chuckle and turn to Paige who is looking at Miles wide-eyed as she quickly tries to hide her flushed cheeks with her hands.

The first night I met Miles, I knew immediately that he had just as much confidence as I did. While I could easily dance in the middle of the room without a care in the world, Miles was always a smooth talker when it came to women. Maybe there was a silent mutual agreement between us, but while we were both single, we never flirted with one another or acted more than just friends. I recently found out he had a brother, so I like to think that maybe to him, I was like the little sister he never had, which could explain why he calls me by my last name. Apart from his brother being older than him by a few years, that was all I knew about the guy.

"Come on! I have a booth for us!" Miles gestures to the raised area of the club and we follow him as he leads us to an empty booth.

Paige slides into the U-shaped seat first, before I slide in next to her while Miles remains standing at the end of the table.

"I'm going to grab you two drinks!" Miles shouts before turning around and heading toward the bar.

I turn to smile at Paige and lean closer, trying to avoid speaking loudly over the music, knowing my voice will likely already be raspy tomorrow.

"So—" I begin, raising my eyebrows quickly as I try to hide my excitement. "I guess it's a good thing you came because it seems like Miles already has you smiling!"

Paige scoffs, then says, "I mean he's cute, but I'm not ready yet."

"I wasn't insinuating that. I just mean it makes me happy to see you smiling."

"Well, this is taking my mind off things so thank you," Paige says, conjuring up a smile.

"Of course! I knew you'd have a fun time here!"

I lean over and give Paige a hug, then I hear a loud cough from behind me through the music. I pull back to see Miles raising his eyebrows as he stands at the end of the table.

"Am I interrupting something?" Miles jokingly shouts, before setting our drinks down on the table.

"Woah, that was fast," Paige says beneath her breath.

He unbuttons his jacket and places his phone face down on the table before scooting into the booth on the opposite side of Paige and I.

"No, just happy that she is here!" I beam.

Looking down, sitting on the table are two martini glasses, both with a reddish hue liquid and a dark colored orange slice on the edge.

"You did get these fast!" I nod my head slowly with approval.

Miles grabs one of the glasses in front of me and slides it carefully across the table over to Paige.

Leaning closer to her, he asks, "So Paige, how are you liking your first club party so far?"

"It's definitely not what I expected," she replies, looking around the room.

I grab one of the glasses and bring it to my lips. The flavor is bold and I'm delighted at the sour and sweet combination, as I'm always a sucker for fruity drinks.

Miles turns to me with a raised brow as he tilts his head, eagerly waiting to see if I like the drink. I quickly nod back with a smile.

I had no doubt Miles would have excellent taste in drinks; he always has. I've never understood how someone in college could possibly know every mixture of drink out there, but he somehow does. And I didn't mind because it meant I was always the eager taste tester for all the new drink varieties he found.

"Did you expect to meet me?" he asks Paige, raising a brow.

When I place my glass back on the table, I see her blushing once again, but a light shining around the edges of Miles' phone distracts me. He notices too and immediately locks his phone without even checking the screen, the light vanishes and he turns his attention back to Paige.

"Well, tonight was the first time I was told I had a party replacement," Paige chuckles.

Miles directs his attention toward me and leans his head to the side with a scowl.

"So, that's what you call me, huh?" he laughs with an approving nod. "Well, I'll take it! Alcord—you should be telling all your friends about me!"

"I'll remember that for next time!" I hold my drink up in the air. "Also, this is delicious by the way! You always know just what a girl needs!"

I glance at Paige who brings the glass up to her lips. She pauses momentarily to shoot me a skeptical look, but I nod, silently encouraging her that she can trust Miles.

Once again my attention is redirected as the phone on the table lights up, but this time, Miles grabs it without hesitation and looks down at the screen. Its bright light illuminates his face and I can see the anguish in his eyes; the unfazed person I know, suddenly distressed about something.

"Everything okay?" I ask, placing my drink slowly back on the table.

"It's nothing," Miles says sharply.

He pauses for a brief moment to consider his tone and places his phone back down on the table. He appears agitated by whatever he just read, but it's only noticeable for a moment as his expression lifts.

"Let's go dance!" he cheerfully shouts.

Sliding out from the booth, Miles stands up and holds his hand out for me to join him. I eagerly jump up and stand beside him as he reaches his hand out for Paige to join. She pulls the glass away, rubbing her lips together in approval of the taste, but she remains in place.

"Aren't you coming?" I ask, leaning onto the seat to get closer to Paige.

"I think I'd rather just wait here. I'm not much of a dancer anyways."

"Paige! I can't just leave you here," I plead.

"No, it's okay! You guys go dance!" she assures me, gesturing for us to leave. "I've got two left feet anyways!"

"You sure? I can show you a move or two!" Miles asks, winking at Paige.

The corner of Paige's mouth tips up and I assume she chuckled, but I can't hear it over the sound of the music.

Ignoring Miles' comment, she gestures with her hand and shouts, "Go! Have fun!"

Paige smiles at me and encouragingly nods toward the dance floor. I smile back, then turn to Miles who holds his elbow out for me to lock arms with him.

"Shall we?" he says, smiling.

"We shall!" I grin, locking my arm with his.

We walk down the steps and a wave of heat comes over me, the musty smell of sweat hits my nose and we become immersed in the movement of people around us, which I'm not particularly fond of. Thankfully, we have a booth in order to get a break away from it all.

When we reach the middle of the room, I immediately start feeling the music through my feet on the dance floor, vibrating with each beat. Miles releases my arm and immediately spins me around in a circle until I'm facing him again. Letting go of my hand, we start moving our hips to the music, jumping when the beat drops.

I love dancing on my own and letting loose to the music, but having a friend by my side makes it that much better, especially when he's just as good of a dancer as I am.

While I turn my head side to side swaying with the music, I start to recognize others around me. Near the stairway we just walked down, I see students I recognize from my freshman writing class and across the floor is a girl dancing who lives just a few rooms down from us in the upperclassmen dorms.

I close my eyes as Miles spins me around again, but as I'm being spun, I instantly hit someone from behind me. While it's common to accidentally run into people in a crowded room, this person may be a bit too close for comfort.

I open my eyes and I'm met with the face of a tall, slightly older man than me. He's wearing a dark colored three-piece suit like Miles, has the same dirty blonde hair, but with a full beard, and from what I can see in the darkness, he has light-colored eyes.

My first thought is that he's cute, but not my usual type. It's always been the dark-haired and dark-eyed types for me, like that bouncer at the door. My second thought— or should I say sense—is that I can smell his breath from here, reeking of alcohol. Almost putrid even.

It's suddenly quiet as if the music has faded around us and I stare up at him. Unbuttoning his jacket, he crosses his arms in front of him and I watch as his pupils dilate. I swallow hard, feeling a shiver run down my spine. I expect his words to be slurred, but as clear as day he says in a low, sultry voice, "Well, Miles always does pick the pretty ones."

As soon as the words leave his mouth, he smirks, but any charm I thought he had disappears.

Pretty? Yes. But if he thinks that line is supposed to somehow be a compliment, he's wrong. *Or rather just drunk.*

My eyes stay focused on him and suddenly I feel Miles' hand let go of mine, shattering the music around me, as I jump back into reality. I hadn't even realized he was still holding onto me.

"Don't," Miles sternly warns.

I look over my shoulder at Miles who is scowling at the man in front of me.

The man chuckles deeply, then tempts him, "Don't what?"

By the look on his face, he's clearly testing Miles. Trying to play games with him for God only knows what reason.

"She's not like that," Miles asserts.

"Not like what?" I frown, quickly turning around to meet Miles' gaze.

"Just don't entertain anything he has to say," Miles says quietly, leaning his face close to mine, while keeping an eye on the man.

"Why? Who is he?" I ask curiously, now looking out of the corner of my eye.

The man doesn't even acknowledge that I'm looking at him and his eyes remain on Miles.

Miles turns his attention away from me and back toward the man. "He's nobody."

I turn back around and a sudden beam of light from behind flashes across the man's face and I catch a glimpse of his piercing blue eyes focused directly on me. My eyes quickly widen, surprised to see such vivid color in them and noticing my expression, he cocks his head to the side.

Once again, he smirks as if he's happy that I'm giving him attention, and when I realize this, I scowl at him.

Taking a step closer to me, he reaches out and my body tenses up as I feel him lightly brush my cheek with the back of his hand. My eyes instinctively close, wishing for this moment to be over as his touch against my skin churns my stomach.

Every part of me wants to run out of this club—which is surprising—considering I'm the type to stay until the party ends, but in this case I'd do anything to get his hands off of me. The only thing stopping me is that I'm not the one to make a scene—especially in a crowded room.

"Don't touch her," I hear Miles growl.

I open my eyes and see Miles grabbing the man's wrist, pulling it away from my face. I can't help but let out a quiet sigh of relief.

The man snatches his wrist out from Miles' hand and in a fist, he holds his hand in the air. Closing his eyes, he takes a deep breath, then scoffs as he opens them.

The corner of his mouth tips up quickly as he utters the words, "You know, he's just like me, yet the only difference is that I can give you the night of your life."

My eyes widen, hearing his bluntness in front of Miles. *Oh god, what other words will come out of that smug mouth of his?*

Once again, I've given him fuel to his fire as he catches my expression. He raises his brow and quickly sneers, "Or maybe a few nights—if you're lucky."

Welp, there it is.

Miles quickly grabs my shoulders from behind and moves me back beside him, further away from this cocky asshole.

"What do you want?" Miles snaps at him and suddenly my energetic friend shows a side I've never seen.

If you watch Miles' chest puff up and a frown grows across his face, you'd think this man across from us assaulted me. *I mean, his words were assaulting enough.*

The guy laughs and then takes a step back, holding his hands up in defense.

"Hey, I'm only playing!" he jokes, before glancing over at me. "Unless she's looking to switch things up."

Miles steps forward, separating me from the man, and I'm no longer able to see him unless I peer around Miles.

"You need to leave," Miles states, crossing his arms.

While I'm confident that I can handle dealing with this man myself, I'm thankful for Miles. I've defended myself from plenty of arrogant men throughout college so far, and this one is no exception. However, it is nice having a guy friend who looks out for me.

The man looks down at his suit and adjusts it before straightening himself up.

He clears his throat, then with a stern face he says, "Can't. Urgent matter."

"What's so urgent that you have to be here?" Miles huffs.

I can tell that he's getting upset and I'm right up there with him because seriously—*who is this guy?*

"It's hard to explain, but you're wanted immediately. Their words, not mine."

Whose words? And clearly it can't be *that* urgent if he has enough time to stop and speak rudely to me.

"I'm not leaving," Miles asserts, holding his ground.

Immediately, the man groans loudly, as if he's exasperated by the situation at hand, then he cocks his head to the side, brows raised.

"Then you've left me no choice."

Suddenly, I see the man's arms wrap tightly around Miles' neck and tug him forward, and before I know it, he's dragging Miles across the dance floor, as Miles' legs try to keep up.

Feeling vulnerable out in the open, I stand there in shock as I look at the rest of the students around me, who appear to be oblivious to what I just witnessed. *Was this a kidnapping?* It had to be, but clearly everyone else is too drunk to notice.

I scan the crowd, spotting them heading for the door, and without thinking, I quickly chase after them. *If nobody else is going to do anything, I'm sure as hell going to.*

I make my way through the bodies of people around me and up to the small stairway. As Miles is forced out through the front entrance with a hard push against his back, I quicken my pace, praying I can stop it before I become a witness to a crime.

Once I pass through the dark hallway and briskly walk by the handsome bouncer, my eyes quickly scan the street for Miles. It's only moments before I catch sight of him being pushed into a black town car by his possible kidnapper.

Without stopping to think, I run over and try to grab the door, hoping I can give Miles enough time to escape. Before I can even reach out, the kidnapper steps between me and the car and presses his hand against my chest, pushing me away.

"Hey! You can't take him!" I shout.

I try to throw a fist at him, but he's too strong as his hand remains on my chest, holding me in place. It's like an old cartoon where the character's legs are racing beneath them, but they aren't moving an inch. My chest puffs out from the rush of adrenaline, and he snickers as he looks down at his hand resting across my breasts.

Leaning in, only so I can hear his words, he daringly whispers, "I'd like nothing more than to stay and find out what my hand feels like under this dress, rather than over it."

As he pulls away from me, the corner of his mouth lifts, a dimple appears, and I feel my heart race by his comment. Am I oddly attracted to it or am I just surprised someone can be this bold? *Definitely the latter.*

I want to yell at the asshole for saying something so candid. Who—in their right mind—would think that line would actually work on someone? *Him apparently.*

His crooked smile quickly disappears as his eyes focus back on mine.

"But, this is a family matter," he insists, then sternly warns, "So stay out of it."

Family matter?

Before I can say another word, he releases his hand and simultaneously slams the car door behind him.

I stand there as if my world around me has slowed and his has not. As the car disappears into the dark and out of my sight, I only have one thought in mind. *What the hell just happened?*

Chapter Two

Lily

Six Years Ago

Trying to make sense of what I just witnessed, I find my way back into the club and over to the booth, where Paige is waiting for me.

"Where'd Miles go?" she asks, clearly not as confused as I am.

I open my mouth to speak, but quickly close it.

What do I even say to her? I don't *think* he was actually kidnapped, but it sure as hell looked like it. Did Miles even try to put up a fight? And who really was that man? He said *family matter*, but family wouldn't act like that. At least not in mine that is.

"Did you hear me?" I distantly hear from Paige, before I hear her shout, "Where'd he go?"

The music almost sounds louder than before as I shake my head, trying to get out of my thoughts.

"He left," I sigh, scratching my forehead before sliding into the booth and next to her.

"He just left?" Paige questions, leaning closer to me so I can hear her clearer.

I blink quickly as I stare aimlessly down at the table, trying to find the words so I can give Paige some sort of explanation.

"He had an urgent family matter," I reassure her, deciding to tell her what I know and hoping it's the truth.

"Oh! Well I hope everything is okay!" she says, leaning back and taking a sip of her drink.

"Me too," I mumble, wrinkling my forehead.

She sets her drink back down and I place my elbow on the table, resting my chin into my hand.

Looking out at the dance floor, I sigh. It feels wrong of me to enjoy the rest of the night and I'm definitely not in a dancing mood. I mean, how could I be when all I can think about is Miles?

Out of the corner of my eye, a light shines and as I turn my head, I notice Miles' phone has been left behind on the table. Being a naturally nosey person, I pick it up and see a single text on the screen.

Spam: You need to leave. Now.

I swipe the screen hoping it will open and miraculously it unlocks.

I scroll through the previous texts from "Spam" and it's clear that the contact name is just a nickname and not actually spam text messages as I read Miles' last reply.

Miles: You can tell them that's not happening.

Whether it's wanting to make sure Miles gets his phone back, tipsy courage, or feeling like this text has something to do with his possible kidnapping, I text back a reply.

Me: Miles left his phone here.

Before I can offer to bring it to him, I get a reply from the number and it's an address. Nothing else.

It doesn't take much convincing to get Paige to leave the club with me and we're quickly in the back of a taxi on our way to the address.

Throughout our friendship, she's known that I've always been too curious for my own good. I've always found one way or another to end up in the wrong situations and find trouble, but luckily she's always been there to keep me in check, and boy, the memories we've made because of it, and this time isn't any different.

The address—located just outside the city in one of the oldest neighborhoods—can't be Miles' house, can it? From what I know, those that live in that neighborhood are rich, and not the flamboyant rich type, but those that are subtle with their money—quiet even.

Nearly forty-five minutes later, the taxi pulls up next to a tall, medieval-looking brick wall. In the distance, I see a large gate that's open, but decide not to mention it to the taxi driver in case this isn't the correct address.

"I'll be right back," I assure Paige as I unbuckle my seat belt. "I'm just going to leave his phone on the doorstep."

She leans forward looking through the front windshield and turns back to me.

"Are you even sure this is the right house?"

I open the taxi door and step out of it before turning to look at the house, now slightly visible over the top of the wall.

"Don't worry. I'll be fine!" I insist with a reassuring smile, but she raises an eyebrow at me, as if she doesn't believe it one bit.

"Well, don't be long, okay?"

I nod to her and quickly turn around.

I'm not sure what to expect, but I have to assume I'm in no danger. If that text was from the same man that took Miles, I'm not scared of him by any means. He may be a possible kidnapper, but he was more of an asshole than a threat. Besides, I won't be on the property longer than a moment.

Walking along the wall down the sidewalk, I turn as I reach the large-gated entrance. It's dark in the front courtyard, but a massive gray mansion is partially lit up by small lights surrounding the property and the windows illuminating from within. The home has a castle-like appearance, with a steep roof and arched windows at the top.

I reach the curved, dark wood front door and stare down at the mat. I had planned on leaving the phone, but

I'm still unsure if the address is correct and I wouldn't want someone to take it. It may be late at night, but if I were Miles, I wouldn't want to spend another moment thinking my phone was missing, so I go with plan B. I hold my breath and knock, assuming the lights coming from within are an indication the homeowners are awake.

Please don't let my curiosity actually kill me.

I let out a sigh of relief as an older gentleman with gray hair, who appears to be in his seventies, answers the door. He is standing with impressive posture, dressed in a black suit with a white vest and bowtie to match.

"Hello, how can I help you?" he asks with a friendly smile.

"Does Miles live here?"

"Yes, this is the Moore residence."

"Oh, good," I chuckle. "I came to return Miles' phone. He forgot it."

I look down at the phone in my hand momentarily, then back up at him. He immediately steps aside, holding the door open enough for me to walk in and I slightly raise my brows, surprised to be let in so quickly. He holds his hand out and gestures for me to step inside and I willingly do so, encouraged by his welcoming smile.

As I step into the large foyer, he closes the door behind me.

"Wait right here please."

I open my mouth to thank him, but he quickly disappears out of sight, presumably to let Miles know that I'm here.

I look around the room as I wait and there's a large wooden staircase with a bright chandelier hanging above me. My heels echo against the marble floors and I suddenly feel as if my short dress is too informal for this house.

I lick my lips as I try to peer down the hallway to ensure nobody is watching, then I take a step into the large living room off the foyer. The tall ceilings are double the height of an average room and the crown molding around the top screams luxury. Facing me is a large fireplace with regal-looking sconce lights and there's moulding on the walls as well.

It isn't more than a few moments from when the man at the door disappeared, but I'm startled as I hear loud arguing from another room. It's unlikely the arguing is from the room next door, due to the way the house echoes, however, they are definitely unaware that I am here.

I stop walking to prevent my feet from creating an additional sound and I listen into the conversation. It's hard to make out everything, but I'm able to hear a few words, especially when the voices grow louder.

"Are you kidding me?" I hear, immediately recognizing the voice of Miles.

"It's non-negotiable honey. We have a reputation to uphold," a woman's voice says to him.

"It was one night," Miles asserts, pausing before adding, "Nothing has happened since."

Unsure of how long I'll be waiting here, I make my way over to the cream-colored couch.

A man with a deep and stern voice adds, "Regardless, you've been poorly influenced and it's time for a change."

Just as I'm about to sit down, I'm jolted back to my feet by the sound of nearby footsteps. I quickly turn around to see the man from the club entering into view in the foyer entrance and while I had hoped he wasn't the contact in Miles' phone, this confirms my suspicion.

"Oh, it's you," he sneers, raising a brow as he turns on his heel to face me.

The man, whose name is still unknown to me, is now dressed more casually, wearing just a button down with slacks.

"You," I say loathingly, as I cross my arms.

"You say that like it's a bad thing," he snickers, his voice just as irritating as earlier. *No surprise there.*

He turns his head to the right momentarily and silence fills the room. The yelling has dissipated and judging by the look on his face, he's heard it as well.

"Isn't it?" I taunt, keeping my face expressionless as he turns back to look at me.

He scoffs, as if amused by my comment.

I watch as his gaze moves across the floor, lands on my heels and I feel his eyes slowly move up my body. While I'd normally be delighted by a man checking me out, the thought that this is the man doing so only makes me despise it.

"Well, you just couldn't wait to see me again," he states as if it's a fact.

He crosses his arms as he slowly steps down from the foyer into the room I'm in.

"I mean, that has to be the reason you're here, right?" he adds.

The corner of his mouth rises and quickly falls, as if amused by his own question.

I quickly exhale then say sharply, "You're the last person I want to see."

He immediately raises both of his eyebrows, as if surprised by my response.

"You can't be here for Miles," he mocks.

Obviously I'm not here for you.

The sound of his steps echoes in the room, breaking the silence around us.

As he stops in front of me, the corner of his mouth rises and once again, I smell the subtle stench of alcohol coming from his mouth.

I swallow hard as I take a step back, trying to create distance between us. I raise my brows, enticing him to mock me more and his smirk fades.

"You know, you'll never have a chance with him," he states.

You've got it all wrong pal.

Unable to read my mind, he continues, "Girls like you don't date guys like him."

An audible gasp from my mouth accidentally breaks through and I can't contain my words.

"Girls like what?" I ask, scowling at him.

"Every one of you is the same. Always after the money," he accuses, closing the distance between us.

With my back nearly against the wall, he leans over me and places his hand on my chin. Tilting my head up so that I can't turn it away, he studies my eyes and I watch as his tongue grazes his lips.

His hand feels like a match burning against my skin, slowly igniting my body the longer he lingers. And for some reason, no matter how much it sears, I can't escape his fire.

Then, he scowls and says, "He may not see it, but I sure as hell can."

A steady anger rises from within me, fueled by the flame he's created and I find a gap to break away from his intense eye contact.

"Excuse me?" I snap, swatting his hand away from my face. *Who does he think I am? A gold digger?*

"Don't act like this is the first time you've heard that. You're not fooling anyone with that dress, Princess."

He reaches down to try to grab onto the fabric of my black dress, but I take a step to the side and out of his reach. My skin boiling from the audacity of this man.

"Fuck you!" I angrily curse, walking around the couch and as far from him as I can.

"You wish, sweetheart," he scoffs, tilting his head. *That ass.*

I bite my tongue, keeping every thought I have in my head from spewing out of my mouth, knowing I've already been gone longer than intended. Without giving him the pleasure of another look from me, I storm out of the room and into the foyer.

As I grab the handle of the door and press my other hand against the wall as leverage, I realize I'm still holding Miles' phone.

Dammit. The whole reason I came to this stupid house.

I can't force myself back into that room with *him*, so I quickly search around me for a place to safely leave his phone, before placing it on the last step of the staircase.

Then, without looking back, I exit the house.

Good riddance to yet another asshole.

Chapter Three

Lily

I look at myself in the mirror, staring at my lavender-colored pajamas and although I'm getting used to the idea of sitting around my apartment and watching rom-coms all day, I know I have another long day of job hunting ahead of me.

When you're just out of college, it's so much easier finding a job. Maybe it's because they see you with that shiny new degree? Or maybe they assume that all the knowledge you learned is still relatively fresh in your mind? However, that's not the case for me anymore. I wish it were, but it isn't.

It's been five years since I graduated and despite having a stable job in education the entire time, faculty cuts will forever be the death of me. More tenured staff stayed, while those like me were termed. Now newly laid off, I'm back on the job market.

I carefully pull my pajama shirt over my head, ensuring it won't smudge my makeup or unravel my perfectly curled hair. Then, I pull down my loose pajama pants, wad the two into a ball and throw them onto my rumpled bed—a bed that will continue to stay unmade until I put some order into my chaotic life.

Walking over to the closet, I grab a white linen long sleeve top and as I'm buttoning it up, I search for a pair of pants to match, before spotting cream-colored slacks.

Stepping back in front of the mirror, I tuck my shirt slightly into my slacks and reach for a set of small gold hoop earrings on my nightstand. As I'm putting them on, I spot Paige, through the reflection of my mirror, standing in the doorway.

"That's cute! So professional," she jokes, crossing her arms as she leans against the door.

I deride at her comment as I put my other earring on before standing up straight to assess my outfit. *Professional enough to get a job.*

"I mean, I can't go job hunting in my pajamas," I say, chuckling, as I look back at Paige through the mirror.

"I mean, you could," she raises her eyebrows, and then adds, "But you probably wouldn't get the job."

I laugh. "Very true."

"Are you ready?" she asks, straightening herself up in the doorway and nodding her head away from the room.

"Ready!" I say, smiling at myself in the mirror.

Grabbing my bag on the counter, Paige and I walk out of the apartment and head to our favorite coffee shop—Hanley's.

It isn't long until we reach The Harper School, a private elementary school that's halfway to Hanley's and also happens to be where I work. *Well, used to anyways.*

Boy, did I love it though, even though it wasn't what I originally planned to be as an adult.

When I was in high school, I nannied part-time for a family with infant twins. A boy and a girl. The family lived in a nice apartment, only a block from my home, and the mother was a stay-at-home parent who just needed the extra help and the father worked long hours as a surgeon. I helped out on the weekends when I could, but it was the weekdays that I was most needed.

When I finished school at three in the afternoon, I would head over to their apartment. The pay was decent for a job that wasn't very hard: I helped bottle-feed the twins, clean the dishes and made dinner when she was especially exhausted. I can imagine it was a lot for one person taking care of two infants, and since they could afford it, they had me help. It didn't hurt either that I was a cheaper option, especially being a teenager at the time.

That job was where my love for children started and as I was heading to my sophomore year of college, I had every intention of becoming a labor and delivery nurse. The twins' father actually inspired me to get into that field. He said it took a lot of effort, but it was all worth it in the end.

And, I already had a knack for taking care of infants, so I might as well help bring them into this world too.

That quickly changed though. As I started college, I still helped when I could despite my dorm being a little further from that family's house. I got to see the twins turn into toddlers and it was incredible experiencing them learning to talk and communicate with me more.

It was at that time that I began to consider a degree in early childhood development. I wanted to be that person that helped children, once they were no longer with their parents, when they were developing at a rapid pace and digesting so much information.

The next day, I switched my major from nursing to just that. Luckily, I was still mainly taking core classes, so I hadn't jumped too far into the nursing program, and my hard work paid off because with only one additional semester of college, I was able to graduate with my Master's.

I quickly found a career as an early childhood reading specialist at The Harper School soon after. I worked in first through third grade and even helped them to develop an afterschool program for learning that not only helped improve efficiency, but definitely left an impression. Unfortunately, not enough of one.

While it may sound unreasonable, I actually thought I would be there until I retired. I had created a home there and truly loved my job. Although I only got five short years at Harper, it still holds a special place in my heart.

As we pass the school, Paige and I finally reach Hanley's and as always, it's bustling with people on this Monday morning. The line nearly reaches the door, but it doesn't take too long to get to the front.

With a friendly smile, the barista, Sophie, pushes two drinks toward us on the counter before we can even say a word.

"Your usual, of course," she says, giving me a friendly wink.

"Thank you, Sophie!" I say cheerfully, handing her my card. I grab one of the drinks and pass it to Paige before taking mine. Sophie returns my card, and I slip it into my wallet.

"Have a good day!" I say as she smiles and waves the next customer forward.

Paige and I walk over to our signature corner table, which is empty as always. I can't explain why it always happens to be available when we arrive, but I call it our lucky table. Paige just calls it a coincidence.

Just as we sit down, I hear a phone ringing from beneath the table and I quickly look around to see where the sound is coming from.

"Sorry! It's me!" Paige says, as I glance up at her holding her phone.

She holds it in front of her and squints her eyes as she checks the contact, before bringing it up to her ear.

"Hello?" she asks.

Simultaneously, I hear a ding from the the bell above the front door. While I normally don't pay attention to every person who walks in, something in my mind compels me to look up and I'm glad I did.

Walking through the door is a handsome thirty-something year old man. He's tall—his head just about reaches the top of the door frame—and he has short, dirty blonde hair that's slightly parted to the side. He's clean shaven and is dressed in a brown suit with a white button down. I'm not sure why but everything about him screams he's in finance.

He looks vaguely familiar, but judging by the look of confusion on his face, he's never been here before. I've compiled a list in my head of who the regulars are at Hanley's, and he certainly is not one of them.

As he scans the room, he quickly nods his head as he spots a barista cleaning up a table near the front window. I watch as he places his hand on the barista's shoulder and they exchange a few words. After thirty seconds or so, he shakes the barista's hand and as he smiles, I quickly lean back in my chair.

Holy. Shit.

The corner of his mouth rises and I feel my heart beat straight out of my chest. His smile is warm and friendly, radiating an energy that pulls me forward in my seat and my cheeks tighten as I feel myself blushing.

If I had seen this man before, I'm confident I would have recognized that smile anywhere. I mean, who could ever forget something like that?

I focus my attention on him as I watch him walk over to the end of the line, which has eased up in the few minutes since we've sat down. He looks down at his watch, then turns to face the room. I immediately look away, feeling as if I was just caught staring. Nonchalantly, I take a sip of my coffee and count to thirty, as I imagine he may be watching me. *Delusional, but possible.*

Once I feel the coast is clear, or that my imagination has stopped spiraling thinking this man could actually be looking at me, I slowly turn my head back his way.

I hear a ding at the front entrance once again, but it's impossible for me to look away as I explore every aspect of him with my eyes. His light brown chest hair peeking through the collar of his button-down shirt. The small, but dark spot behind his left ear, I assume is a birthmark, his square jawline and the single dimple on his cheek.

And as he quickly turns around to look behind him, I get a brief glimpse of his vibrant blue eyes. Light blue like the sky, but deep, dark blue like the sea around the irises.

I slowly draw down his face and I'm once again enlightened with the sight of his dashing smile in a much closer view.

I feel a piercing in my chest and as I blink slowly, there's a realization that hits me as I swallow hard. I've been caught. That smile is directed toward me and I'm no longer in my imagination bubble as his eyes peer through me, leaving me breathless.

While I am usually confident in my own skin, I suddenly feel vulnerable with his eyes on me. I blink quickly, freeing myself from his gaze and timidly smile back, before directing my eyes to Paige.

My curiosity gets the best of me as I peer out of the corner of my eyes and see him still watching me, eyes focused and my heart racing. I turn my head to look at him more directly, but his attention is abruptly pulled away as Sophie motions for him to step forward.

Then, Paige's voice echoing draws my attention to her.

"Hey! Did you hear me?" Paige asks, tapping my hand.

Moving around in her seat, she retrieves her bag from the floor and lifts her drink from the table as she stands.

"I got called in early. I have to go," she says, holding her arms out. "Good luck with the job hunt!"

I quickly stand and pull her in for a quick hug.

"Thank you! See you back home!"

She turns around and walks away and I follow her with my eyes as she heads for the door. When she makes her way out, my eyes veer off to the left where the man is now sitting down at a table. And unquestionably, he's staring directly at me.

While I planned to use my time wisely and search for jobs on my laptop while sitting here, I doubt I will be able to focus with *him* there gazing at me with those alluring blue eyes and that compelling smile.

Nope. Definitely not.

While I've seen attractive men at this coffee shop before, I never felt like I was being pulled toward any of them, like I was craving their presence, among other things.

Until now.

Trusting that being a regular here helps protect my belongings, the little voice in my head shouts at me to get up. I grip the table as I stand and I know, it's now or never.

I take a deep breath as I prepare to face this desirable man and then I rub the top of the table with my fingertips. Likely for nerves, but I tell myself it's to generate some extra luck. Then, lifting my hands from the table, I walk over in his direction.

One night with someone like him won't hurt.

Chapter Four

Mason

Nobody told me how challenging owning a business would be. Even after being basically groomed my entire life to take over, I'm still not used to it, not even after three months into the role.

Is it because I still have so much yet to figure out? Or is it because my father is still breathing down my neck, waiting for me to make a mistake?

He claims he's retired, yet he doesn't trust that I know what I'm doing. Why pass down the business when he still wants to be so involved? I mean, I get it. This business has been in our family for 137 years, so like his father before him, it's normal he wants to ensure it continues to grow and adapt for more decades to come.

Being the oldest, I was first in line to take over and my brother was supposed to be by my side. *Supposed*—that was the plan anyways.

I went to Mayfair, a prestigious college upstate, following in the footsteps of every other person in my family. As I would eventually be the face of the Moore Corporation, I had to be on my best behavior. I couldn't be unhinged as I had a duty to fulfill—or at least that's what my father said.

I still had my fun though. On the surface— especially to my parents—I was Mr. Perfect, getting straight A's, studying in the business program and preparing for my future endeavors. Yet, I still found a way to enjoy the typical college experience.

When your family is in the liquor industry, you get to know your product, and bourbon was my drink of choice. Even better? The new-found confidence that came with it.

I wasn't the type to approach women, and even to this day I'm not, but if you get quite a few drinks in me, I become a self-proclaimed playboy. And like every guy who thinks he can get any girl he wants, I was that asshole. I'm not ashamed to admit it. I was.

But you can't be one forever, especially when you are still single in your thirties, and even more so when you are about to take over a multi-million dollar business. So, I learned to control my liquor consumption and my cocky attitude left with it. Or maybe I just grew up?

I put all my focus into preparing to take over and learning every aspect of the spirits industry. I analyzed what worked and looked at what we could improve, so when the time came, I was ready.

But my brother? My brother didn't join me when it was time for our father to step down. No, he got off easy. And while he had the privilege to make his own choices, I didn't.

He got to pick his school and chose Barrett Square, far from elite and smack dab in the middle of the city. He got to be a typical careless college student and got drunk every weekend—or so I thought.

That changed during his junior year, following an incident. Once you turn 21, you start exploring the options out there, and once you find a drink you like, you stick to it. However, you have to watch yourself. *Carefully.*

And if you're from a family like ours, you especially have to take precautions; I always did. One slip and you will seriously harm the family's reputation—and he did just that.

One thing led to another, and while those memories of mine are still foggy, I do remember it got out of control. So much so that my parents started making the choices for him. He switched to Mayfair, sobered up and got his act together. Was it by his own will? Maybe. My guess? No.

While this incident may have been small, it made all the difference. Think about it—wouldn't it be ironic to have a Sober Sally helping to run a spirits corporation? Yes. That's the only answer.

Fearing he would go off the deep end in that case, my parents gave him an out. Stay out of trouble and you don't have to get involved in the family business. They made an irrational decision based solely on a college student doing what college students do. But he got to make the decision and he was out. And then, everything fell on me.

As I stepped into my role, a crucial business expansion was already in the works; you never grow bigger if you don't take the risks.

My father had spoken to an Italian-based distributor prior to stepping down and now it's my job to seal the deal. Once everything is signed, we will soon have a company we can trust to bring our product into European markets. There's just a few more necessary steps before the deal is done, but I look forward to our family company finally branching out to another continent.

But right now, I'm trying to complete my own plan for the business, which includes upgrading our office buildings here in the city. We may be a 137-year-old corporation, but that doesn't mean our employees have to work in buildings that look like they are from the 19th century, so that's where Ryker Blackwell comes in.

"He's one of the good ones," I hear my mother's words echo in my head.

That was one of the main reasons I reached out to him in the first place. He's new money, so he isn't like the rest. He's been working his way up to becoming one of the leading real-estate executives in the city and didn't just get it from his father's trust fund. He worked hard just like my family did when we started the business, so I know he'll be able to get us what we need.

It's a quarter past seven and I'm early, surprisingly enough. Traffic is usually a bitch on a Monday so I skipped my morning coffee and left as soon as I could. Yet, here I am, thirty minutes early because everyone else in this city decided to be late today so traffic wasn't a nightmare.

My driver dropped me off five minutes ago, but as I look up at the building, I read the numbers: 1258—numbers that should read 1268. *Shit!*

Well, it doesn't help to be early if you aren't even at the correct building.

I quickly look around and spot a coffee shop on the street corner and head toward it. Maybe someone in there can point me to the correct building, because it's clear that phone directions won't help either, since even the driver got the location wrong.

As I walk in, there's a ding above the door and the smell of coffee fills my nose. It's quieter than I expected, despite all the occupied tables and the line of people.

I look around the room, hoping to spot an employee to ask for directions—something I'd rather not do, but have no other choice. I know I could ask any customer, but I hate to bother them while they enjoy their morning coffee. At least an employee would be more willing to help.

Off to my right, I notice a young man wiping a table down and he glances at me. I nod at him, hoping to get his attention, before walking over.

"Hello," I say, placing my hand on his shoulder.

He turns to face me and straightens himself up, lifting his damp rag from the table.

"Hi. Can I help you?"

"Yes, sorry," I stutter, looking over my shoulder toward the entrance and then back at him. "I was hoping you could give me some directions."

He agreeably nods as he crosses his arms.

"Yeah, where are you needing to go?"

I scratch my temple. "I was looking for the building across the street marked 1268, but I'm only seeing 1258. Do you happen to know where that is?"

He chuckles, "This has been happening a lot lately." He points toward the window. "It's that white building right there."

I turn in that direction, and two buildings down from where I was standing on the street is the white one. *Really?* I should have at least tried walking around out there before asking for directions. Well, might as well get a coffee while I'm here then.

I turn back to him and hold my hand out.

"Thank you! I appreciate it."

He grabs my hand and shakes it, "Not a problem at all."

I grit my teeth, feeling the moisture from the rag in his hand and quickly smile at him, acknowledging his help. Then, I walk over to the end of the line with only four people ahead of me and wipe my hand against the side of my pants.

Pulling my wrist up toward me, I look down at my watch. *7:19.* Enough time to enjoy my coffee before I need to head back across the street.

Stepping forward in line, I look around the room for an empty table, hoping to find a place to sit once I have my drink in hand.

As my eyes scan the room, they quickly land on two brown-haired women sitting at a table in the corner. One is talking on her phone, but the other? Something about her catches my attention and now, I don't want to take my eyes off of her.

Her hair masks part of her face, but the small glimpse of what I can see, holds my gaze. I marvel at her beauty, curious if she's even aware it's hidden.

As she brings her drink up to her lips, I sip in a breath of air. For the first time in years, I feel my heart race and there's an instant rush throughout my body that is indescribable.

I take in every piece of her as each millisecond passes. Her hair concealing what I'm so desperate to see. As if some unworldly power takes away my torment, she lifts her fingertips up to her face, pulling back a strand of her hair and tucking it behind her ear.

She's beautiful in every way. *Mesmerizing even.*

And then, her eyes are on me, so intense, their green hue reminiscent of a forest being cascaded in rain. Green eyes are common, but on her? They'll take your breath away.

I try to turn my head away, knowing that I shouldn't stare, but I can't help it. Watching as she studies every single part of my being. Blissfully unaware that I've been doing the same to her.

As she traces my face with her eyes, I can no longer contain the smile I've been painstakingly holding back. And finally, she becomes aware.

She's bold—I can already tell, judging by her unfaltering focus. But as she notices me smiling at her, I sense that I shook that confidence. Then, she quickly turns away, as if she's been caught in her act.

Just as she's about to bravely turn and face me again, I hear, "Next!"

I blink suddenly as I jerk my head toward the barista at the counter.

"Hi. Just a black coffee please," I ask quickly, wanting to look back at the woman as soon as I can.

"Name?" she says, holding the cup up in front of her.

I give her my name and then pull my wallet out before handing her my card. She swipes it and then returns it to me.

With a quick smile she says, "Have a nice day!"

I return the gesture and glance behind me, but I'm unable to see the woman again, blocked by a few people in line behind me. I shake my head and walk over to an empty table by the entrance, hoping I'll have another chance to get a small glimpse of her. As I sit down, I feel my attention being pulled in her direction and while I have to force myself not to stare again, I'm incapable of doing so.

I've been so focused on other things that I've neglected to date in the past three years. My parents have nagged me constantly about settling down, and there isn't a doubt in my mind that if they could, they'd just pick someone for me. However, all I can do is keep insisting that someone will come into my life and tell them that I just haven't found the right person yet.

Now, for the first time in a while, I'm looking at someone who I'm interested in. No, *captivated* by. And by some irrational feat, she's heading straight toward me.

"Hi," she says. "Is this seat taken?"

Before I can answer, she sits down.

From across the room, it was easier to look at her, to memorize every part of her in case she just walked out the door and I never saw her again. But, here she is and now every nerve in my body is tensing up.

"I'm Lily," she beams. "Lily Alcord."

I sip in a breath of air as the corners of her mouth tip up and my heart starts racing once again.

"I'm—"

"Wait, hold that thought." She quickly holds her finger up in front of us before I can continue. "Let's see if she gets the name correct!"

Straightening herself in her seat, she nods her head toward the barista who's walking out from behind the counter. I turn my attention in that direction.

"Chai tea latte for—" the barista pauses, squinting down at the cup. "Batman?"

I silently laugh. *That can't seriously be the name that someone put on their cup.*

"That's definitely wrong," Lily guesses, taking the words straight out of my mouth.

She turns back to me and grins before adding, "What do you think?"

I open my mouth, but no words come out. I'm immobilized by the fact that she is sitting here and I fear I may say something foolish. It's already a miracle that she walked over to me, something I never would have had the guts to do myself.

"Like who would name their child Batman?" she laughs as she looks at me for a moment and then back at the barista.

A man walks behind Lily and up to the barista, slightly frowning as he reaches for the cup.

"It's Damon."

Lily and I both quietly chuckle before looking back at one another. Then, she raises her eyebrows and sneers, "See. Told you."

It's cute how proud she is for being right and I can't help but find it attractive as hell. If I weren't out in public, the snarky comment would make me slightly hard, but I push the thought away.

"Black coffee for—" The barista shouts, pausing.

I blink quickly and turn my attention to her standing at the end of the now obsolete line. Simultaneously, I raise my eyebrows and put my hand into the air before she can say my name as she rotates the cup. She acknowledges me with a nod and walks over to my table.

"Here you go," she says, placing the to-go mug on the table.

Lily looks up at the barista with a smile, before looking back at me with a scowl.

"You know, it's more fun if you wait for them to say your name," she sneers.

There's a brief pause from her, as if she's waiting to see if I understood her humor.

A short smile forms on the corner of my lips and appearing relieved, she chuckles, "But I'll let it slide."

I take a breath and finally find the words to say, "How'd you know she was going to mispronounce their name?"

"Isn't it obligatory for a coffee shop to mispronounce your name?"

I chuckle. "As far as I've heard."

Looking down, I place my hand on the side of the cup and feel the heat radiating from it. As I look back up after observing my name on the front, hidden to Lily's eyes, I lean forward.

"So, what's your botched name?"

Her face is suddenly expressionless, as she thinks, until she shakes her head.

"I don't have one." She frowns as if disappointed.

I furrow my brows and click my tongue.

"Oh, I'm sorry—"

She quickly shakes her head and smiles. "It's alright."

I raise a brow and she sees the confusion on my face.

She chuckles and then tilts her head. "I may have had one at some point, but by now, it's been far too long for me to remember what they called me."

"So, you come here often?"

She laughs and quickly places her hand over her mouth to hide her smile.

With my free hand, I scratch my temple, afraid I just embarrassed myself in some way.

"What?" I ask.

She coughs, choking back the lingering laugh and takes a deep breath in.

"Nothing," She says slyly, before coughing away her giggles once more. "I've just never heard that line actually be used in person."

"What li—" I pause, quickly understanding. "Oh!"

I shake my head, thoroughly embarrassed and hear her soft chuckles from across the table.

Slowly nodding, I squint my eyes at her and playfully scoff as I say, "I see what I did there."

She teasingly bites her lip.

"I'm a regular."

Well, that explains.

"And you aren't—" she says, grabbing onto the top of my cup. I lightly release it and she twists it toward her and leans forward as she reads, "Mason."

She lets go of my drink and tilts her head to the side, waiting for me to reply.

"No, I am not."

"Well Mason," she starts, sitting up in her seat. "What brings an outsider into this coffee shop?"

"Outsider?" I ask, raising an eyebrow.

That's the first time I've been called that. Feels like something you'd say to a tourist, so I never would've expected to hear it in a coffee shop of all places.

"You're right. That's not the right word," she states, looking up momentarily and then back at me. "Non-regular? First timer? I'm not sure what you'd call it."

"There's a first for everything," I say, enthralled by her quirky humor.

She raises her eyebrows as if a lightbulb has gone off in her head.

"Well first timer, how's this for a first?" She takes a quick breath in and smiles confidently. "Since I have no idea if I'll ever see you again, you're going to take me on a date."

I feel myself fall back into my seat, shocked by the bluntness of this woman.

Damn. She's forward.

"Excuse me?" I chuckle the words out, thinking I imagined the statement.

"You heard me," she asserts, holding her head up high.

Nope, she said it. And just like I thought earlier, she's confident. Never in my life have I met a woman like her, but oh, how I like it.

"Well you got me there. That's definitely a first for me," I say, raising my brows.

She quickly straightens herself up and with a wide grin she quietly adds, "I knew it."

I bite my cheek, trying to hide my growing grin, and caution her, "But, you don't even know if I'm single."

She furrows her brows and looks down at the table for a moment, as if she hadn't considered what she'd do if she'd encountered that issue. She shakes her head and looks back up at me.

"Well?" she leans forward slightly raising her brows. "Are you?"

I chuckle deeply as I nod, "Yes. I am."

She straightens herself up again in her seat and I can see she's pleased with my answer. Then, she quickly looks around at the tables near us before leaning over to tap the shoulder of the woman behind her.

"Hi! Can I borrow that?" she asks, pointing to something after the woman turns around.

I lean to my side and see a pen resting on the woman's table. The woman nods and hands the pen to Lily, who faces me again as I lean myself back into place.

Grabbing the top of my drink again, she slides it toward her and writes something on the side of the paper koozie. Placing the cup back on the table, she turns around.

"Thanks!" she says, handing the pen back to the woman.

As she faces me, she bites her bottom lip as she carefully slides my cup across the table.

"There," she says with a smile.

I anxiously smile back, curious what she wrote, and look down at my cup. Turning it slowly around so the writing faces me, I pull it up to me and see a number written on the koozie. And not just any number. No. *Hers*.

I'm speechless at that moment. Not only did this beautiful woman just give me her number, but she's already insisted that I take her on a date. These were two things I did not have on my bingo card for today.

As I try to muster the courage to say something that doesn't sound foolish, I slightly glance at my watch out of the corner of my eye and I see the time. 7:47.

"Shit," I mumble abruptly and immediately regret the words that come out of my mouth as I see Lily confused by my words.

"Sorry!" I say, quickly trying to recover as I shake my head. "I'm actually late for a meeting."

She tilts her head to the side, and questionably raises a brow, as if she doesn't believe me and I'm just making an excuse to leave.

"You know, you could have said no when I asked."

I place both of my hands on the edge of the table and lift my fingers up as I lean forward.

With a smirk, I playfully snicker, "I don't think you'd let me."

She licks her lips, as if she wants to say she agrees and then, she confidently smirks back. I lean into my seat and after a moment of silence, a ding above the door shakes me back into the bustling noise of the room.

"I really do have to go though. I'm sorry."

She takes a deep breath and then her smirk turns to a smile.

"No worries. You know how to reach me," she brags, holding her head up high.

I stand up from my seat and button my suit jacket, before grabbing my coffee from the table. She looks at me with one brow raised, as though she's waiting for me to speak.

"I really wish I could stay," I say, frowning.

Truly, I wish I could. My heart is still racing and I don't want it to stop.

"Don't worry. I'll see you again on our date," she assures me. "Goodbye Mason."

"Moore," I quickly add.

"What?" She quickly replies, curiosity written on her face.

"Mason Moore," I reiterate.

She tilts her head slightly and hums to herself, before smiling.

"Goodbye, Mason Moore."

I shoot her a quick smile, before turning on my heel and heading out the door.

As I walk toward the white building across the street, every part of me wants to go back to talk to her more, but I know I can't. I have a business to run and getting these office buildings is part of it.

But, this won't be the last time I see her. We are going on a date. That's unquestionable and that's one I wouldn't miss for the world.

I may not have the confidence to go up to a random person and ask them out, but she sure as hell does. And every part of that was the most attractive thing I've ever seen a woman do.

So, if I play my cards right on this date, I may never want to let her go.

Chapter Five

Lily

"So, how'd the job search go?" Paige asks, setting her stuff down on the counter.

I chuckle. "Another doozy today."

"Darn," she sighs, as she walks over and sits down next to me on the opposite end of the couch.

I point the remote at the tv and turn it off, before straightening myself up and turning toward her.

"It's a good thing our rent is so cheap," Paige teases, rolling her eyes.

"Hey!" I say, pushing my hand against her shoulder. "How was I supposed to know I was getting laid off?"

"You didn't," she admits and I can hear the sympathy in her voice.

She pauses for a moment before smiling widely. "But, it does relieve some added stress though, right?"

"Very true!" I say, nodding in agreement. "I will forever be thankful that we got this smokin' deal!"

After graduating, Paige and I searched for apartments throughout the city and found the one we are living in now for an incredibly low price—shockingly low, in fact.

Now, I don't know how our neighbors found out about the rent or when the rumors started, but I guess word got out four months ago.

I had just gotten off work when I ran into our neighbor, Tia, from across the hall. We had gotten to know her fairly well over the years, as she was around the same age as us, and she always gave us juicy building gossip.

Well, that day, the gossip was about us—more specifically—me. She had found out about our rent and insisted I tell her how we got it.

When she first asked, it was unclear why she was actually asking though. We paid our rent like everyone else —nothing special. But when she explained that she had heard our rent was a third of the rest of the building's, I was just as shocked as she was. We knew it was low, but we were oblivious to the fact that everyone else was paying so much more.

The gossip though? Tia had heard a rumor that I slept with the landlord. Ridiculous, yes. Even more so, considering I had never even met the landlord and still haven't to this day. But, when I denied it, she didn't believe me.

So now, everyone thinks I hook up with the landlord to get our low rent. Maybe in college I would have done something like that, but definitely not now. Yes—I may sleep around here and there, but even if sometimes I'm unlucky and end up only having one date, I always hope it leads to more.

No matter how we actually got the deal, I'm relieved we don't have to stress about money right now. I can't imagine how much more on edge I'd be if I had to worry about not only finding a job, but also us being able to afford our apartment.

It didn't help that I had a distraction today—a good one, that's for sure, but I'm not any closer to finding a new job than I was yesterday.

"What are you thinking about?" Paige asks, tilting her head.

"Well, I didn't have luck with a job, but I did find some luck somewhere else."

"What do you mean?" she asks, furrowing her brows.

"Someone else," I correct myself, trying to hide my animated reaction.

Paige's eyes widen and she leans back slightly into the corner of the couch.

"Wait, what?" she shouts. "When?"

"Actually, right after you left Hanley's."

"And I missed it?" she huffs, rolling her eyes before focusing her attention back on me. "Well, are you going to tell me about him?"

"He's handsome," I start, pausing and looking off into the distance as I trace an image of him in my mind.

I look back at her and continue. "Dirty blonde hair and striking blue eyes," I pause again, thinking of what to tell her. "He was sitting at the table near the entrance and I just decided to go up to him and sit at his table."

I hold my breath, waiting for her reaction.

"And?" Paige asks, placing her hand on the couch cushion as she leans forward.

"Well, this won't surprise you, but I asked him out," I chuckle.

Paige leans back, chuckles quietly and nods, "Yeah, I'm not surprised! You know what you want and you go for it."

I laugh. "I basically used the same trick on him that I did on you back in elementary school."

"You mean, how you told me we were going to be friends and I had no choice?"

She raises an eyebrow at me.

"No," I scoff, trying to hide my lie.

She playfully scowls at me as she shakes her head. "The oldest trick in the book."

I purse my lips and look away for a moment before glancing back at her out of the corner of my eye.

"Are you going to tell him he has no choice but to date you too?" Paige asks, crossing her arms.

"Hey!" I shout turning to face her as I push her shoulder again with my hand. Her arms flail from her chest as they uncross.

"I have to go on a date with him first," I say, pausing before chuckling the words, "But maybe."

"Well, when's the date?" Paige asks.

"I'm not sure yet, I'm waiting—" I pause as I hear a ding from my phone.

Both of us look down at the couch to where my phone is laying face down. We both look up at one another simultaneously and I smile. *Please be him.*

I pick up my phone and see an unknown number pop up on my home screen. I look up wide-eyed at Paige before looking back down at my phone.

Swiping it open, I pull up the text and it reads:

Unknown: Is this the girl who confidently told me we were going on a date?

I feel a smile grow quickly on my face. No hello. No introduction. Just a single sentence. But I know it's Mason.

It may seem out of the ordinary for a woman to ask a man out, but I always try to act on impulse. Why not? Would he have even gone over to my table, had I not? Either way, I don't regret it. Not a single bit.

I decide to flirt back, playing his game:

Me: It might be. Why do you ask?
Mason: Well, I was afraid of what she'd do to me if I didn't text her back after she gave me her number.
Me: Well, you got the right girl. Must be your lucky day!
Mason: Must be, especially since I met you.

I feel my cheeks tightening and I'm certain that I'm blushing, just like back at Hanley's.

While I chose to give Mason my number, Paige can attest that I'm the worst at texting. I could be in the middle of a conversation and then forget to reply for three days. She says it's my only true flaw.

So, the sooner this date is planned, the less I'll have to worry about forgetting to text back. Besides, getting to know someone is easier in person.

> **Me:** So, when's our date?
> **Mason:** You tell me!
> **Me:** How's Friday night?
> **Mason:** Friday works with me.
> **Me:** I'm thinking we should get a drink. Know a place?

What's a better date than getting drinks? It can be intimate, yet still easy to engage in conversation.

> **Mason:** Actually, yes. I do. I can pick you up around 7?
> **Me:** Pick me up? Do you have a car in the city?
> **Mason:** Well, no, but—
> **Me:** That's good, parking would be a nightmare! I'll meet you there instead, just send me the address.

He may be handsome, but I'd rather find my own way to our date. If we don't connect, at least I'll only need to be there for an hour or two, and can head home.

That's the beauty of dating. You meet someone, go on a date and if it doesn't work out, at least you tried.

Mason texts me the address of a hotel and according to my map, it's only a 10-minute walk from the apartment. Hotel bars are definitely fancier, but still provide the same intimacy as any hole-in-the-wall place. *Good choice on his part.*

I glance up at Paige and I can't hide the wide grin on my face.

"It's all set," I beam, attempting to hide my smile.

"How exciting!" she cheers, raising her brows quickly.

As I'm about to put my phone down, I hear one last ding from my phone and it's a text from Mason. Like the start of our texts, it's one sentence:

Mason: I'll be waiting.

Mason

God, why am I so nervous? There isn't a thing I know about this woman, yet it feels like she already has a hold on me.

Is it the thought of seeing her again? Or the possibility of what could be? Because thinking of her makes me feel like I can't breathe and my heart races too fast.

I changed my suit three times and already feel myself sweating through this one as I walk into The Rose Pine—a luxury hotel.

It isn't my first time here. With a company as big as ours, our product is supplied to nearly every hotel, club and restaurant in this city and hundreds of others. When I was shadowing my father, I found that it was best to visit some of the locations we supply to, ensuring the quality. This hotel is one of them.

I don't know what it is about this location specifically though. Maybe the moody atmosphere? Maybe the tall booths that provide you your own space, or help you avoid those around you? But, I come here often and on my own.

She asked to meet me here, but I have ten minutes to spare as I walk through the bright lobby over to the bar. I may have been late for my meeting earlier in the week, but there isn't a chance in hell that I would be late tonight— even by five minutes.

Call me a recluse or just out of luck, but being single has taken its toll on me. It's been three years since my last date and I can barely remember the circumstances of it, let alone what the girl looked like. So maybe that's why the nerves are getting to me tonight.

My parents are so eager for me to find a lifelong partner. They feel that running a business is best conducted with someone by your side.

I, too, desire a partner by my side, truly. Someone to share life with, to fall in love with, and to create a family with, someday. I didn't choose to be single running a multi-million dollar business, but here I am.

Life has its own way of playing its little games with you. So considering the circumstances, there has to be a reason why Lily came up to me at that coffee shop and declared that I was taking her on a date. The same time my parents are pushing for me to settle so badly. I've never believed in fate, but maybe it's the time I start?

I won't jinx myself though. I can't. I may have been looking forward to this date all week, but there's two sides to everything. All I can hope is that she will still be as interested in me as I was the moment I saw her.

I unbutton my suit as I sit down at the bar and raise a finger in the air to get the bartender's attention. John, a bartender that knows me well, gives me a short nod before walking over.

"Hello Mr. Moore. What can I get you tonight?"

He wipes the inside of a wine glass with cloth, then turns around and hangs it under the shelf behind him before facing me.

"Bourbon. Neat," I say, politely smiling.

He nods and turns around, just as I look down the bar. A man and a woman are sitting at the opposite end with two cocktails in front of them. I look around the rest of the room and it's a relatively quiet night for a Friday as the tall booths lay empty around me. Only one closest to the lobby is occupied.

"Here you are sir," I hear as I turn back toward John, who places my glass down on a small napkin in front of me.

I open up my suit jacket and retrieve my wallet from my inside pocket. As I hand a card to him, I say, "Keep my tab open."

He nods again and takes my card from me before replying, "Of course."

I reach for my drink and look down at it. The transparent brown liquid swirling in the glass. The memories of when I drank too much still linger—or at least the ones I can remember. But that's the past, and now, I understand my limits. So, when she invited me for drinks, I wasn't the least bit concerned. For me, I wanted to remember every part of this night.

As I take a sip of my drink, my eyes are distracted as I look over my glass at a figure walking through the lobby. *Her.*

Her dark brown hair is curled, she's dressed in a dark, red dress that hugs her curves paired with black heels.

As I lower my glass, my eyes move back up her body and up to her sweet face. She's smiling gently and her eyes wander as she searches the room around her. One again blissfully unaware that I'm captivated by her.

After a moment, she turns in my direction and makes her way over to the bar. She hasn't spotted me yet, so I watch as she gracefully walks over. Her hips move back and forth under her tight dress and her breasts bounce with every step.

It's impossible to turn away as I adjust myself in my seat, trying to ignore my growing erection—one that I'll have to be forcibly ignoring throughout this date because of her. But fuck if I can help it, one look at her will bring it back throughout the night.

As she draws closer, her eyes shoot up to mine and I see her face brighten, instantly filled with joy at seeing me here.

I turn toward her in my chair as she stops in front of me.

"Is this seat taken?" she playfully asks as the corner of her mouth tilts up. The same first words that she used at that coffee shop.

"Only for you," I reply with a smirk.

She slides into the chair next to me and John walks over, as if just on cue.

"Hello miss, what can I get you tonight?" he asks, placing a small napkin down in front of her.

"Do you have something fruity?"

She raises her eyebrow, pursing her lips as if in thought.

"Yeah we have a few things. Are you looking for something sour or sweet?"

"Erm, I'm not sure," she says, shifting her focus to the table, then up to me. "Maybe—"

She pauses her sentence and furrows her brows at me, and judging by her expression, I must have an unsettling look on my face. One that I didn't realize I was even making until now.

"What?" she teases.

I quickly nod my head and pretend to be unobservant as I claim, "Nothing."

She places her hand on my forearm that's resting on the counter. Her warm touch against my skin makes me throb beneath my pants and I swallow hard, reminding myself I need to reply.

Nervously chuckling I add, "It's just—"

"I know. I know," she says jokingly as she rolls her eyes. "I'm that typical girl that looks for something that's girly, right?"

She pauses to raise her eyebrows, then turns to John as well.

"Right?" she says, directly towards him.

Looking back to me, she frowns and says, "I just don't know what else to order."

I'm taken back by her statement as I raise my eyebrows. If this industry has taught me anything, it's knowing what a good drink is and I sometimes forget that not everyone shares that knowledge.

"May I?" I carefully offer, holding my hand out. She agreeably smiles as she nods her head.

I turn toward John who is still waiting patiently.

"An aviation please."

He nods his head and says, "Good choice sir," before walking away.

A few minutes later, he returns with the drink and placing it on the small napkin in front of her, she appears impressed as she looks at the glass.

"Oh! My favorite color!" she beams as she twirls the cocktail skewer holding the brandied cherry above the purple liquid.

"Purple?" I ask, tilting my head.

"Yes," she nods, then adds with a smile, "If this tastes good, it may very well be my new favorite drink—not for the color alone."

I chuckle deeply as her fingers slide down the sides of the glass onto the stem and she lifts it to her lips. I hold my breath as she takes a sip.

The aviation uses a creme liqueur that we supply, which is why I'm familiar with it, so I'm hoping the floral flavor gives Lily what she's looking for.

Pulling the glass back from her lips, she delightfully says, "That's good." Turning to me, she adds, "That's really good."

I softly scoff and tell her, "I'm glad you like it."

"You know your drinks," she states, raising her brow with a slight smirk on her lips.

"Yeah, I—" I pause, thinking of what to say, "— You could say so."

I nod as I give her a quick smile.

I only know about drinks because of the industry, but I choose to keep that to myself. Better left unsaid.

I've found out that in the past, you can never be too cautious about who to trust. It's surprising how many women have thrown themselves at me as soon as they found out I come from wealth. I don't flaunt it by any means, besides my suit—a necessity in my mind—but when word gets out, it's hard to hide from it.

I don't believe Lily is like that though, but I always have to be careful what I share and with who. But, I'm an optimist. If Lily is anything like I believe she is, then I won't hesitate to spoil her—not to show off my money, but because I want to share what I have with someone who truly matters.

"So, tell me about yourself Mason," she says, taking a quick sip again from her drink. "What do you do for work?"

The dreaded question.

"Marketing," I say, teetering on the truth.

Not a complete lie as we've done our own marketing since the beginning, but it's also not entirely the truth. When I meet people I don't know, this is my easiest go-to answer, not only because it's not far from the truth, but it rarely begs for additional questions.

"Interesting!" she says, appearing curious. "What got you into that?"

I swallow hard, not anticipating her to ask follow-up questions.

"My father," I reply, leaning forward slightly, waiting to see if she'll ask more about it.

"Are you close with him?"

As anticipated, the topic steers away.

I straighten myself up again, clear my throat and then tilt my head back and forth.

"You could say so." Once again, not the entire truth, but hopefully enough to steer the topic away further.

She takes another sip of her drink and then gulps, as if her next question is coming out of her head before her mouth can catch up.

"Do they live near you?"

"Yeah, not too far."

I leisurely take a sip of my drink.

"That's good! And are you from here?"

Pulling my drink away, I smile softly as I lower it back down to the table.

I lick my lips and say, "Yeah, just outside of the city."

She opens her mouth to ask another question, then her eyes quickly grow wide.

"Are you alright?" I ask, frowning.

She takes a quick breath in and says, "Oh my God, I'm talking too much aren't I?"

I chuckle deeply as I shake my head.

"No, not at all."

She scowls as she presses her lips together, as if she doesn't believe me, then looks down at her drink momentarily. When her eyes meet mine again, she has a half smile on her face and she shakes her head.

"I'm sorry, my mouth just keeps going."

I could think of something else it could do.

I adjust in my seat once again, turning slightly toward the bar, which helps me to dismiss "those" thoughts, and think of something else.

I turn my head to look at her and clear my throat.

"I don't mind, I promise."

She raises a brow and I can sense she doesn't believe me.

"Your replies say otherwise."

"In what way?" I scoff, raising a brow back, thinking that was a quick turnaround.

"They all tend to be pretty short answers," she points out, taking another sip of her glass as she keeps her focus on me.

Maybe they are short because I'm a little distracted. Can you blame me?

I shift my body back toward her and rest my leg over the other. Grabbing onto it with my spare hand to keep it in place, I lean forward.

"I'm just not much of a conversationalist."

I lean back into my seat once again as she sets her glass back down on the table and tilts her head to the side. This time, she leans closer.

Through almost a whisper, she says, "You know you could have said no to our date."

I lean forward and whisper back, "And why would I have done that?"

She licks her lips and straightens herself up, holding her head high as she looks off to the side, then back to me.

"Well, people generally give short answers when they aren't interested in someone. You know, if you aren't interested, I could save your time and mine."

She's ridiculous for thinking I'm not interested in her, because my God, I can't even take my eyes off of her. I chuckle in disbelief and she quickly turns to me with wide eyes.

Shaking my head down as a grin grows on my face, I look back up at her.

"You truly are something," I hum quietly, then louder with a smirk I say, "I can promise you, I'm very interested."

She smiles slightly at my reply, then the frown returns to her face.

I take a quick breath, then tell her, "It's just me. I assure you. I'm just not one for words."

Her face softens.

"Yeah, I could see that when we first met," she jokes as she nods in agreement.

"You know, I'd much rather know about you anyways," I say, lifting my drink into the air and raising a brow.

She leans back into her seat, crosses her legs and holds her drink up into the air.

"What do you want to know?" she asks curiously.

"Everything," I smile.

She looks up and away, and the corner of her mouth tips up as if she's thinking.

Trying to make it easier—for her and myself—I go with the first question that pops into my head. Ironically, it's the same one she already asked me.

"What do you do for work?" I ask, taking a sip of my drink.

"I'm unfortunately unemployed at the moment."

I furrow my brows slightly, hearing the sadness behind the words, but the moment she notices my expression, she thinks she needs to explain more —because she quickly continues.

"No, it's not like that. Well it is—kind of," she says with haste as she shakes her head. "It's a long story, but basically I got laid off; I'm a teacher in early childhood development. I got a phone call one day saying I was being termed. I honestly didn't expect it, but it happened. So, I got let go. And now I've been on the hunt for a new job, and honestly, I feel bad for my best friend Paige—who I live with—because she's the only one with a job. Luckily though, we don't pay a lot in rent so it's actually not too horrible, but—"

She catches herself before she's able to say another word and blinks quickly. Frowning as she looks down momentarily, she gazes back up at me.

"Was." She corrects herself. "Was a teacher."

"I'm sorry to hear that."

She takes a deep breath and smiles, trying to cheer herself up. "It's okay."

She purses her lips, and then quickly continues, "I've actually been trying to find another job. So far, no luck, but—"

I chuckle as she continues and the corner of my mouth tips up. Her slight rambling is not only adorable, but I'd happily let her talk all night if she wanted to and I wouldn't mind one bit.

And I did just that. I let her talk.

As the night carried on, she was so eager to talk and I was just as eager to listen. And to make sure that nothing —including myself—would ruin the night, I carefully watched how many drinks I had.

I'm not much for words, and some would even call me an introvert, but for her, I think I'd do anything.

I only spoke a few sentences at the start of the night, mainly just to let her know I was listening, but she didn't seem to mind. I was happy to hear every word she spoke, and every story she told me was intriguing.

As I sat there though, I felt myself engaging more in her stories, sharing my thoughts, and despite the lack of drinks in me, I could no longer remain quiet and the only explanation for that was *her*.

I feel like I already know this woman and she will be the one to break down the walls I built so high, the one to pull me out of my shell, the one I can be my true self around. *And I can't wait for that moment.*

Chapter Seven

Lily

Three hours, four drinks and feeling like this man now knows everything about me and all I want to do is leave.

But not on my own.

He didn't seem like the type to say yes at first, considering he's more reserved than I'll ever be, but by the end of the night, when I asked him if he'd like to come back to my place, he quickly agreed.

"Can I get the check please?" I ask, getting the attention of the bartender as I reach for my clutch on the chair next to me.

"Don't worry," he tells me. "I've got it."

I furrow my brows, but it's masked by my hair, as I keep my attention turned down, attempting to open my clutch to quickly grab my card.

I asked him on this date, so it's only right that I pay for myself too.

"No, I can't have you pay for my drinks. I've had twice the amount you did," I insist, looking up at him.

"Please. Let me," he offers, stopping me as he reaches for my hand.

I look down at his hand, nearly covering mine. His palms are soft and his hand is warm. Even though we've talked for hours, this is the first moment that he's touched me and it instantly sends heat between my legs. Suddenly, I feel the urge to leave sooner, and I choose to let the discussion go. *Not this time, Lily.*

"Okay," I agree, thanking him with a smile.

"Okay," he smiles. He lets go of my hand and turns toward the bartender and says, "We can close my tab. Thank you."

The bartender quickly retrieves his card from behind the counter and hands it to Mason, who tucks it into his suit.

As Mason stands up, he buttons his jacket and holds his hand out, raising his eyebrows. I smile as I grab his hand and pull myself out of the chair.

"Lead the way," he says, gesturing toward the lobby.

It's a brighter night out as a full moon looms in the sky and as we walk back to my apartment, his hand stays in mine the entire way.

Despite the drinks, I stay relatively quiet. Maybe it's because I've already talked his head off at the bar? Or maybe it's the anticipation of what's coming soon?

As we walk through my apartment door, I sit down on the small bench by it and immediately start unstrapping my heels. Mason walks in after me and closes the door behind him.

Paige doesn't spend many nights at her mom's apartment, but she had told me earlier in the day that she was. If she was here, I wouldn't have invited him back.

"Well, this is it," I say, blowing my hair out of my face as I look up at him. "It's small, but we love it."

"It's—" he pauses, looking around my dimly-lit apartment. "Nice." He nods as he smiles down at me.

I slip off both of my unstrapped shoes and slide them under the bench.

It's already moody in my apartment as I stand up with a smile before turning toward the living room.

As I take a step forward holding my arm out, I say, "I can show you—"

Before I can finish, I lose my breath as I feel his hand grab ahold of my wrist and with one swift pull, I'm turned around facing him. His other hand wraps behind me and lingers just above my ass as he pulls me closer to him.

I don't even have a moment to look up at his face before his lips are on mine, engulfing me in his delectable flavor.

I didn't expect it, but his lips taste smoky. Not the disgusting smoky taste of cigarettes or weed. *No.* The taste of his mouth is sweet and toasty, like a marshmallow you roast over a campfire. I know it's from the bourbon he was drinking and as common as bourbon is, I can't get enough of it on him.

Reaching up onto the tips of my toes and pressing my breasts against his chest, I dive deeper into his kiss. Wrapping my arms around his neck, I push my tongue slowly into his mouth to get more of his addictive flavor.

As our tongues wrap around one another between momentary breaths, I can feel the heat between my legs rise again. An ache that was growing back at the bar that will soon be uncontrollable, but I have to wait for him. Wait for his move to—*fuck.*

His hand slides down over my ass and he assertively grabs it, sending me the signal I need. I position my lips around the bottom of his mouth and as I pull away, I suck on his lip. *Hard.*

With my face now inches from his, I finally see his eyes in this dim light. They are vibrantly blue even as his brows shadow over them.

I playfully smirk at him, and by some inaudible signal, we distance ourselves by a foot and immediately start removing our clothes. *As. Quickly. As. Possible.*

As I unzip my dress, he removes his jacket and reaches for his tie, but before he can fully remove it, my red dress is on the floor, wrapped around my ankles.

I'm nearly naked as I stand in front of him in my matching black lace set. Biting my lip, his fingers slowly stop fidgeting with his tie and he directs his eyes to my lips. The corner of his mouth tips up and as if I've given him permission, I watch as his eyes drop down to my chest.

"You looked so beautiful in that dress," he says, as his eyes gaze slowly down my body and back up to my eyes. He cocks his head and with a mischievous smile he adds, "But you're even sexier without it."

I feel my cheeks blush and before he can make the next move, I grab him by his tie and tug him toward my bedroom.

"This way, first timer," I wink. A slight nod to what I called him at the coffee shop.

His voice drops and he says, "Not for this."

Entering through my bedroom door, I smile as I look down at my neatly made bed, thankful that I finally cleaned my room up. I wasn't entirely expecting to bring him back here, but I definitely wasn't going to risk it being messy. Who knows what he'd think of me if he saw that?

Letting go of his tie, I turn around and sit on the edge of my bed, placing my hands on the side of me. I watch as his eyes fall down to me again and I teasingly smile as I cross my legs, eager to watch him finish undressing.

He playfully smirks back and I see the dimple on his cheek appear. I don't know what it is about dimples, but they can make a man a thousand times sexier and I will die on that hill. I mean seriously, who can blame me?

He loosens his tie more and pulls the end out from the loop, before dropping it to the ground. He's quick to unbutton his shirt and as it's halfway removed, I get a glimpse of his chest.

There isn't much hair, but it's enough that I anticipate my fingers being able to slide through it in hopefully a few moments.

Undoing the last button, he slides his shirt off and it drops to the floor. I don't know why, but I pictured him having a six-pack and powerful biceps. Probably due to the one too many rom-coms I've been binging lately. However, he's still in outstanding shape. He is quite lean, and while his stomach isn't a six-pack, it's toned and I'm still immensely attracted to his body.

I bring my eyes back up to his and they are still just as vibrantly blue—even under the weak lighting in my bedroom. I lean slightly forward, pressing my breasts together as I tighten my arms on my side. I watch as he clenches his jaw and his Adam's apple rises and falls as he swallows.

With a single suggestive look with a raised brow, I tempt him to come closer. I want to feel the warmth of his body over me; his hands touching every part of me. I want to feel him deep inside me. Playing out every thought that raced through my head on the walk over here, finally coming to life.

The corner of his mouth lifts and as I had hoped, he obeys.

Taking a step forward, he places his hands on the edge of the bed and leans over me. Our eyes are fixed as our bodies hover within inches of one another.

As his face hangs over mine, I feel the intense energy between us. An immense fervor already generating as our bodies prepare for the inevitable.

I stick my chin out slightly and our lips nearly touch once again. Suspended in the air as we wait for a trigger to release us. The tension builds with every second until suddenly a muted gasp escapes my lips and the silence breaks.

His hand slips behind my neck as his lips press against mine. The restraint I thought I could hold onto takes over as I'm consumed by the sweet flavor in his mouth, and I'm unable to contain the muted moan I hoped to keep to myself.

I feel him kick his shoes off as a thud echoes against the floor. My fingers force themselves off the edge of the bed and immediately get to work on his belt, unbuckling it as quickly as I had removed my dress only minutes before.

The zipper on his pants effortlessly slides its way down and my hand brushes over the throbbing bulge beneath it, and the thought only heightens the growing desire that builds inside of me between bated breaths.

I quickly grab the top of his pants and pull them down, bringing everything with it. I'm unable to get a glimpse, but feel his erection whip out of his pants as they fall to the floor and I'm nearly breathless by the thought.

Grabbing a hold of the back of his neck, I pull him down on top of me. His weight pressing against my half-naked body as my head is engulfed by the surrounding covers.

He quickly positions himself over me as he balances on one elbow. He slides his other hand out from behind my neck and moves it slowly down until he's cupping my breast. His fingers dance across the lacy fabric and his thumb finds its way to my nipple, hiding underneath. He brushes it gently and the sensation sends a shiver all the way to my toes, which I irresistibly curl and I press my chest up, aching for me.

As he brings his hand slowly down to my stomach, the pleasure throughout my body increases and I'm tickled by the tips of his fingers, making my body tremble beneath him. His hand reaches down further, and I feel his finger inch its way beneath the fabric.

My heart is pounding out of my chest as he inches closer to the spot where my body is radiating the most heat. Slowly, he slides in his two fingers and pushes them deeply in until his knuckles rub over my bundle of nerves. My breath shudders and my head falls back, nearly breaking our lips apart. I can't help but tighten my eyes as he moves them around, prompting me to only kiss him more intensely and my nails to dig into his neck.

The swirling of his fingers within me builds the wetness between my legs with every motion, creating a pool of moisture that rests in his palm. My hands release his neck and move down the sides of his body until they are on his hips. I move a hand down further, wrapping my fingers around him and feel his immense stature—all I want is for him to be inside me.

As if he can hear my thoughts, he carefully slides his fingers out from within me, my arousal dripping from them as he drags the side of my underwear past my hips, pulling them down. When they reach my calves, I carefully, and reluctantly, kick them off and onto the floor.

I scoot myself slowly up the bed, our lips never parting, as Mason follows. I widen my legs, allowing him to position himself between them and his chest presses against my breasts as he balances his weight on both of his elbows.

Pushing my hips up, I feel his erection brush against the inside of my thighs and a chill runs through my spine. I take a deep breath with anticipation, thinking of him pulsing inside me, hitting every delirious spot until my body reels with pleasure, but he abruptly pulls away from our kiss.

He raises an eyebrow as he looks down at me.

"Are you—" he starts, but I interrupt him before he can finish.

"Yeah, don't worry," I assure him, knowing where his question will lead, but also not wanting him to pause a second longer.

"Okay good."

He leans down and places a single peck on my lips before pulling back slightly. I can feel his warm breath against my chin as he holds his position above me.

Grabbing a hold of himself while shifting his weight onto the other arm, he slowly presses the head against my entrance. I feel my heartbeat pulsating through me and my body bracing with anticipation as he holds himself in place between my legs.

Lowering himself on top of me, his lips make their way back to mine. He kisses me calmly and with intention, as if to savor the moment, but all I can think about is the fire building between us.

Slowly, I feel him ease his way inside me and I hear him let out a slow, exhaled, breathy moan. I squeeze my eyes shut and slowly inhale as he pushes deeper, surprised by his girth as he stretches me.

Suddenly, the gentle kisses start to deepen and turn more passionate, leaving me breathless with every press of his lips to my skin. Before I even realize it's happening, he pushes all the way to the hilt, instinctively forcing a moan out of me as he fills me.

Wanting more, I let my spine curve and feel him deepen himself, my grip tightening on the covers beneath me as my neck arches back, breaking our lips apart. Without hesitation, he brings his lips slowly down my neck and the kisses send delectable tingles through every part of me all the way down to my fingers and toes. Tiny, little pieces of pleasure that make my heartbeat fasten and intensify with each passing moment.

But now, all I want is for his lips to be back on mine and for him to consume me. For me to taste him again as his delicious tongue swirls inside of my mouth, possessing every inch of it.

I grab the back of his neck and pull him deeply back into a kiss, savoring his flavor that's already becoming a craving—a high I don't want to fall from. His hair is soft against my fingertips and as we move against the bed, the soft sensation only heightens what the rest of my body is starting to feel.

Thrusting my hips, I wrap my legs up and around his back, pulling him in deeper. His breath shudders between us and as he rolls his hips, his movement fastens, but remains steady. I'm immensely hot and sweaty, but I ignore it, focusing just on us. The two of us dancing in this delectable act.

Bit by bit, he rapidly hits all the right spots, sending beautiful chills straight down to my bundle of nerves and with every movement, I wait for the gratification that will soon come for both of us.

Our breathing quickens, I can feel his erection throbbing, his body jerking, my toes starting to curl beneath me, and I start to tremble by the waves of force. My head starts to spin as my focus shifts from skillful concentration to monumental passion and my body finally contracts around him, unable to hold it in.

I'm overcome with gratification, as my body blissfully releases itself. I cry out in pleasure, my eyes rolling to the back of my head and my legs shaking over him. It isn't a second more that he follows, lowering his head onto my shoulder as his body tenses. I hear a deep grunt echo from his throat and he thrusts his hips forward before letting out a few remaining pushes until it becomes overwhelmingly intense for us both.

Everything is ringing around me and I barely realize his forehead now resting against mine as I smack my lips together, feeling the dryness in my mouth and nearly breathless from the thrilling release. The distant noises of outside slowly resurface and I'm soon able to hear the mixture of our shallow breathing, breaking the silence in the room. I keep my eyes shut, but we take slow, meticulous breaths to calm ourselves, slowly making our way down from the high after what felt like a marathon.

When our bodies finally ease into relaxation, I lower my legs and he pulls his head back while carefully pulling himself out of me, and rolling next to me on the bed. I blink quickly as I open my eyes and calmly turn to him, seeing his stark blue eyes staring back at me with a soft smile.

"Want to stay the night?" I whisper, smiling shyly.

He takes a short breath in and as he lets it out, he smiles back.

"I'd love to."

He leans over and gives me a quick peck on the lips and I let out a soft chuckle.

"What?" he asks curiously.

"Nothing."

I try to contain my grin before leaning over to kiss him again. *It isn't nothing though.*

One-night stands are a means to satisfy a need. To fulfill a craving. If you actively go out and search for someone to have sex with, then you'll find someone pretty easily—or at least that's how it's generally been for me.

But I don't love one-night stands, I actually hate them. Is there anyone that realistically likes them? It's not intimate, nor is it meaningful since the person is a stranger.

Each time, you can always hope that it'll be different. In this world, how often do you meet someone that you have incredible chemistry with, and the sex is great? Unfortunately, not often in my book.

I want more than just one date, one night and one morning after, but if the cards don't stack up, then there it is again – another one-night stand.

However, this time feels different. *Good different.*

I didn't expect it, but he's already like a drug—a craving I don't want to lose and one I'm desperate to keep.

This time doesn't feel like just another night that I'll forget about. Another night that'll stay in the past. Another night that I won't have to look back on.

No, not even close.

Chapter Eight

Lily

I hear a quiet vibration in my head, one that persists and refuses to fade. Asleep, I thought it was a dream, but as my body starts to bring itself to wakefulness, I realize that isn't the case.

The sound grows louder and louder until I feel myself drifting back into consciousness as the vibration turns into a distinct ringing.

Blinking as I adjust to the light coming through the window, I quickly realize that it's morning. I don't even remember falling asleep, let alone when it happened.

Pulling my hair out of my face, I shake my head in an attempt to stir myself awake. My eyes grow wide and with two more slow, meticulous blinks, the blur of the room finally sharpens into focus.

I search around for the ringing sound and I'm pleasantly welcomed by the sight of Mason sleeping soundly next to me. I had almost forgotten he had stayed the night, and a rush of memories flood my mind.

What I thought would be us closing our eyes and drifting off to sleep turned into hours of kissing and rambling about God knows what until just before dawn. It was an experience unlike any I'd ever had and surely far from what I expected.

He's handsome—even while sleeping—and the image of him wearing a suit from the night before is quickly replaced by this image of him. Messy hair, five o'clock shadow, and his shirtless body next to me.

I quickly shake my head and focus back on the problem at hand: A ringing phone. I push myself up from the bed and look around the room. The ringing is muffled and I remember that my phone is still in my clutch by the front door which—I realize—would be too far away for me to hear.

As I pull the sheet off, I stand up and walk over to my closet, grabbing a pair of gray sweatpants from the top drawer and sliding them on. I walk toward my open bedroom door and as I reach it, the ringing grows further from me. *Definitely not my phone.*

Turning back around, I crouch down to the ground and wait for another ring to come. When I hear it, I quickly get onto my hands and knees, listening to the sound grow louder as I make my way towards the end of the bed.

Reaching the edge, I crawl over Mason's jacket and shirt, I see his pants partially hidden under my bed and the muffled ringing coming from that direction. I rest my elbows on the floor and lean under my bed to pull his pants out, my back arched and my ass raised.

"Well, isn't this a good morning already?" I hear from above me, as Mason lets out a deep chuckle.

The sound jolts my body up into the bed frame, sending a throbbing pain to the back of my head.

"Ow!" I yelp, grabbing his pants as I pull myself out from under the bed.

"Oh, shit!" Mason curses, quickly pulling himself to the end of the bed as I sit up on the floor, holding the back of my head.

"Are you okay?" he asks, putting his hand over mine.

I look up at him and his messy hair falls over his face slightly. He just woke up, but he doesn't have that 'I just woke up' look by any means. *Lucky him.*

As for me, I can't even imagine what I look like right now. Some smudged makeup and messy hair surely.

I shrug my shoulders and then chuckle, "I'm probably dying."

The dimple on his cheek appears as he smiles quickly before he leans closely over me.

"Let me see," he commands and I can sense the concern in his voice.

He removes my hand from my head, and I lean my neck forward so he can see where I bumped myself. His fingers move through my hair as he assesses the damage.

"No bleeding luckily," he confirms, moving his hand away as I straighten myself back up.

"That's a relief," I chuckle.

He furrows his eyebrows and asks, "What were you doing under your bed anyways?"

I blink quickly and then look down at his pants that I'm holding over my arm, then look back at him.

"You know, it's where I do my best thinking," I sarcastically boast as I rub the back of my head and raise my eyebrows. "But, I won't be able to concentrate now."

He laughs momentarily as I put my hand into the pocket of his pants and pull out his phone, resisting the urge to look at it.

"Actually, your phone was ringing and it woke me up," I admit, turning back to him as I hand him his phone.

He looks down at it and scowls.

"Sorry about that," he frowns. "Looks like I missed three calls."

I push myself off the ground and take a step forward. His eyes look up from his phone and glance at my half-naked body in front of him.

"So, are you going to call back or—" I flirtatiously ask, as I wrap my arms around his neck.

He brings his eyes up to mine and before the smile spreads on his face, I quickly lean over and plant a quick kiss on his lips. As I pull away, I wink at him as I playfully tilt my head.

"No, he can wait," he says, quickly setting his phone on the edge of the bed and wrapping his arms around my waist, pulling my body between his legs.

I lean in again and press my lips deeply into his. He no longer tastes smoky, but surprisingly, he doesn't taste like stale morning breath either. *Damn, how lucky is this guy?*

As his tongue swirls in my mouth, a surge of emotions flow through me as I match his rhythm. I pull one knee up and over his leg and rest it on the edge of the bed, preparing to straddle him, and then the ringing of his phone parts our lips.

He quickly looks down at it then back at me, shaking his head.

"I'll get it later," he says, releasing my waist to quickly click the side of his phone to end the ringing. "There's something more dire to take care of right here."

Wrapping his arms back around me, he grabs a handful of my ass and I squeal as he pulls me up onto his lap with one swift pull.

He moves one of his hands slowly up my back as his eyes land on mine and as it reaches my neck, he pulls me in close. Capturing my lips with his, I can feel the pool of moisture soaking my panties and his growing bulge pressing against the fabric that separates us. *Why did I even put on pants honestly?*

I lean closer, pressing my breasts against his chest hoping to push him backward onto the bed, when a ringing from his phone interrupts us yet again. *Are you kidding me?*

We both let out an exasperated groan as I pull myself off of his lap and stand as I withdraw my arms from around his neck.

"I think you should answer it this time," I chuckle.

He takes a deep breath.

"Do I have to?" he asks, raising a brow.

Wriggling my hips, I slowly step back, pressing my breasts together between my arms as I lean forward and our eyes stay focused on one another.

"Only if you don't want any more interruptions."

He pulls his hand down his face, his eyes scanning my body, and he lets his mouth hang open as he releases his hand. His eyes narrow, as if to weigh his options, but finally with a huff, he says, "Okay, but I'll be quick."

Taking a deep breath, he grabs his phone as he stands up from the edge of the bed and takes a step closer to me. Towering over me, I watch his chest rise and fall between us before he gives me a quick kiss.

He adjusts himself, trying to hide the growing surprise I'm already fully aware of, and he answers the phone as he walks out of my room but stays in my line of sight.

"What's so important that you have to call—" he immediately snaps, looking down at his phone momentarily before putting it back up to his ears, "—four times?"

Judging by the tone of his voice, it doesn't sound like a work call, or at least that's not how I would talk to my boss—if I still had my job. However, who would seriously call so early in the morning on a Saturday? And four times for that matter?

As he listens to the caller speaking, I sit on the edge of the bed and look down at my breasts. I adjust my bra, pushing my breasts up in the cups, then look back up at him.

He's scowling toward the living room window and his arm is crossed over the other holding the phone. I can't help but wonder what the conversation is about, but I'm too preoccupied staring at the more important things: his strong and toned arms; his slightly curly chest hair leading down to a happy trail just above his belt line; and his blonde hair that I already plan to mess up when I get the chance to run my fingers through it. *It needs a bit of messiness in the morning.*

He slightly turns with his back facing me and I see a defined line going down his spine. My eyes move back to his rugged shoulders and I have to forcibly cross my legs, trying to suppress the tingling sensation spreading straight to my core.

I never got a full glimpse of his naked or—for that matter—semi-naked body last night, but everything I see now is pleasing to the eye. Maybe a little too pleasing as this image will now be stuck in my head once he leaves. That is, *when* he leaves.

"I'm leaving now," he firmly huffs over the phone.

Well, there goes my hopes.

"I'll try to be there as soon as I can," he groans, before hanging up.

I take a deep breath as he makes his way back into the room.

"You're leaving?" I ask, feeling my forehead wrinkle.

I quickly stand up from the bed and walk over to my closet.

"Unfortunately," he sighs as he clicks his tongue.

As I grab a t-shirt and walk back out, he's sitting on the edge of the bed pulling on his pants.

"There was a last minute meeting that I need to go to," he says, standing to pull his pants up to his hips.

"On a Saturday?" I scowl.

"Yeah, unfortunately," he says, buttoning his pants.

"Ah, so it was a work call then?" I ask, trying to confirm my suspicions.

"Actually, no."

He grabs his shirt off the floor and puts one arm through the sleeve.

"It was my younger brother, Miles and he—"

Miles. I've only met one person with that name before and that was back in college. He was always so fun to be around. A good friend at the time, until he suddenly disappeared. Rather fast for that matter too. I think maybe he switched schools, but I'm not sure.

He also was big into his bourbon and dressed sharply. *Like Mason.* And had dirty blonde hair. *Like Mason.* And his last name was—

"Wait," I say, interrupting him. "You said, Miles?"

"Yeah, my brother," Mason says, looking around the floor of my bed for something.

"Your brother is Miles Moore?" I repeat, trying to confirm how he knows him. And praying he isn't who I think he is.

"Yes, why?" he hesitates, raising an eyebrow as he walks over to his shoes on the floor.

I quickly throw my shirt over my head and cross my arms as I ask, "Blonde hair? Good dancer?"

Sitting back down on the edge of the bed, he slides one shoe on, then the other and scoffs.

"I mean yes, but I'd say I'm the better dancer between the two of us."

Fuck. If there's anything I remember about that night when I last saw Miles, it was my run in with a particular person. Fuzzy memories to say the least, but I would have recognized him, right?

I anxiously look up and down at Mason. Did I seriously just sleep with that dick from six years ago? The one that was so smug, thinking I would just fall to my knees for him. *No, it can't be.* Mason is different. He's kind and sweet. It can't possibly be him.

I look up at his face and as I glance back and forth at his eyes, I suddenly recognize the man from my past. The same familiar features that I somehow failed to notice. The very man I swore would never touch me again, even with a ten-foot pole. *How could I have missed it?*

"Is this a joke? Are you trying to mess with me?" I nervously chuckle, turning my head to the side.

It has to be some prank. Right? *Please say yes.*

"What? No," he insists, standing up quickly as he holds his hands out in front of him. He takes a step toward me, but I take a step back.

"How do you know him?" he asks, raising a brow.

"This is unbelievable," I say, rubbing my head as I start to pace back and forth in a panic. "I can't believe I seriously fell for your act."

I stop and turn to him for a moment.

"You really played the part perfectly, didn't you?" I snap, hearing my voice crack slightly.

When his eyes meet mine, I quickly stare down at the ground, not wanting to give him the satisfaction of having my attention.

I can't believe he's acting like he didn't have this all planned out. I knew he looked familiar at Hanley's, even his last name, but how could I not see who he really was? How could I not see through those blue eyes and remember that man from before?

"I have no idea what you're talking about," he argues, stepping forward and grabbing the sides of my arms. "Tell me what you think is going on."

Of course he's going to act like he doesn't know what I'm talking about. That's what they always do—every asshole who's come my way. *Always playing games.*

My eyes finally lift from the floor as I turn to face him, scowling.

"Don't play dumb," I fume, my lips forming into a thin line. "You knew I didn't fall for that asshole version of you back at the club and when I didn't recognize you at Hanley's, you thought you'd finally get a chance."

I nudge my shoulders, brushing his hands off of my arms and they fall to his side. He wrinkles his forehead and immediately takes a step back, aware now that I don't want him touching me.

I give him a thin smile as I snicker and say, "Well, congratulations. You got what you wanted."

"The club? What club?" he frantically asks, scratching his head as he holds his other hand out.

"The club from six years ago when you dragged Miles out," I shout. "You were at his house when I dropped off his phone."

Mason furrows his brows and looks down at the ground.

I sarcastically add, "Ring a bell?"

After a second, he looks back up at me with pressed brows. "Wait, that was you?"

He sounds doubtful, but I know it's a lie and he hasn't actually forgotten who I am. It's all been a game to him as he's toyed with my emotions. Making me think he's this amazing guy, just for him to come out and say he got me. *Oh, you got me good Mason.*

"You need to leave," I firmly demand as I cross my arms and take a step away from him, distancing myself even more.

"I honestly had no idea," he mumbles, shaking his head. "Let me try to explain."

I see the slight sorrow behind his eyes—or maybe regret, but it doesn't matter to me, not any more. I don't want to hear anything else he has to say. All I want is for him to leave.

"You've done enough," I warn, turning away from him, as I focus on another area of my room to distract myself.

I feel his eyes on me, but I can't look at him. The regret and disgust I feel is already overwhelming.

He takes a deep breath before I hear his shoes against the ground as he turns around. Out of the corner of my eye, I see him walk to the side of my bed and grab his jacket off of the floor before facing me again.

He opens his mouth, but quickly shakes his head, choosing not to say anything before exiting my room. Then as I hear the front door close, I let out a sigh of relief; happy that he's gone.

Another game of deception and lies—one that I never realized had even started. At least now, the game is over, yet he played his game and won.

Chapter Nine

Mason

Well, fuck.

How unbelievable that of all the women in this city, I happen to find one who I've already met? And in less than ideal circumstances.

This is just great.

Just when I thought I found someone that I truly connected with and I was actually doing well at keeping my mouth shut, the old me fucked it up.

I thank the taxi driver and hand him a twenty before walking through the revolving doors of the building. I quickly check my watch as I take a deep breath, then nod with a thin smile to the lobby attendant who nods back as I walk toward the elevator.

I wait for it to arrive and look at my reflection staring back at me on the polished doors.

I look like a disheveled mess. Of course I do. How else would someone react to news like this? And it doesn't help that someone scheduled a meeting without my knowledge. *What else can go wrong?*

I run my hand through my hair, fixing the small pieces that are still sticking up from this morning, then straighten my jacket.

Trying to make myself somewhat presentable, I glance up at my eyes in the reflection. The whites of them are partially red and I also have a five o'clock shadow.

Clenching my jaw, I take a deep breath and try to collect myself, but quickly shake my head. *Nope.*

I was hoping I'd find some way to ease this new pain, but nothing works. I look like shit, and I feel that way too.

How badly did I fuck this up?

Every conversation, every kiss, every part of her body that I touched just felt *right.* Could I have fucked it all up so badly in my past that she'll never talk to me again? That I'll never get to see her beautiful smile or hear her voice again? *No, I can't let it be.*

I blink quickly as the elevator doors open and I step inside. Clicking the button for the 37th floor, I glance up and the mirror on the ceiling shows my reflection again, but this time all I see is the asshole I once knew. I scowl at his face, with that smug smile, then quickly force myself to look down.

Six years ago, I was a mess. I was drinking, acting out and pretending that nothing else in the world mattered —except for me and my desires. I didn't have any regard for the repercussions that came with the way I acted, and it was a personal lifestyle that I regret. But that's not me—well it was, but not anymore.

That's the person I buried three years ago. I made the decision to prove to myself that I was better than that and I did. *Now, if only Lily could see that.*

The elevators open and I pause before stepping out, placing my hands into both of my front pockets. *Hold up.*

I quickly dig around my pockets, feeling only emptiness surrounded by expensive fabric. Pulling my hand out, I grab my back pocket and I can instantly feel the hard outline of my wallet. But, that's all. Just my wallet. One last check in my jacket pockets, and still nothing. *Where's my phone?*

Before I can retrace my steps in my head, I hear the elevator doors moving. My eyes shoot open and I throw my arm forward to stop them from closing. *I'll figure it out later.*

I step out onto the floor and make my way down the wide hallway. As I reach for the doorknob to my office, a hand pulls at my shoulder and forcibly turns me around.

"Hey man," Miles sighs, patting my shoulder. "Sorry about all the calls," he pauses, clicking his tongue before shaking his head. "But they just left."

I rub the back of my neck, stretching it toward the ceiling as my chin tips up, feeling the tension quickly build.

"Shit," I curse under my breath before rolling my head back to Miles.

"Yeah, didn't mean to blow up your phone. I guess nobody knew they were coming."

Whether the meeting was planned or not, it wouldn't have made a difference in how this morning had gone. Well, I guess Miles wouldn't have called me, but the truth would have eventually come out. Either today as it did or later.

I look down at the doorknob resting in my hand and then look back at Miles.

"Do you know what the meeting was about?"

"Not a clue," Miles frowns. "Sorry."

I pat him on the shoulder and give him a thin smile.

"Well thank you for trying to give me a heads up."

"Not a problem."

As he gives me a reassuring smile, I feel my stomach drop as I'm reminded of how cruelly I used to treat him. How much my actions hurt those I loved. I really wish I could take it all back.

I open my mouth to ask him about Lily, but decide to keep it to myself. He would give me advice and if he did, it'd be on a girl he knew six years ago. I know her now, but to him, she's just a distant memory, just like I was in her mind.

"Good luck in there," he adds, before I turn and open the door to the office.

My office is brightly lit by the morning sun through the tall, large windows that overlook the city. It contrasts with the dark ambiance that the rest of my office gives off. The wall adjacent to the door has shelving filled with books, knick knacks and a plant that my mother insisted I keep. My wood desk sits in front of that and closer to the door are several chairs, in autumn-colored shades. Lastly, there are two couches, one of which my mother and father are sitting on.

"Hi honey," my mother greets me with a soft smile.

The corner of my mouth lifts, almost forming a smile, but it never appears as I turn to my father, who has a blank expression on his face.

"Son, where's your tie?" he demands with a scowl. "You should always wear a tie if you plan to wear a suit."

I look down at my shirt, which is buttoned almost to the top, only to realize I am, indeed, missing a tie. I hadn't even noticed—but of course, my father did. I shake my head and decide to ignore his comment because there's more pressing issues at hand.

"Do you want to explain to me why I wasn't aware of this meeting today?" I casually ask, unbuttoning my jacket as I walk around the chair closest to me and sit.

My father holds his head up as I rest my arms on each side of the chair.

"The meeting didn't involve you," he says sternly. "The Bombardis flew in and had a proposal for us so we set up a meeting with them."

"The Bombardis?" I growl, quickly clenching my jaw to contain my anger.

I rub my hand across my face and feel my nostrils flare beneath it, and take a deep breath to try to control my voice level.

"I'm in charge of this company now and I'm handling that deal." I quickly stand up to scowl down at my father. "How does this not involve me?"

"Sit down, son," he demands, waving his hand downward.

I feel my shoulders tensing up and squeeze my hands into a fist against the side of my body.

"You know I can handle this," I snap.

"It's not like that honey," my mother reassures calmly.

I glance over at her sitting on the couch and slowly unfist my hands, recognizing my temper is upsetting her.

"Then why are you setting up meetings behind my back?" I ask through gritted teeth, trying to steady my breathing.

"It wasn't business-related," my father claims, looking at my mother quickly and then back at me.

I look over at my desk—still as neat as I had left it, and rub my forehead. Looking at my parents from beneath my brows, I take a deep breath as I take a step over to it, hoping the distance will calm me.

Turning around as I reach the front of my desk, I argue, "If it wasn't business-related, then why did Miles call me so many times?"

I drop my hand from my forehead and furrow my brows as I see my mother chuckle quietly through a smile. My father turns to her and catches the end of her smile as it fades away, then looks back at me with a frown.

"Miles isn't involved in the business," he insists.

I put my arms out in front of me. "So it *was* business-related?"

"No," my father says sternly, as his forehead wrinkles. "It's none of your concern at the moment."

"None of my concern?" I sneer as I cross my arms in front of me. I scoff and reiterate, "So a meeting with the Bombardis—our soon-to-be partner—is none of my business?"

"You'll understand soon," he says with a nod as he turns to my mother and carefully places his hand on her knee.

"Seriously?" I snap, unwrapping my arms and pushing myself forward.

My father ignores me and then quickly straightens himself up on the couch as my mother grabs ahold of his hand. They look over at me and I take a step closer, leaning forward to look directly at them.

"Well?" I ask, raising my brows.

"Speaking of business, you need to go to Italy next weekend," he bluntly states.

"Are you kidding me?" I laugh, rubbing my hand over my chin as I turn away from them.

I don't understand the urgent need for me to go there now when we've been able to handle everything from overseas. Why? Why does it have to be now? Especially when I'm in the middle of figuring out how to win Lily back—if that's even possible.

"Yes," he commands. "You are the face of this company now, and you need to get to know the people we are doing business with. Learn about them and their culture."

I furrow my brows, as I turn back to face them.

Rolling my eyes as I shake my head, I say, "I don't think learning about their culture will be the deciding factor in getting this deal."

"It won't, but we have a plan in place. Just trust us," my father pleads, as the corner of his mouth rises momentarily. Possibly even a grin. Something I seldom see from him.

Trust them? When they went behind my back to have this meeting in the first place?

I stare down at the floor with a scowl, then slowly look back up at my mother, who tilts her head. I inhale slowly, then find it in me to smile at her.

"Sure," I lie. "I'll try."

My mother grins widely as she stands up and walks over to hug me.

"Honey, you're doing great with the business," she says, embracing me. "We know you are."

"Thanks, Mom," I say, letting out a sigh. She may think so, but I'm certain my father doesn't.

My mother pulls away and follows my father, who is already waiting at the open door.

"Enjoy your time in Italy," he says, grabbing my mother's hand as they walk out of my office.

I stare at the closed door, then click my tongue as I turn to walk around my desk. As I sit down, I lean my head back in the chair and stare up at the ceiling.

I don't know what my parents are up to, but that's the least of my worries. *At least for now.*

We've been looking to expand into Europe for quite some time as well as grow our customer base in the European market. The high tariff on spirits being exported to Europe is the reason we chose a company we knew is just as established as we are; someone that understands how the industry has changed over the last century, but is still able to produce our products with the same high-quality ingredients—if not better.

To guarantee the Bombardis become our European distributor, it's vital that I do whatever is necessary to get on their good side, especially after missing this meeting. *Well, that's what I'm going to keep telling myself anyways.*

So, for the sake of our company, I'll be headed to Italy next weekend. In addition—as my father says—I damn well better make certain that I win them over. *Learning their culture.*

I lean forward and glance over at the books on the shelves. I've only read a handful of them and the rest sit there waiting to collect dust for God knows how long because in this business, I'll never have time.

I sigh, then look down at my desk as I open the top drawer. Pulling out a thin binder, I stare down at the unfinished business proposal in front of me. The one I created for the Bombardi Family to sign.

I turn to the fourth page in the binder and see the incomplete sentence I last wrote. I pick up my pen off the desk and press it against the page. Licking my lips, I scowl down at the paper thinking, but my pen stays in place.

Fuck.

I quickly lay my pen down onto the desk and close the binder shut as I shove it back into my desk drawer.

If I want to guarantee that everything is running smoothly with *my* company, I'm going to have to seal the deal next weekend, which means I'm going to need this proposal done by then. *It has to be.*

I glance over at the large window and hear the subtle ticking of the clock on my bookshelf.

How can I? Will it even be possible for me to think about business when she'll be at the front of my mind?

Placing my hands on the edge of the desk, I push myself away and walk over to the window. I rest my forehead against the warm glass and stare down at the cars slowly moving down the street below.

I know I fucked up. There's only myself to blame, but can I even rectify it? Can she look past the former version of myself that disrespected her so much?

I didn't recognize her at the coffee shop, just like she didn't with me. Would she even believe that?

A part of me knows I have the ability to just walk away and forget about her—just as she did with me six years ago. I could just step out of her life and erase everything that happened between us, but every part of me fights that feeling.

Her personality and sense of humor drew me in. Her witty replies and the endless hours that we talked, losing track of time. Those are the moments that matter—not the one moment from the past. Those are the moments I want to fight for.

One date and she's all I can think about—all I want to think about. But I just need her to forgive me, to forgive my past self and only see the person in front of her.

I don't have a plan yet, but if I can rely on my past experiences where I do my best under pressure, I will think of something. I only hope five days is enough time.

Chapter Ten

Lily

"What are you doing?" I hear, startling me momentarily as I lift my head and shoulders slightly and glance up to see Paige leaning against the doorway.

I'm relieved that it's Paige back from her mom's, but also slightly disappointed that it's not Mason. Obviously it's not him. Why would it be? He doesn't live here and I'm mad at him. *Right?*

I take a deep breath and then plop myself back onto the bed, once again staring up at the ceiling.

"Nothing," I sigh, lying between my teeth—something I know I shouldn't do.

God, I wish I was doing nothing. Nothing would be by far the best thing I've done the past four hours. Instead, my mind has been racing endlessly. Nothing I think about seems to get me out of this stupid trance I've put myself in, and nothing seems to cure the hopelessness I'm feeling or lift my defeated mood.

The last thing I want to think about is the first thing on my mind. *Him.* Why? Beats me, but I cannot stop myself, not even for a second.

Maybe it's my eyes dancing around as I watch the ceiling fan above me, or the dream I have yet to wake from, but my mind keeps circling back to him—specifically to Saturday morning.

Was I harsh? *Maybe.* Did he deserve it? Yes. Well, at the time I thought that was the right answer, but now I can't be sure.

"Seems like your date went well," Paige chuckles.

I blink quickly as I focus back on the ceiling fan. I had completely forgotten she was still standing in the doorway of my room.

I lick my lips. *Fine? Well?* How else would I categorize it? If anything, it didn't go well. Not at all.

Dandy? Sure, let's go with that. It's better than explaining the rest of the situation to her. Wait. Did she even ask a question? How would she know how it went?

I prop myself up onto my elbows and frown at her.

"What?" I question.

"Your date," she repeats, raising a brow. "It must have gone *really* well." She puts emphasis on that word and I'm completely lost by her implication.

Her eyes drop to the floor, then lift back to me and she raises her brows with a seductive look. What is she getting at?

I turn my head slightly, furrowing my brows before slowly pulling forward to the end of the bed and looking down. *Nothing.*

I glance up from below my brows at Paige again, then grab the side of the bed with both hands, so I'm practically bending over upside down. Once I'm able to see beneath my bed, I finally notice something. The "something" Paige has been eyeing. *What is that?*

Reaching under, I grab the end of it and out comes a gray piece of fabric. I don't recognize it at first, but as I straighten myself back onto the bed and cross my legs beneath me, I realize it's Mason's tie and that he must have left it behind. My eyes widen at the sight and I quickly ball it up in my hands and throw it over to my dresser. *I'll throw that away later.*

"I don't know what you're talking about," I lie, putting on a fake smile as I look around the room and avoid eye contact.

"Okay," she laughs. "Whatever you say Lily."

Paige rolls her eyes, then turns around, exiting into the living room and out of sight.

Two hours. It's been two hours now that I've been going back to that night six years ago. The pretentious confidence he had. The infuriating words he spoke to me. That smug smile he planted on his face when I reacted. And now, I can put a name to his forgotten face. *Mason.*

I may not remember everything about that night, but there was one sentence that stood out, 'Girls like you don't date guys like him.' He said it to me with so much disgust, it'd be hard to forget that detail from the night.

I scratch my head and I still wonder what it means, especially now. He chose to go on this date with me and he chose to stay. If there was a moment he didn't want to, he could have left. So while those words still confuse the heck out of me, I can only think of what has happened now— w*ho* he is now.

No matter how hard I try, that face no longer repulses me like it did once before. That arrogance I remember from then is slowly replaced with the quiet, soft-spoken man I spent hours talking to. Those irritating words are washed into the back of my head by his compliments that now make me want to smile. As for his smile? That hasn't changed, but I'd be lying if I don't say I picture him semi-naked standing in front of me now.

I was shocked, yes. Did I expect the man that I just slept with to be the same man from a grotesque memory in the depths of my mind? *No.* I can't wrap my head around the fact that he's different from back then. But I have lingering doubt, is it all a ruse?

I turn my head to the side and with my thumb I click my phone screen that's been resting in my hand. The screen lights up and for a moment I'm hopeful, but nothing. Not a single text from him.

For all I know, when he realized who I was he decided to never speak to me again. It could also be that I easily talked his head off? I won't rule it out.

I fall back onto the bed, resuming my continuous staring contest with the ceiling fan. Suddenly, a dinging sound shoots my body straight up and I look down at my phone. *Still nothing.*

As I look around, I quickly see a light shining from beneath a t-shirt of mine on the floor. I roll myself off the bed and lift my shirt, where a phone lays with a black screen.

I lick my lips as I gently rub my fingertips together, then lift it from the floor. Sitting down slowly onto the edge of the bed, I turn the phone over, recognizing that it's Mason's. *Damn, how many more things of his am I going to find here?*

Reminding myself that it made a noise, I turn it back over and the screen lights up, immediately pulling my head up toward the window.

I rub the side of the rubber phone case, eyes narrowing as I keep my head turned, and while I know I shouldn't be looking down at someone else's phone, curiosity is begging me to take a peek.

I glance at the doorway of my room, waiting for Paige to step in and tell me not to be my nosy usual self, but she doesn't appear. Taking that as a sign, I scoot myself up to the head of my bed and rest my back against the white wooden headboard. Pulling my knees to my chest, I place the phone—which now has a black screen—on my knees.

I rub the phone case again, moving my thumb up to the lock screen button on the side. I take one more glance at the doorway as I wait for Paige to intercede, but when she doesn't, I take it as a sign to see who texted him. I mean, it can't be that bad.

Wrong.

As I click the button, my eyes automatically focus on the screen and I see a text from an unknown number. The words are all written in Italian. Definitely didn't expect that, but lucky for me, I took a year of Italian in college and I'm able to translate.

> **Unknown:** Ciao, bello! Sono felice di iniziare questo viaggio con te.

Ciao. Well that one's easy. It's hello. *Bello.* I've heard that one before. It's like the bell of the ball. The most beautiful. Or, the most—*handsome.*

I sip my breath in quickly as I look down at the phone. I've heard Italians are energetic and friendly people who are passionate with their words, but clearly this woman —presumably—is more than just a friend, but that doesn't sit well with me.

I study the rest of the words on the phone and can only make out the short words, but not the rest. *Clearly I'm a little out of practice.*

I pick up my phone on the bed and translate the rest of the text, which says: I'm happy to start this journey with you.

Journey? Now that certainly doesn't sound like something a friend would send.

That bastard! His seduction skills travel beyond borders. I wonder what language I'll need to translate next.

Just when I was starting to think that I was too harsh on Mason for not giving him a chance to explain, I see this.

Is he dating multiple women? I honestly wouldn't put it past him at this point since he's clearly still in that playboy mindset.

I know I shouldn't have read his texts, but it's now apparent he is still that same self-centered jerk that I met before. A womanizer at heart judging by this text. Lucky for me though, I saved my own heartache by not trying to make it right with him.

Honestly, it's infuriating that I didn't recognize him at Hanley's. I can only be mad at myself for not seeing through his nice guy act.

I clench my hand, squeezing the phone tightly, and a quick thought crosses my mind which suggests that maybe I should break it. If I did, then at least I wouldn't have to worry about him reaching out to me again.

I blink quickly as I inhale deeply, then calmly lower his phone down to the bed, before I decide to slam it into the sheets.

I lean my head back against my headboard and close my eyes, trying to think of where I should go from here. I can't just keep this man's phone, but I also don't want to be near him when it's returned because I can't predict how I'll react. I was confident six years ago when I stood up for myself against the way he treated me, but things have changed. I've now slept with this excuse of a man, which makes all the difference.

Opening my eyes, I quickly lean forward and grab my phone from the middle of the bed.

I may have a deep hatred for his brother, but all I can hope for is that I still have a friendship with Miles. And lucky for me, I still have his number.

Chapter Eleven

Lily

As each person walks by, I wonder if I'll still be able to recognize Miles.

Despite the blonde hair and extremely blue eyes, I didn't even recognize Mason. I'm not sure how I didn't either. *My mistake.* At least I keep telling myself that. For all I know, the memory of Mason from six years ago was wiped from my brain, leaving no room for any shadows of his past self.

That smile though, is unforgettable. How could I have forgotten that—*what am I even saying?* The last thing I want to think about is *him*.

Surely though I'll recognize Miles. He doesn't leave a distaste in my mouth when I think of his name. In the short time I knew him, he never once treated me unkindly or acted like we weren't friends.

While my plan will be to ultimately return Mason's phone to Miles, I can't push away the lingering questions that are popping up in the back of my mind. *What happened to him?*

If I remember correctly, that same night six years ago was the last time I ever saw him. I reached out—as any friend would do—but never heard back. Not once. Well, that is until yesterday when I texted him after all these years. Was I the one that did something wrong? *I sincerely hope not.*

I definitely didn't expect these past twenty four hours to play out like this, to learn a cruel truth about someone I thought I knew, or that I'd reach out to someone I thought I would never see again. Two extremes in my mind and I never imagined they would involve people from the same family. Especially not two brothers who I had completely opposite kinds of relationships with.

Leaning back on the park bench, I sigh.

"What?" I hear a voice scoffing. Jolting my eyes open, I hear him add, "Are you really that disappointed to see me?"

I look up at a man standing behind me and to my surprise, I recognize him immediately. *Miles.*

He's aged slightly in the past six years and has small wisps of gray in his beard, but still has his same slicked back dirty blonde hair. Just as before, he's still sharply dressed, wearing a casual black suit with a dark brown wool coat over the top.

My wide eyes return to normal and he smiles down at me with that recognizable smile and it's at that moment that I see he's still exactly as I remember him.

"Miles," I say confidently with a smile, following him with my eyes as he walks around the bench.

Standing up as he reaches me, I hesitantly open my arms to give him a hug, even though I'm unsure if he'll return it after all these years apart. I can only assume he's been upset with me since he never returned my calls.

I pull my arms back slightly as a small frown forms on my face, but he quickly leans forward, returning my hug.

When he pulls back, he cheerfully says, "Lily, it's nice to see you."

"You as well," I chuckle timidly.

Maybe I didn't do anything wrong? Or maybe he's forgotten?

I give him a thin smile, then motion away with my head.

"Want to walk?"

"I'd love to," he says.

We both put our hands into our coat pockets as we step onto the path and head into the park. It's a slightly chilly day, but the sun shining between the trees above us adds a bit of warmth.

As I consider the right words to say, it's quiet for a moment before we both turn our heads toward one another and open our mouths. As the words begin to come out, we both chuckle.

"No, you go," he insists, turning slightly as he motions his hand still in his pocket.

I take a deep breath and let the words out that I've been thinking about for the past 24 hours.

"I didn't think you'd come," I confess.

He stops on the path and looks at me with a scowl, then immediately laughs.

"I didn't think *you'd* come!"

I take a step back. *Wait, what?*

"Why didn't you think I'd show up? I was the one that reached out."

"Of course," he jokes, pressing his tongue to his cheek. "But I thought maybe you were mad at me after all these years for disappearing and decided to get back at me by not showing up."

I raise my brows in response. *He thought I was mad at him?*

"I wouldn't blame you. I wasn't a good friend. And if you didn't show up today, I would have definitely deserved it."

I try to find the words, which creates a short silence between us, but I can't contain it as I burst into laughter.

"Miles, I thought *you* were upset with me!"

A look of shock washes over his face and then he joins me in laughing.

"What? Never!"

He quickly removes his hand from his pocket and wraps it around my back, squeezing me tightly into his side.

"You think I'd miss a chance to meet up with an old friend?" he asks, raising a brow, as he releases his arm from behind me. "Definitely not."

Well that's a relief.

"So—" I turn slightly toward him as I tilt my head, "—I have to ask. What happened?"

"That night?"

I nod and he sighs, looking down at the ground as he kicks a small pebble out of the path. He kicks it again as we catch up to it and then takes a deep breath.

"It was the weekend before that night," he pauses, then looks up at me with a half smile. "It may have been the only night you didn't join the party."

Six years feels like a lifetime ago. I don't have the slightest clue as to why I didn't meet up with him that weekend, but it had to be for good reason. I wouldn't have missed a party, unless I absolutely had to.

"Must have," I assume as I lean in, eager to hear the rest of his story.

"Well there was this guy, Gage. A friend of the family. He came down from Mayfair and I was thrilled to have him experience the true party lifestyle, so he joined me at a house party just outside of the city."

Miles stops walking and runs his hand through his hair, then turns to look at me from beneath his fingers.

"The thing was, we drove there versus getting a ride. That was our mistake."

Miles shakes his head, then looks down at the ground, pressing his foot down on top of the same pebble as before.

"I don't remember what happened. I was in the passenger's seat of his car and the next thing I knew, I woke up in the hospital. We were both fine, didn't have a scratch on us, but word got out. Quickly."

He glances back up at me, then continues down the path. I quickly take a couple of steps to keep up.

"Now his family has the kind of money that if something happens, they can make sure nobody finds out. And that's what happened. But, there were doubts from others about my brother and I taking over the family business. Especially from my parents."

Family business? Mason never mentioned anything about that. He said he was in marketing. I remember him telling me that as clear as day.

Miles looks at me quickly and I raise an eyebrow, pushing for him to continue.

"Well, jump to the night we went out, my parents and I had an argument and told me that another incident couldn't happen," he pauses then corrects himself. "Wouldn't happen."

I quietly scoff to myself, but Miles, raising an eyebrow, hears it and asks, "What?"

"I was there that night."

"What do you mean?"

"I heard the conversation. I didn't understand what was going on, but I remember hearing about an incident that could ruin your family's reputation."

It all makes sense now. He didn't choose to leave and disappear. He was *forced* to. I know we are supposed to agree with what our parents say, but in this case, I'm not sure how something so small could seriously cause any damage. Car accidents happen. They don't ruin reputations.

"Wait, how could you have heard that?"

"You left your phone at the club and I came to give it back to you."

Miles raises his eyebrows as if a lightbulb just went off in his head, then he mumbles, "So that's how my phone got back."

"I wanted to make sure you were okay too, but I never got the chance to ask you since your brother was such an ass to me."

I shake my head, only remembering details here and there from that night.

Miles crosses his arms and nods his head in agreement.

"He was drunk that night. He's always an asshole when he's drunk. Well should I say, *was.*"

"Was?" I question curiously.

"Yeah, not to change the subject, but when it got closer to him solely taking over the company, he really made a change," Miles chuckles. "I honestly hated him before. Even had his name in my phone as 'Spam' because I didn't want to talk to him."

I awkwardly laugh, knowing that I had checked his texts and saw that contact and that now explains the odd name. I mean, it's definitely a good joke, naming it for someone you don't want to speak to.

"Now, he'll only have a drink or two," he adds, scratching his head. "Honestly, I haven't seen him act like that in years."

"You mean the whole 'dragging you across the club' act?" I joke, nudging his shoulder.

I definitely think that night Mason could have been a little less harsh, and a little less of an asshole.

"Yeah, that was a bit much, but I think he was just pissed off that my parents told him he had to come get me that night."

I stay quiet, wondering if that was the main reason for his behavior. Could he have truly only acted that way because he was drunk? That would also explain why he barely drank while we were out. Making sure he didn't let his own personal demon out, as it would then quickly get out of control, or possibly ruin the date. The memorable date I enjoyed a little too much.

I shake my head, dismissing the thought as quickly as it appeared.

Filling the silence as we walk, Miles mutters, "So, I'm sorry I never reached out. It was definitely a big change for me and I should have let you know."

"No, it's okay," I say softly. "You didn't expect that to happen."

"I appreciate that," he smiles. "I truly do. Honestly, I may have hated it at first, but it definitely helped. You were a good friend though. I always remembered that."

I smile while taking a deep breath, feeling a fondness knowing he has good memories of me.

"Speaking of friends, are you still close with that friend of yours from the club?" he asks, titling his head. "What's her name again? Paige?"

"Yeah, Paige," I nod. "We still live together actually!"

"Still best friends I assume?"

"Always!" I beam and then nudge his side with my shoulder. "You know, she's still single."

I look at him with a suggesting look and he chuckles as he glances back at me.

No matter what, I'll always try to set my best friend up—and who better than Miles? He's clearly doing well. Maybe the two of them will hit it off?

"I appreciate the offer but—" he raises his left hand and wiggles his finger with a black ring on it. "—I'm actually married."

"What!" I yelp excitedly. "Congratulations!"

He chuckles. "Thank you. Thank you."

"I'm so happy for you!" I shout, leaning over to give him a quick side hug. "How'd you meet?"

"It was about two years ago," he grins. "Crazy how fast it went by. She was—well, still is—my brother's accountant."

"For your family's marketing company?"

I immediately grit my teeth as the words spill out. *Shit.* I have yet to mention the date I went on with his brother and I'm already mentioning things he told me. Things I *shouldn't* know.

"Marketing?" Miles asks, scowling before shaking his head. "No. My family is in the spirits industry."

Excuse me? That is definitely not what Mason said to me. He clearly said marketing. I know that for a fact. Was he lying then? *I wouldn't put it past him.*

"Wait, what?" I stop on the path and hold my hands up as I raise a brow. "The spirits industry? Like alcohol?"

"Yeah," he confirms, furrowing his brows. "I thought you knew? Didn't I ever mention it back in college?"

I tilt my head and scratch my forehead. Did he or is my memory foggier than I thought?

"No, you didn't," I reply slowly.

"Oh, my bad. I thought I did," he chuckles. "Yeah, I met my wife, Alice, on one of her first days at the office and I don't know, we just clicked."

"That's nice," I hum with a smile.

I turn to look away, but can't help but ask, "You said she was your brother's accountant? What does he do specifically?"

"Mason?" Miles smiles and as if he's happy for the words to come out of his mouth, he proudly tells me, "He's the CEO."

I open my mouth, but quickly close it, trying to contain my shock. Now this really is making no sense. If Mason was the CEO of his family's business, wouldn't he have told me?

142 | K. Jaspersen

I shake the thought from my head. Why do I even care what Mason said? I don't care about him anyways. *Right?* Right.

"And are you also involved with your family's company?"

"No, not at all," Miles chuckles, then adds, "I've been sober almost six years now. I don't think I could be involved even if I wanted to."

I turn and scowl at the ground before he quickly adds, "No, I'm actually a professor over at Mayfair."

A teacher? Of all the jobs I imagined my wild friend having, this was definitely not one of them.

"No way!" I gasp excitedly. "I'm also a teacher!"

"I figured you were," he smiles, tilting his head. "I remember you were studying in education."

"Was a teacher," I say with a sigh. "I recently got let go so currently I'm not working."

"Oh, I'm sorry to hear that," he mumbles before clicking his tongue. "But just because you aren't working as one now, doesn't mean you aren't one. Don't put yourself down."

"Thanks."

"The right job will come soon! I know it."

I smile shyly as I look down at the ground again, then inhale deeply before looking back at him.

"What a small world though that we both ended up being teachers."

"Truly is!" he says with a smile. "I was majoring in business since I thought I'd be joining my brother in running the company, but once I moved to Mayfair, I switched my major and got into teaching."

I nod trying to pay attention before quickly biting my tongue. I know I shouldn't bring him up, but I can't help it.

"So, speaking of your brother," I pause, then swallow hard. "I have a confession."

Miles stops walking and frowns at me just as we reach a small fountain where the path turns into a gravel walkway.

I quickly look away from him and take a step toward the fountain, sitting down on the ledge.

"This sounds serious," Miles jokes, as he follows and sits across from me.

"So, I didn't just text you to catch up," I start.

"Okay," Miles says in an uncertain tone.

"I'm happy we've caught up though!" I quickly add, hoping he doesn't think that this was all with ill intention. "But, I have something for you."

I reach into my bag and pull out Mason's phone and hold it out in front of Miles.

"Your phone?" Miles guesses, his forehead wrinkling.

I look down at it and then back up to him.

"No, it's actually your brother's."

"Mason's?" he asks, scratching his temple.

He looks away for a moment and then back at me, frowning.

"Why do you have Mason's phone?"

"Well, that's the thing," I cautiously say, licking my lips. "We actually went on a date on Friday night."

"Wait, really?" he gasps, jerking his head back. "Didn't expect to hear that today."

"Yeah, really," I say as he grabs the phone from my hands and looks down at it.

"How'd you two meet? Well, besides when he acted foolish six years ago."

"We met at this coffee shop near my apartment and I asked him out."

"Damn," Miles chuckles deeply. "Bold move Alcord."

I smile, remembering his nickname for me, then continue. "We went on a date and it honestly went really well. I really liked him."

"Hey, that's awesome!" Miles nods with an encouraging smile.

I sigh. "But I didn't recognize him. Like at all."

"So?" he asks, raising a brow. "What's the issue?"

"Well, I can't date him. I just can't."

I throw my hands up into the air and explain, "He pretended to be nice and sweet to me and I know he's faking it."

Miles walks over and sits down next to me on the ledge.

"Where is this coming from?"

I purse my lips, looking up slightly, then look back at Miles.

"Well, back to that night at the club. He was an asshole to me. He's obviously still one now."

"Hey," Miles laughs. "That's not him anymore. As I mentioned earlier, I haven't seen him act that way in years."

"But, how do I know?" I anxiously ask as I furrow my brows.

"Did he say anything cruel to you on your date?"

"No," I cautiously answer.

"Did he do anything to you that would make you think he was still the same person he was before?"

"No," I quietly confirm.

Miles scoffs. "Then he's changed."

I scowl and look down at Mason's phone in Miles' hand, remembering the text from yesterday.

"I wasn't snooping, I promise, but there was a text from some woman in his phone."

Miles looks down at the phone and then back up at me.

"The texts were in Italian and she mentioned a journey with him," I spill. "That doesn't sound so innocent, but you believe I should trust him?"

"You know, you shouldn't snoop," he sneers, sternly raising a brow.

I nod my head back and forth, then chuckle, "Curiosity got the best of me."

His face softens.

"Once again, nothing to worry about," Miles laughs. "The company is doing a business deal with an Italian distributor. They have a daughter who fancies Mason, but that's it. From my impression so far, their family is very outspoken, but I promise you, he's not interested in her at all."

If Italian women are as beautiful as the Italian men I've seen in the movies, then I'm shocked he's not interested. But maybe he truly isn't that playboy after all.

"But—" I open my mouth, but Miles stops me.

"Trust me. He's changed. I can promise you that," Miles nods with an encouraging smile.

Can I trust what Miles is saying? I was dead set on ignoring Mason if he reached back out after I had planned to return his phone. I didn't want anything to do with him, but now? Miles wouldn't lie to me. He knows his brother better than anyone, so it must be true.

Unless Mason's a phenomenal actor who's about to receive an Oscar for his astounding performance, he's not the person I once knew. *Thank god.* It's not everyday that you meet someone like him. Or should I say *re-meet* someone.

I can't think of the last time that I met someone whose calm and reserved personality meshed so well with my loud, outgoing self.

I take a deep breath and a smile begins to grow on my face. "Okay. I believe you."

"I'll get this back to him," Miles says, holding up the phone in his hand, before tucking it into his coat pocket.

Miles looks up from beneath his brows and stares intently at me. "And when I do, you have to make me a promise."

"What kind of promise?" I answer, hesitantly.

He straightens himself up and raises a brow. "If he reaches out, you can't ignore him."

I glance away, avoiding eye contact as I quickly search for an excuse. "But he lied to me about being in marketing."

I turn back to him and lick my lips, hiding my smile.

"That's what he tells everyone he does," Miles says through a laugh. He raises a brow and adds, "I mean, it's not really a lie. There is a lot of marketing that is necessary for the business."

"But why didn't he just tell me he ran your family's business?"

"Honestly?" he tilts his head back and forth. "There's a lot of people out there that will try to find a way into our family."

"What do you mean?"

"The details aren't important, but I know you aren't like that."

I click my tongue and say, "Maybe it'd be better if we just go our separate ways. You know, it may be for the best."

Miles chuckles. "Let me tell you something."

I lean forward, eager to hear what he says.

"I can't remember the last time that Mason has been on a date, so if he went on one with you, you must mean something to him."

Could that be true? I know I was the one to ask him out, but as I've said before—*he could have chosen not to show up.* Did he think there was something special about me at Hanley's?

"Really?" I grin, lifting my eyes up to his.

"Really," Miles says without hesitating. "So will you promise me?"

I swallow hard, then exhaling I nod, "I promise."

Miles gives me a playful grin as he pulls his shoulders back. I quickly stand and hold out my hand for him to grab. Grabbing it and pulling himself up, I smile and nod my head toward the path.

As we start walking, I can't hide my curiosity as I say, "Now, tell me more about your wife, Alice."

Chapter Twelve

Mason

After leaving the office that day, I retraced my steps and knew that I left it at her apartment. I knew it in my gut, but I didn't want to admit it to myself that quickly.

A part of me wanted to go back over there and try to talk to her, but I knew she wouldn't want that. I'd just be shut out. Another part of me would rather just get a brand new phone, hoping to avoid any additional conflict.

I eventually settled on asking her for it back later in the week, when things hopefully had settled down a bit. Then, late Sunday night, I'm surprised to see Miles knocking on my front door.

"Bad timing?" Miles jokes as he looks down at my boxers and then back at me. "You awake?"

"Miles?" I ask groggily. "I'm up now."

I rub my eyes then turn to look at the clock on the wall behind me. *Eleven o'clock.*

"What are you doing here so late?"

"Sorry man," Miles mutters, his eyes narrowing. "Can I come in?"

I rub the back of my neck and exhale deeply as I slowly open the door. When it's just barely wide enough for someone to walk in, Miles quickly ducks under my arm and walks past me.

"Wow," he says, stepping into the living room. "Looks like you've changed a few things since the last time I was here."

I blink slowly and rub my hand down my face, feeling the heaviness in my eyes after being woken up.

"Miles."

"Oh! Nice fireplace. I don't remember you having a fireplace the last time I was here. Is that new or—"

"Miles," I say louder and it gets his attention.

"Sorry," he chuckles, walking back over to me.

He shuffles through his pockets, pulls out a phone and holds it out to me. I raise an eyebrow as I reach for it.

"Thank you?"

Of all the interesting things I can say Miles has done, buying me a new phone and bringing it to me at eleven o'clock at night is definitely high on the list. Why? *Fuck if I know.*

Miles smiles widely with a bright-eyed look on his face, while I'm over here exhausted and feeling weary. Why the hell is he so happy anyway? I swear this guy never sleeps. Didn't in college when he was out partying and apparently, still doesn't even today.

His eyes glance down at the phone in my hand and I frown. Does he want me to say thank you again?

"Open it," he smiles.

I glance down at the phone, then back up at him from beneath my brows. He gives me a head nod, gesturing for me to continue, and I click on the lock button with my thumb. It immediately lights up the home screen and I see a familiar photo of the ocean. *Wait, it's my phone.*

I scratch the back of my head as I scowl at the phone and the questions start to race in my mind.

First, where? Second, how? And third, I need an explanation.

"This is my phone," I state, as my mouth hangs open.

"Yeah," Miles nods happily. "You're welcome."

I immediately picture Miles climbing through Lily's apartment window and retrieving my phone himself. Honestly, I wouldn't put it past him. However, I didn't even mention my date with her so that's highly unlikely. Yet, that begs the question, where did he find it?

"No," I say, my lips thinning. "Tell me where you found it."

"Brother, that'd be too easy," Miles says scoffing as he turns and walks away from me.

Great, now he's playing games.

I cross my arms in annoyance as he jumps over my couch and sits back with his arms widely spread across the top of the cushions.

"Wow. This is a comfortable couch. Alice insisted on a leather one, but I wish we had one like this."

I clench my jaw. Not only am I tired, but I definitely don't have time for this.

"No," I say quietly, shaking my head.

He leans forward and peers toward the kitchen.

"What kind of food do you have here?"

Alright. That's enough. If Miles doesn't spit out whatever he has to say within the next minute, the throbbing vein in my forehead will surely pop.

"Tell me how you got my phone or leave," I sneer. "Because I'm fucking exhausted."

Miles glances back at me, takes a deep breath, then pulls himself up from the couch.

He huffs and then says, "Fine. I'll spit it out."

Thank you.

"But you have to say please first."

Are you kidding me?

"Really?" I grumble, raising a brow.

"I could just leave and you'll never know how I got it. If that's what you want then—"

"Fine," I huff, taking a deep breath as I roll my eyes. "Please, will you tell me how you got my phone back?"

"Gladly," he smiles with his head held high as he walks around the couch. "I got a text from an old friend and we happened to meet up early today."

"Wait," I gasp. "Lily reached out to you?"

I instantly feel my cheek tighten as the corner of my lips rise.

"I can't confirm nor deny," he chuckles. "But let's just say that I cleared up everything for you."

My smile thins and I scowl at him.

"Great," I say sarcastically. "What did you say to her?"

"Hey, I did you a favor," he suggests, holding his hands up in front of him. "Nothing you can't thank me for later, but let's just say she is willing to talk now."

Well shit. That sounds like he blackmailed her to talk to me. He squints his eyes as he sees me think.

"And no, it wasn't blackmail. She actually wants to hear you out."

What? How did he—

I open my mouth to speak, but quickly close it and rub my temple as Miles walks past me. I turn around as he opens my door, then looks back at me for a moment.

"You're welcome," he smirks, then walks out, closing the door behind him.

Chapter Thirteen

Mason

Is there a limit to how many texts I can type out and delete before finally sending one? I've been contemplating what I should even say—or if she'll even reply.

How can I even explain it all? Would she even believe me?

When I left her apartment, or rather when I was forced to go, I hailed a taxi to the office. In the short drive, I thought about how she felt at that moment. The feeling of betrayal when she found out who I was. The thought that I was only nice to her because I wanted to sleep with her. Ridiculous, but not true by any means.

I may have been that asshole to her six years ago, but she won't get anywhere close to that guy again—I'll make sure of it. But, that can only be considered true if I can win her back, show her who I am now, and how I feel about her.

Whether I believe in love at first sight—or love at second sight in this case—one thing is abundantly clear—I won't let her go that easily. Not now, and maybe not ever.

As soon as Miles brought me my phone, I pictured myself writing up the perfect text to send her, but now after hours of ideas circling in my head, I know that can no longer be my plan.

As I walk up to her building and stare at the doors from the sidewalk, I can only hope that she'll be home and I'll get my chance to explain. And if not, maybe this bouquet of flowers in my arms will win her over instead.

Rubbing a hand down the side of my pant legs, I take a deep breath. As I release it, I step onto the small stairway and look up at the long list of names on the wall, each with a button next to them. My eyes slowly move down the list until they land on hers. *Bingo.*

I quickly click the buzzer next to her name and it starts ringing. *Shit.* I don't have the slightest clue what to say when she answers, but I'll have to make something up. And fast.

I clear my throat in anticipation as the ringing continues. *Or if she answers.*

My eyes search the street, looking for some idea of what I'll say to her. Any idea really. But, before any words form in my head, the ringing stops. Could she possibly know it's me and she's ignoring me?

I let out a sigh and shuffle my feet on the ground, knowing that I'm going to have to resort back to Plan A— sending a text.

Just when I'm about to take a step down the steps, I hear the door click behind me. With a glance over my shoulder, I see a delivery man exiting the building. I turn on my heel and grab the door just before it's about to close. Well, here goes Plan B—or is it C?

I walk swiftly through the lobby toward the elevator, and just my luck, the doors are already open. I smile as I step inside and lift my finger to the buttons, but hover in front of them. *Shit.*

On Friday, we had an impromptu make out session in the elevator, and I focused on everything but the floor she lived on—I definitely had more important things on my mind. Now I realize what I should have done was look at Lily's apartment number next to her name outside. Why I didn't check it is beyond me.

"Hold it please," I hear, just as the elevator doors are about to close.

Instinctually, I reach my arm out, stopping the doors from closing. I hold my breath and my eyes grow wide as I get a glimpse of long, brown hair. *Not right now. Definitely not right now.*

As the doors open, I let out a sigh of relief as I see the face hidden behind the hair is not, in fact, who I thought it was.

The short, dark-haired woman stands at the door holding a small pile of mail, and as we make eye contact, she smiles.

"Thank you," she politely replies as she steps inside.

My eyes follow her as she walks in next to me and turns around before the doors slowly close in front of us.

"Floor 32 please," she adds, as I turn my head slightly.

I look back at the buttons, where I see my hand still raised in the air and I quickly click the button for her floor, lowering my arm back to my side.

Out of the corner of my eye, I look at this woman and I can't help but notice the similarities. Same height or a little bit shorter, brown hair, and she looks to be in her mid-to-late twenties as well. Maybe she'd be willing to lend me a hand?

Lily's apartment building is rather large and from my experience, I wouldn't be able to tell a neighbor from someone on the street. Who's to say she won't either?

She looks up at me and frowns, before motioning to the buttons.

"Aren't you going to click one?"

I press my lips together and immediately stare straight ahead, hoping she'll just ignore me. My best bet is to stay quiet and just wait until she leaves, then I can take a peek outside the building entrance at the apartment number.

"Okay?" she says slightly annoyed as she turns back forward.

I check her facial expression out of the corner of my eye and she's scowling straight ahead. *Great.*

I'm about to look away, but I glance down at the mail she's holding and it immediately catches my eye. My mouth slightly falls open as I look down at the top white envelope in her pile with black handwriting. And now, I truly believe in pure luck as I see her name.

Lily Alcord.

Chapter Fourteen

Lily

Who waits five days to text someone back after a first date? Well technically only four since two of those days he didn't have his phone, but still.

I've gone on dates with quite a few men in the past. One night together and then they're gone the next day. And of course, the underlying message is always clear when they don't reach out again: *They just aren't that interested.*

Maybe it was delusional of me to think that we actually had a meaningful connection? Or even something that would warrant us a second date at least.

Sure, he was a jerk to me six years ago, but I made a promise to Miles to give Mason a chance if he reached out. I wanted to give Mason the opportunity to make things right, to show me the side of him that Miles claims is now the norm.

Miles seemed so sure that Mason would be quick to text me after getting his phone back, but it's already Wednesday. At this point, I doubt he ever will.

And what's worse? This has me thinking that I am the one that did something wrong, that I may have ruined the date in some way. I'm thinking if that is the case, well then I'm better off without him.

I shake my head at the thought as I roll up my mat on the floor.

I knew I needed to get my mind off everything, so when I woke up this morning, I went on my phone and signed up for a yoga class a few blocks away.

When I was working full-time, I really only ever got the opportunity to go to yoga on the weekend, which came with a downside—the classes were packed full of people.

I'm not sure why I expected the weekdays to be the same, but it was refreshing to see such a small class this time. I actually preferred it. It seemed that the quieter ambiance definitely distracted me a bit.

When I first started going to yoga, I expected it to be simple stretches and a relaxing activity. Just something to do when I had a little extra free time. *Nope.*

Yoga was definitely not easy. It involved strength combined with a good amount of balance as well, which meant it was a lot more challenging. However, I loved it. Some poses are easy, and when I started going to hot yoga, which involves the room being at a sauna-like temperature, it became my favorite workout.

As I walk outside, I'm delighted to see that the sun has finally come up, and it's still a cool morning. Even though I wiped off the beads of sweat on my forehead, and the back of my neck before exiting the building, I still feel the aftermath of the class. My spandex workout clothes stick to my body and I feel the underlying dampness running throughout my hair. As I make my way home, the morning temperature cools me off, just as I had hoped it would.

Rounding the corner to my block, I flinch, nearly dropping my yoga mat from under my arm, when I spot Mason standing outside of my building. *Shit.*

Pulling my now-frozen body quickly back and out of sight, I can only hope he didn't see me down the sidewalk. I press my fingers against my temple and look down at the ground.

Of all the moments he could choose to show up, now is not one of them. I have been hoping to see him again, but now my hair is a mess and I probably stink from sweating. I wanted to look cute when I saw him again, specifically if we go on a second date, but not like this. Definitely not like this.

Raising my head up slowly, I turn to check my reflection in the building's window. *Okay, not as bad as I thought.*

Placing my yoga mat on the ground against the building, I undo my ponytail and flip my head upside down as I run my fingers through my hair. Collecting it all back into a ponytail, I fix the stray hairs and as I look back into my reflection, I'm happy that my hair looks somewhat more presentable.

I lift my arm slightly and sniff myself. *Phew, now bad.* My eyes gaze up and down my reflection and I cup my hand in front of my mouth. Letting out a breath, I inhale through my nose. *Also not bad.*

Satisfied with my presentation, I grab my yoga mat back off the ground and tuck it under my arm. If not now, then when?

I take a deep breath as I round the corner and make my way down the sidewalk toward Mason.

As I draw closer, he catches me walking toward him out of the corner of his eye and turns to face me. He's wearing a cream-colored long sleeve button down shirt, navy slacks and a pair of brown shoes. To add to my surprise, he's holding a large bouquet of flowers wrapped in brown paper. I give him a soft smile and he returns it with a large grin.

I keep my eyes on him as the distance between us closes and then briefly glance at the flowers in his arms— white lilies. *My favorite for obvious reasons.*

As I reach him, I open my mouth to speak, but he takes a step forward, stopping me.

"Before you speak, I need to say something to you."

I obediently listen, while eagerly waiting to hear what he has to say.

"I've thought about how I acted in the past a million times over, regretting every poor choice I've made and awful word I've said. That was someone who didn't know the consequences of their actions, someone whom I'm ashamed to have been. But that's not me. Not anymore."

Mason looks down slightly at the sidewalk as he appears to collect the rest of his thoughts. He looks back at me with his beautiful blue eyes, and I watch as the dimple on his cheek partially appears with his soft smile.

"I can't think of any other way to say it, but I have not been able to stop thinking about you since I saw you at that coffee shop."

He rubs the back of his neck and I open my mouth again to speak, but he quickly continues.

"No matter how hard I tried, I couldn't turn my attention away from you that day. You were beautiful in every way," he pauses, then adds, "You are."

The corner of his mouth tips up.

"There was something about you that seemed familiar, but that's not what I saw. To me, you were a beautiful stranger on the street. I recognized someone with a hell of a spirit and radiating confidence, but I didn't realize that I had seen it before. I didn't recognize you."

His brows draw together and he sighs.

"But remembering you now, I can't believe how arrogant I was to you. I know you don't believe me, but that's the truth. You didn't deserve it. You never did, and I'm sorry for that."

I offer him a small smile as I maintain steady eye contact with him and he returns the expression, but I can see it in his eyes—a pained look of regret.

Without knowing he'd be here, I had already forgiven him in my mind on the walk home. Whether I'd have seen him again or not, I truly believed what Miles had said—that Mason had changed. And if I got to see it from his eyes, I'd be lucky because even Mason's relationship with his brother had changed, shifting from solid hatred to a close bond.

It's not easy to acknowledge your past mistakes; everyone has made them—whether big or small. And as I can see, he's deeply wounded by his past actions and trying to make amends. Lucky for him, I'm willing to give him that second chance.

"You don't have to say anything," he mutters, breaking my thoughts.

I quickly look up from the flowers in his hand, realizing I had broken our eye contact.

"Are those for me?" I ask softly, as I reach out to touch the brown paper around the flowers and my hand brushes his.

He blinks suddenly and nods his head.

"Yes. They are."

He holds out the bouquet of lilies and I set my yoga mat down on the ground before grabbing them. Burrowing my nose into the petals, I inhale. Not only do they share my name, but I have always loved their scent.

I smile softly as I pull back my face and gaze up at Mason.

"How would you know that these are my favorite?" I chuckle, raising a brow.

"Lucky guess," he smiles as his face softens.

I glance down at the flowers before looking back at him.

"There's nothing to apologize for," I admit, putting my hand out as I place it on his wrist. "Truly."

He opens his mouth to speak, but quickly closes it.

"Hey," I say quietly. "It's in the past. Let's move forward with the future."

He takes a deep breath and a smile grows. His gaze explores my face and I suddenly feel his hand slowly running down the side of my arm. He lowers the bouquet with his other hand, and I feel his hand shift from my arm up to my face. Cupping my jaw, I watch as his eyes glance to his thumb on my cheek.

"You're still beautiful in every way," he says in a low voice and I close my eyes slightly, basking in his touch.

His thumb gently brushes back and forth across my cheek and I almost feel compelled to remind him that I can't possibly be that pretty after a sweaty workout. *But as long as he thinks so, that's what counts.*

When I open my eyes, his hand tugs the back of my neck forward, and his lips clash with mine.

My body had grown tense during our conversation and I hadn't realized it, but now I relax into the kiss knowing we've reconciled.

His soft lips on me are a stark reminder of how much I enjoyed kissing him on Friday. Something I could easily get used to. The sweet and gentle ones, as well as the ones that make me want to rip his clothes off.

He slowly pulls back, stopping just inches from my face.

"I don't want this to be how our story ends," he expresses, pulling back with a smile as he straightens himself up, "It may have been a rocky start, but I promise our story will change from here," he pauses and then adds, "I want to take you somewhere if that's alright."

Finally, a second date! I've been eagerly waiting for him to ask me.

"Like on a date?" I playfully ask.

"Erm, yeah."

"Oh! Let me guess!" I say, excitedly. "A restaurant? Maybe a stroll through the park? Am I close?"

He deeply chuckles and then I see a small glimmer in the corner of his eye.

"Actually, I want you to come on a work trip with me."

I can't help but frown. That's definitely not what I envisioned for our second date.

"Oh," I sigh. I quickly try not to appear disheartened by the suggestion and offer a soft smile. "I guess that could be fun."

He leans slightly forward as his eyes scan my face, then pulls back.

"No, it's not what you think," he shakes his head. "I want you to come to Italy with me."

Italy? He can't be serious, right?

"Like Little Italy?" I question. *That has to be what he means.*

"No," he laughs. "The country."

I sarcastically scoff. "I mean, that would be amazing, but I can't afford to go there. You know I don't have a job at the moment."

Then, in a serious tone he says, "Don't worry about that. I'll take care of everything."

I squint my eyes as I study his expression.

"You're kidding," I joke.

He raises a brow as he tilts his head and my eyes grow wide at his lack of response.

"Oh my God. You're serious."

He gives me a reassuring smile and I quickly shake my head.

"No, I can't let you do that."

His brows draw together, as if he's disappointed and I frown as I look down at the ground.

No, I definitely can't let him pay for me. That's insane.

Looking back up, our eyes meet again and I see the yearning behind his. As if his eyes are begging me. *Pleading.* He wants me to go and his expression is saying it all.

Several thoughts start racing through my head. I am currently jobless, so I have the time. I really like this man and since I know his brother, at least he's not a total stranger any more. Lastly, and what makes it even more interesting, is the fact that it isn't every day that you have the opportunity for a trip like this—even if it is just him going for work.

"Please," he eventually adds, noticing me searching for an excuse in front of him.

"This is crazy," I say sternly.

He chuckles deeply and shrugs his shoulders.

"I mean, what do you have to lose?" he chuckles.

I look up and slide my finger across my lip. *I mean, nothing, unless you murder me.* I quietly scoff at the thought then shake it away.

His brows draw together and he appears to be patiently waiting for my response as a small smile crosses his face. Squinting at him, I purse my lips, then slowly look up and down at him. *Nah, he isn't capable of murder.*

I anxiously laugh and then quickly take a breath in and out.

"Okay, yes, but just let me move some things around and I'll figure it out."

A large grin strikes his face suddenly as he hears me agree.

"When are we going?" I ask, raising a brow.

"Friday," he says slowly with a brittled laugh.

My eyes grow wide. "Friday?"

"Yes."

I lean forward slightly, checking that the words he said weren't somehow miscommunicated from two feet away.

"Like this Friday? Two days from now?"

"Yes," he nods.

I shake my head and press my fingers against my temple. *That's way too soon! I won't be able to get the money by then.*

I turn away and start pacing back and forth in front of him. After a moment, I stop and throw my hands up into the air.

"I'm sorry. I can't go," I decide.

Mason leans in closely to me and places his hand on my forearm, stopping me in place.

I turn my body towards him and with a smile, he softly says, "Don't worry. I've got it."

I open my mouth to speak, but he quickly lays a peck on my lips before I can let out a word.

As he pulls back, I'm quiet. I doubt he'll take no for an answer at this point, so I might as well just keep my lips sealed. I mean, it's not every day that a devilishly handsome man invites you to Italy. *Right?*

Chapter Fifteen

Lily

I can't go to Italy with him. I barely know the man, and I've only gone on one date with him. *One date!*

Am I crazy? *Must be.*

Did I get a concussion from hitting my head under the bed last week? That has to be it. That's got to be the only explanation.

Why else would I say yes? I may like the man, but who's to say he won't murder me while I'm in another country? Nobody would even know. Well, except for Paige. But what if she thought that I was going through a jobless phase where I had suddenly decided to move to Italy? *It's a possibility.*

Yet, Miles wouldn't allow that. He would have said something if he knew that his brother was a serial killer. *Right?* So I have to assume I'm in the clear, but that doesn't make this any less deranged.

I pace back and forth in the living room, and turn my attention toward the door when I hear it open. I stop in place and cross my arms as Paige steps inside.

"Where have you been?" I frantically ask.

Paige scowls at me as she slowly closes the door behind her.

"The store?"

"I've been waiting for you!" I admit as I take in a shuttered breath. "We have a lot to discuss."

I quickly walk over to her as she places several plastic bags on the countertop. I place my arms on the opposite side of the counter and lean toward her.

"Oh, these are beautiful."

Paige tilts her head as she looks at the bouquet of lilies I've arranged in a vase on the counter.

"Who are they from?" she asks curiously.

"So you know that guy that I went on a date with on Friday?" I stammer as I bite my lip.

"Yeah, Mason?" she asks, raising a brow.

"Yeah, Mason. Well he just asked—" I pause and wrinkle my forehead. "Wait, what did you just say?"

"Nothing, go on," she insists, scratching her head.

I stare at her, but she avoids eye contact as she casually takes her groceries out of the bags.

"No," I cautiously say. "I never told you his name."

Paige looks up as if to think, then turns her attention back to her groceries.

"Yeah, I'm pretty sure you did. I think it was after I noticed someone stayed the night."

"No," I assure her, taking a step around the counter. "I definitely didn't tell you. I'd remember."

"Maybe you forgot," she suggests without raising her head up.

I tap my foot as I cross my arms. "Alright, spill the beans."

She's quiet for a moment and I add, "Now."

"Fine!" she hollers, throwing her hands up into the air. "You got me! Mason and I have already met."

"What?" I ask. Did they meet at the club as well? I could have sworn she stayed at the table the entire night. "When?"

"Earlier today actually."

Phew. That's a relief.

She smiles as if she's hiding something then she chuckles. "He was looking for you."

"I know, he was waiting outside our building" I smile, then cock my head. "But when did you meet?"

"He came by and I offered to let him wait for you in the apartment. I tried making small talk, but I think he may have been uncomfortable waiting around. Actually, I think it only took two minutes for him to decide to leave and wait outside. He seemed like a nice guy, but he was awfully quiet. Definitely different from you."

"He's definitely more reserved, but once you get to know him, he opens up."

"So, what'd he ask you?" she says, raising her brows.

I frown, forgetting my train of thought. "What?"

"You said he asked you something?"

I narrow my eyes. *How could I forget the biggest thing on my mind at the moment?*

"You won't believe this, but he invited me to Italy."

I hold my breath, eager to hear her reply.

"Italy? Like Little Italy?" she asks skeptically.

I chuckle. "That's what I said! But no, the country."

"He asked you to go to Italy?" she scowls. "No, you're lying."

I quickly shake my head. "No, it's the truth."

"Italy? The country?" she hesitantly repeats as if she still can't believe it. "When?"

"Friday."

"Friday?" she shouts as her eyes widen. "Are you crazy?"

I scratch the back of my neck and squint at her through an anxious smile. "Possibly."

"That's insane Lily. Even for you," she says, and I hear the concern in her voice.

I take a deep breath and throw my hand into the air. "You're right. It's crazy."

She shakes her head and her face softens. "Well, are you going?"

"What? You just said it was insane," I counter.

"I mean, it is," she says. "But how often do you get invited to Italy? You have to go."

"I thought I did all the convincing in this friendship?" I joke.

"Not this time," she laughs. "This time, I'm telling you. You. Have. To. Go."

I attempt to hide my head between my shoulders, but I'm unsuccessful. "Well, I may have already said yes."

I tightly close my eyes, and prepare for her disappointing speech, but she remains quiet. Feeling the silence heavily weighing on me, I lift my head up and slowly open one eye to see Paige scowling. Then, her expression eases and a large grin appears, instantly making me open my other eye.

"You're going to Italy!" she beams before turning toward the fridge.

Sighing with relief, I cheer, "I am!"

She lowers her head to glance into the fridge, but I watch her body stiffen before looking over her shoulder.

With an anxious look she adds, "Just make sure you have him send me a photo of his driver's license though. I can give it to the cops if you go missing."

"You think I'll be kidnapped?" I laugh.

She straightens herself and turns to me, one hand still holding onto the fridge door.

"That's what happens with handsome men," she warns.

"You watch too many true crime documentaries."

"And you watch too many romantic comedies," she shoots back.

"Hey!" I chuckle. "I can't help that I'm a hopeless romantic! I'm just waiting for a man to come swoop me off my feet."

I glance at the flowers once again, then look at Paige, her eyes glaring through me with concern.

"I'll be fine, I promise," I assure her.

"Better safe than sorry," she says, shrugging her shoulders.

I shake my head, then slowly turn my attention to the floor as unwelcome thoughts creep in.

"Maybe this is crazy," I whisper before bringing my hand up to my mouth as I shake my head. "I. Am. Crazy."

Chapter Sixteen

Lily

Droplets of rain trickle down the awning as I watch from the comfort of the complex lobby inside. I can feel the cold air escaping through the slit of the glass doorway and it sends chills up my spine.

Traveling on a rainy day is never ideal, traffic starts to pick up, and as people run late, delays at the airport are to be expected. If I were looking for the perfect excuse not to leave today, this would be it.

It's definitely comforting knowing I'll be leaving the weather behind me today, but I can only hope that the weather in Italy will be nicer—warmer even. Regardless, I packed for it all.

I look down and wiggle my toes within my sneakers, trying to warm them up. The cold finds its way in there even through the thick fabric.

I smile as I tighten my shoulders, relishing the warmth that my clothes provide me, even if my shoes aren't up to par. I'm wearing my go-to airport outfit that gives me the comfort I need for any plane ride – a pair of black lounge pants, a black long sleeve top and a denim jacket.

There are three things I hate about plane rides: The tight quarters, the endless hours of trying to get comfortable, and the far-from-ideal food they serve. Now, I can't imagine how much worse it would be if I had to wear tight jeans that dug into my stomach, but I can't complain too much this time, considering I'm heading to my dream destination for a week.

As I gaze through the foggy glass at the wet ground outside, I notice a black car pull up and park in front of the entrance. I sigh, knowing it's not for me.

I look down at my phone resting in my hands and check the time. *4:28.* I expect him to be arriving in a taxi soon, but there isn't a doubt in my mind that he'll be a little late due to the traffic. *It's always the traffic.*

I flinch as I hear a knocking against the glass door in front of me. Wide-eyed I look up and see Mason cupping his hands against the door, attempting to see inside as the foggy glass obscures him.

From what I can tell, he's wearing a black wool jacket over a dark suit, which is definitely not the most ideal outfit for a long flight, but it is a business trip, so I'll give him the benefit of the doubt.

His eyes search the room, and when he spots me, a smile grows on his face as he steps back and waves for me to come out.

Holding the railing, I push myself up from the steps I'm sitting on and grab my rolling suitcase. I walk to the door and open it slightly, letting the bitter cold fly through the doorway, making me shiver as it stings my face.

"Hi," he says softly, taking a step back from the door. "Are you ready to go?"

"Yes," I nod, inhaling as I brace myself for the rush of the outdoor breeze and cold.

Mason pulls the door open wider and extends his arm as I roll my suitcase in front of me.

"Here. I've got it," he insists, grabbing the handle.

"Thank you," I smile, crossing my arms in an attempt to keep the warmth from escaping me.

I take a step outside as he walks down the steps. His body leans slightly to the side as my bag weighs him down, but he quickly carries it to the back of the black car.

My brows draw together. Maybe he couldn't get a taxi in this weather? Or did he decide to drive himself? He said he didn't have a car, but that could have been yet another one of his white lies. So, if it's his, it's pretty bold to own a car in the city.

He loads my bag into the trunk and after closing the hood, he jogs over to me as he tries to avoid getting even wetter from the rain.

"I didn't expect a bag so small to be so heavy," he chuckles as he reaches me under the protection of the awning.

He shakes his head, attempting to dry his hair and wipes droplets off his forehead with the back of his hand.

"I didn't want to forget anything," I chuckle back. "But I also wanted to make sure it fit in the overhead so the airline wouldn't lose my bag for any reason."

Mason scoffs quietly as the corner of his mouth tips up. "Good thinking."

Grabbing the umbrella that's resting against the floor-length window, Mason opens it up and holds it over him. With his other hand, he reaches out and I slide into his arms.

The warmth radiating from his body immediately erases the chills that were still tingling my arms, and I nuzzle closer.

Huddling under the umbrella, we walk down the steps in unison and over to the parked car. I expect him to open the passenger door, assuming he's driving, but he opens the door to the back seat.

Holding the umbrella above me as I slide in, I'm startled when I see a man sitting in the front seat.

"Oh, hello," I say, acknowledging him.

Okay, so he didn't drive here. Maybe it's one of those fancy black car services? Seems like it could be one of the perks of the business.

I see his reflection in the small rear view mirror and he smiles up at me, but remains quiet. Then, Mason opens the opposite door and slides in next to me.

Leaning forward he says, "Alright, let's go."

I look over at the man in the driver's seat as he nods and puts the car into gear. Mason leans back in his seat and turns to look at me.

"You ready?" he asks.

I nod with a smile as our car drives off.

Chapter Seventeen

Mason

Pulling onto the tarmac, I'm tempted to look outside, but the windows are fogged over. I'm aware I don't need to see outside to know the rain has picked up—I can hear it pounding against the car roof.

I grab the umbrella from the pocket in the car door and open it as I slide out. It does little to shield me from the rain—I can still feel the mist against my cheek as it falls in at an angle.

I walk around the car and open the door for Lily, who smiles at me as she steps out.

"Let's hurry!" I insist, pulling down on the handle and hoping to get it as low as I can to keep Lily dry. "It's pouring out."

Ducking under the umbrella, we quickly run to the stairs leading up to the plane. I stop at the bottom step and gesture for her to go first, but she's no longer next to me.

I quickly look around and see her standing a few feet behind me, staring up at the plane. Without thinking, I rush over to her, covering her once again under the umbrella as I slide my arm around her.

"What are you doing?" I ask, looking down at her as I wrinkle my brow. "You're getting soaked."

She continues to stare straight ahead with wide eyes and her mouth slightly open.

"When you said not to worry about paying, I thought that it may have meant you had an extra plane ticket."

She blinks quickly and then slowly adds, "Like in economy."

I lick my lips, then see her pupils dilate as they remain focused forward.

She swallows hard and quickly stutters, "Not that we'd be leaving in a jet!"

I feel a sudden jolt of happiness race through me. She may not realize it, but from that response alone, I can tell she didn't have a clue that our family was so financially fortunate.

I chuckle and she blinks rapidly, snapping herself out of a trance, and looks up at me with her brows raised.

"Come on," I say, gesturing toward the plane.

I pull her forward, her feet dragging briefly before she lifts them, and we take a couple of steps. As we near the plane, she lifts her head, her mouth still wide open in awe.

"After you," I say, nodding my head toward the door.

She takes a step and slightly trips, but I catch her arm, and her attention turns down as she focuses on walking up. Following closely behind, I shake the umbrella out before entering the plane.

I turn around and nearly run into the back of her as she stands frozen in the walkway.

"Where is everyone?" she asks without turning around, assuming she's examining the cabin.

"Who else are you expecting?" I joke, placing my hand behind her back as I escort her over to one of the seats. "Maybe everyone else is late? Here, have a seat."

She sits down slowly in the large leather chair and leans back, closing her eyes as if she's being absorbed into the seat. A muted chuckle escapes my throat and after a moment, she opens her eyes, blinking suddenly, before scowling up at me.

"Miles told me you weren't in marketing," she admits.

"I mean, we do marketing too," I say, teetering my head back and forth as I look at the plane ceiling to avoid eye contact.

Then, I hear a puff of air come out her nose as if she doesn't believe me and when I look back at her, the corner of her mouth slowly tips up.

"He said you'd say that too," she jokes, playfully biting her lip.

I open my mouth to speak, but she quickly adds, "Don't worry though. I don't blame you for not telling me.

I can only imagine how stressful it is to take over a family business."

I nod in agreement. "Yeah, at times."

I take my coat off and drape it over my arm as I take a step toward the stewardess in the aisle behind us. She reaches out to me and I hand it over to her before stepping over to a chair across from Lily.

Unbuttoning my suit jacket to sit down, I glance over to see she has her elbows resting on the armrest and she's leaning towards me.

"What?" I chuckle deeply, seeing her prolonged eye contact.

She frowns and then looks down as she grabs the center of her denim jacket.

"If I had known you would be dressed so nice, I would have picked something different to wear."

I furrow my brows, placing both of my hands on the armrests as I sit down.

"What do you mean? You look beautiful."

She purses her lips as she looks down at her legs, lifting each one up, back and forth.

"I'm wearing sweatpants," she groans, looking back over to me with pursed lips.

"I like sweatpants," I tell her with a smirk.

She tries to hide her smile I see peeking through, but that doesn't hide the redness appearing on her cheeks.

The stewardess walks between us down the aisle and to the front of the plane. She seals the door shut and quickly returns to the back of the plane.

I glance back at Lily and she's staring forward.

"What?" I ask.

"It's just us? Nobody else is coming?" she questions, raising a brow.

"Apparently not," I lie, attempting to sound shocked despite knowing that nobody else was joining us all along.

"Why am I under the impression that this little family business of yours is not so little?" she asks, as she narrows her eyes at me.

"I'm not sure what you mean," I coyly say as I shrug my shoulders.

I look up just as the stewardess hands me a glass of champagne, thinking it's perfect timing—I'm not sure I want to explain it all right now.

"Thank you," I say, giving her a small smile before turning to look at Lily, who is scowling at me with her head tilted.

"Please don't tell me you own this plane too."

I shake my head and lie, "I don't own this plane."

"Okay, sure," she mutters, holding the words like she can see directly through my lie.

The stewardess takes a step over to Lily and hands her a glass. She takes a sip from her glass, then turns to me holding her drink up.

"Is this the normal treatment on a private plane?"

I lean back into my seat and look at her over my shoulder, shrugging as I lie again, "I wouldn't know."

Turning my attention back to the front, I raise my eyebrows and take a sip just as I feel the plane start to push forward. When I pull the glass away, I playfully scoff, then add, "I'm a first timer too."

Chapter Eighteen

Lily

I blink suddenly as I'm jolted awake by rocky movement, and my first instinct is to look over at Mason.

The cabin is quiet, and the lights are all dimmed, except for one brightly lit above Mason, making his hair appear almost gleaming. Unaware I've woken up, I smile softly at the view in front of me. This man, blissfully unaware that my attention is focused on him.

A shuffling noise draws my attention down, and I see he's holding a piece of paper in his hands. After he finishes reading the page, he lifts the small pile of papers on the tray table in front of him and slides it into a stack, moving it to the back.

Lifting another page to study it closely, I see his eyebrows arch, and he looks like he doesn't want to miss anything while he reads.

I squint at the page, attempting to read it, but it's too far away for me to see clearly. I press my forearms against my chair's armrest and as I lean forward to try to get a closer look, I hear the leather under my arm squeak.

Almost immediately, Mason's head rises and as he turns, I quickly face forward, pretending to still be asleep.

I take a deep breath, but my heart starts racing, feeling as though I've been caught looking at something I wasn't supposed to. Mine may be closed, but I can feel his eyes are glued to me. Is he wondering if I saw anything important? I hope as far as he's aware, I'm still sleeping.

Thinking he'll eventually return to his work, I take a deep breath, calming myself from the slight adrenaline rush. As I hear him shift in his seat, I assume he's back to focusing on his paperwork and the coast is clear. *I haven't been caught.*

Opening one of my eyes slowly, I hold my breath as I turn slightly to look at Mason. As I suspected, his attention is focused back down at the table.

Shifting myself back into my seat, a chime from overhead suddenly startles me and when I turn back to Mason, he's looking my way. Our eyes meet and a soft smile forms on his face, which quickly tips up in the corner. *Damn it, he knows.*

My eyes grow wide, then I quickly look up as I hear, "This is your Captain speaking. Sorry, just some momentary turbulence."

Out of the corner of my eye, I notice Mason's attention is still on me. I press my legs together in my seat, feeling a slight tingling and shaking my head, I turn to him nonchalantly.

"Can you point me to where the bathroom is?" I ask with raised brows.

His smile remains steady and he nods his head to the side, gesturing toward the back of the plane.

"In the back."

"Thank you," I softly smile as I stand from my seat.

I grab the top of the chairs with each hand and make my way down the aisle, steading myself in case of additional turbulence. I see a dimly lit green sign at the back of the plane, indicating the bathroom and walk in, closing the door behind me.

As I close the door and a light flickers on, I turn around and my eyes widen.

"Are you kidding me?" I gasp, raising my brows to look around the room.

Expecting a normal airline bathroom, I'm completely awestruck by the size of this one. Two of my own apartment bathrooms would fit into this one alone, and there'd still be extra room. Is this how all private planes are?

Stepping over to the large mirror that covers the entire wall, I turn on the sink nozzle and quickly wash my hands under the water. The sweet smell of oranges fills my nostrils from the soap, and as expected, the towels have a plush-like softness to them.

I take a deep breath as I place my hands on the edge of the marble counter, looking at myself in the mirror. This may be very well the furthest date I've ever been on from a first date with someone. *Give or take 4,500 miles?*

I bite my lip as a smile grows on my face and my cheeks grow red. I don't know what to expect from this trip, but I have no doubt it'll be memorable.

My eyes flash to the door in the reflection of the mirror as I hear a creak and it slowly opens. Did I really go into a bathroom and forget to lock the door behind me? *Probably.*

Mason quickly slides through the small opening and with his hands behind his back, he closes the door. A quick click confirms he's locked it.

Once again, my eyes grow wide as I look back at myself in the mirror, before turning to look over my shoulder.

"What are you doing?" I yelp, turning around to face him. "You can't be in here."

He raises one brow. "Who says I can't?"

Maybe me for one?

He takes a step forward as his eyes search my face, waiting for a response. I take a step back, feeling the undeniable tension between us filling the room, and immediately feel my ass press back against the counter. I turn my head slightly and place my hands on the edge, before looking back towards Mason.

For a man who is so reserved, he sure is bold. But then again, it's not too difficult to become comfortable with someone once you've slept with them.

My chest rises as I part my lips to reply to his remark, but no words come out.

Maybe I don't want him to leave.

He takes another step forward, inching closer until he's hovering over me. I gaze up at his blue eyes, and they appear to darken as our eyes stay locked.

"Shall I leave?" he tempts me, as a smirk forms on his face. *No, please don't.*

I bite my lip subtly, hoping he can read my mind where I'm silently confessing to myself that I'm willing to take the risk, but is he?

I feel his hand reach for my face, and just as he cups my jaw, his thumb grazes my mouth. The momentary touch against my lips sends a sharp, electric zap, creating a physical spark between us. My heartbeat quickens beneath his thrilling touch as a mix of fear and a sensational delight rises within me—fear of being caught and delight at what's to come.

Just as I wonder if he can also feel my heartbeat pounding through my cheek, he stops his movement.

His voice grows low as he leans forward, narrowing his eyes and says, "You're a curious one, aren't you?"

I furrow my brows and playfully ask, "What do you mean?"

He deeply scoffs as the tip of his mouth rises.

"Did you think I wouldn't notice you looking over my shoulder as I worked?" he states, raising a brow.

I tighten my lips and look off to the side, trying to hide the guilt I know is written all over my face.

Learning back slightly, he adds, "I wouldn't mind if you did."

I look back at him and tilt my head, feeling slightly less guilty about snooping than before, but not enough to admit it.

"Still don't know what you're talking about," I tease with a devilish smile.

"No?" he asks playfully, tilting his head down to look me directly in the eyes.

I slowly shake my head back and forth, as I look up at him from beneath my brows.

"You shouldn't be in here," I bluntly admit, but aching for him to stay.

"Who says I can't?" he taunts.

I glance over at the locked door, then back at him.

"We'll get in trouble for both being in here."

"I won't tell if you won't."

I watch as he presses his tongue against the back of his front teeth, his crooked smile widening—like he's blatantly disregarding the rules.

Looking down at his parted lips, I quickly lick my own, feeling the dryness from the cabin air. My lips always seem to be dry on planes, yet I seldom remember to bring chapstick. Looking at him, his lips aren't dry at all. In fact, they look as though they are begging to soothe mine.

I bite my lip playfully as I shift my focus back to his eyes. His smile fades, he narrows his eyes at me and leans forward, pressing his weight against my body, forcing my ass deeper against the counter. It almost hurts, but I barely feel it—because all I can think about are his lips on mine.

I try to pull my hands away from the edge of the counter, but with his weight against me, my arms behind me are locked in place. Squirming slightly, I manage to free one hand, but he quickly places his free one on top of it, holding it down.

I glance down at my hand, then glare up at him.

"Hey!" I say sternly, wanting to be in control. "I wanted to ki—"

He swiftly cups his hand over my mouth, stopping me from finishing my sentence. I stare up at him wide-eyed, both shocked and excited by his boldness.

He looks off to the side out of the corner of his eye, then as he leans in closer, his eyes focus back directly on me.

"Shush," he says as a momentary smirk rises in the corner of his mouth.

He pulls himself slightly away from me as he looks over his shoulder momentarily, which helps to release my other hand where it was trapped from behind my back.

Then, looking back at me, he licks his lips and gives me an alluring smile before playfully adding, "Don't want us to get caught, do you?"

I quickly inhale through my nose as my legs slightly tremble beneath me at the suggestion. He may have appeared hesitant when I saw him at the coffee shop, but now, he's unapologetically daring.

I slowly shake my head in response, feeling my bundle of nerves aching as his hand moves down from my mouth. Rotating his hand and lowering it to my chin, his thumb brushes over my bottom lip. I expect yet another spark, but instead the touch intensifies the growing sensation between my legs.

Exhaling, his thumb pulls at my bottom lip, breaking my lips apart as he continues bringing his fingers slowly down my neck. Despite having my hands free and trying to consider where to put them, I'm frozen as I tilt my head back and instinctually close my eyes.

Soon I feel the soft brush of the back of his index finger move down my neck. Slow, yet teasing, in every way. Before I know it, the touch vanishes, replaced by the warmth of his breath against my skin. I feel his hand steadily wrap around the back of my waist, and as he pulls me tightly against his body, my eyes shoot open and I wrap my arms around the back of his neck.

Staring up at the bathroom ceiling, my eyes flicker as his lips finally touch my throat, but he places a painstakingly slow kiss against my skin that does nothing to deplete the growing urges I'm feeling. I take a deep breath and as his lips pull away, I'm certain he knows how I feel as my breath shudders and my veins pulse in my neck. Waiting and feeling his warm breath still close to me, is turning into a slow and agonizing delay.

He pulls me tighter against his body as he nuzzles his face into my neck and I can feel the fabric of his suit pants become tighter between my legs. Breathing deeply, his lips lightly brush against my skin, which sends a shiver up my spine that is impossible to ignore.

Finally, I feel the urge inside of me take over and I can no longer wait. Especially not when every touch of his lips intensifies the heat building straight to my core. I want more. *Now.*

Arching my breasts out, hoping he'll take the hint, his lips meet my skin again, but this time, it's not a subtle kiss. His lips quickly start to flow over my throat as he devours me and I close my eyes once again, leaning my head back, not caring if he leaves a mark. It's exactly what I want right now, but unfortunately it's not what I *need* right now.

With impulsiveness, I pull my head back even further, breaking the seal he's generated between my skin and his lips, I wrap my hand around the back of his neck. Pulling his face u[to mine, I don't give him a second to catch his breath as I press our lips deeply together.

His other hand slowly moves from my back, up my arm and behind my neck. I feel him pull back slightly, drawing in a breath of air, before breaking my lips apart with his tongue. His fingers dig through my hair and he starts to consume me. Between heavy gasps of air, he explores every part of my mouth that I'm sharing with him, and I devour back his sweet, delicious taste.

Releasing my head, his hands slide down to my ass and he presses my hips tightly against him. I feel the pulsing below his belt and with a quick sway of my body, his hands reach down behind my thighs, pulling me up onto the counter.

As our lips break apart, he glances down at my lap and glides his hands back up to my waistline. He attempts to move his hand below my waistband and back over my ass beneath the fabric, but barely gets a handful before stopping.

"You've been teasing me all day with these sweatpants," he growls under his breath.

"Teasing you?" I chuckle as I tilt my head.

He quickly kneels down and looks up at me from beneath his brows. With a crooked smile, he directs his attention to my waist, and his fingers delicately curl around the elastic band on the top of my sweatpants, tugging at them. Using his shoulders as support, I lift myself just enough off the counter for him to pull them down further and past my knees until I watch them fall to the floor. He brings his hands slowly up the sides of my thighs and brushes his hands up and down, sending exciting chills down my spine.

Taking in a breath of air, my chest rises too fast as I eagerly await what's next.

Smirking, he says, "Yes, teasing. They were concealing just a little too much."

I feel my cheeks tighten as I try to hide my growing smile, just as his attention turns back down. He glides his hands onto the top of my lap, then slowly slides them between my legs, sending a vibrant sensation through me as he slowly parts them.

Suddenly overwhelmed, I quickly press my legs together trapping his hands between them and immediately, he looks up at me with a raised brow.

"Do I make you nervous?" he asks, a slight thrill in his voice.

I shake my head slowly, keeping my eyes locked on his, but really, I'm silently nodding yes.

He huffs as if amused by my blatant lie, and then adds, "Are you sure about that? Because I've been waiting for an opportunity for us to be alone again, and now that we are stuck on this plane, I'm going to take advantage of it."

I inhale sharply, taken aback by his bold statement as I try to hide the rush of attraction that hits me. His eyes lower to my lips and I look down to catch the start of his dimple forming, paired with a playful smile. Before I can glance back into his eyes, my legs are suddenly spread apart once more as he rises from the ground and wraps his hand behind my head, pulling me into a deep kiss.

I wrap my arms around his neck, devouring his kiss as waves of emotion run through me. In the back of my mind, fear of being caught heightens every sensation as my adrenaline rises and a deluge of pleasure builds from within.

I bite his lip hard, overwhelmed by the intensity and feel him twitch momentarily between my lips, but he never breaks away.

Briefly releasing his hand from behind my neck, I hear him fidget with his belt. *Hurry up I internally scream.* After a few seconds, I realize it's not nearly quick enough, and it becomes a distraction that needs to be dealt with. *Sooner rather than later.*

Releasing my hands from around his neck, I slide them down his chest. Anticipating my next move, he pulls his pelvis back, giving me enough room to assist. He places his hands on each side of me on the edge of the counter as I quickly get to work.

Grabbing both sides of his belt, I quickly unlatch it and then pop the button out of the hole on his pants before working on the zipper. As it reaches its end point, I start to pull his pants down, but get distracted by his erection trying to break free. I clench my legs against the side of his thighs, feeling a pool of moisture building, and I move my hands back around his neck.

Bringing his lips back to mine, he places one hand onto my lower back and the other glides down the side of my thighs, then moves between my legs. His finger dances over my thong, painstakingly teasing me while sending an exciting chill up my spine as the fluttering movement adds to the blissful sensations I'm experiencing.

Without pause, his finger pulls the wet fabric to the side, and with a quick tug against my back with his other hand, my bare ass slides forward on the counter. I sip in a breath while I have the chance, and as I reach the edge— and before I can exhale—his fingers slip inside me. I pull my lips from his briefly just as I hear a quiet ding above me —which I immediately disregard—and focus on his movement, while feeling the tip of him brush against the inside of my leg. Curling his fingers inside me, my grip tightens around his neck and I flutter my eyes, feeling his thumb brush over my bundle of nerves.

Suddenly, a shift in the cabin jolts us slightly off balance, causing my eyes to briefly spring open. His hand —which pulled out and released my thong during the abrupt interruption—slides my thong to the side again. Then, before the plane can settle, he quickly thrusts himself inside of me. The forceful impact makes me nearly breathless and feeling him push his way to the hilt, I can't help myself as I let out a soft moan.

The plane shifts once more and I close my eyes again tightly, feeling him throbbing inside me, pushing deeper as gravity brings him forward. My breasts press into his chest as he catches himself against the mirror, and I'm oblivious to the moment his hand let go of my thong and slid out from between my legs. He attempts to steady himself, removing his hand from beside my head, and I feel my ass being gripped tightly as the plane jolts again, sending a thrilling mix of pleasure and pain through me.

Slowly adjusting on the now-titled floor, he continues to thrust, managing to hit every delectable spot, and heightening every sense within me. The lingering scent of orange-scented soap mixes with the sweetness of his breath, flooding my senses. The ambient sound of the plane shutters his low grunts, but I'm still able to hear the faint commotion of someone just outside the door—presumably the stewardess.

Through his soft lips, his deep, strong bated breaths against my skin begin to engulf me as my heart races, threatening to break free. I gasp for air, overwhelmed as my emotions take over, the intensity rising. Everything all at once—overpowering yet consuming. It's like being underwater, yet he is the force that pulls me back to the surface to breathe. The only lifeline I'll ever need.

Pressing into the most intrinsic parts of pleasure inside of me, the plane tilts again, pushing my hips forward as I willingly beg for more. With one hand firmly on my ass, he squeezes it hard, acknowledging that carnal need, and with the other hand, he slides down my thigh and wraps it around the back of my knee. Pulling my leg firmly up to the side of his body, he pushes himself deeper than I thought he could with a swift movement that now forces my lips apart from his.

Keeping my eyes closed, I pull my head forward, as I concentrate on the heightened pleasure, every deep thrust and every delicious pull. He mimics me, pressing his forehead against mine, and while steadying himself as he holds my leg he continues to push into me. He's careful with each movement, but steady on beat, as our bodies create a rhythm.

My lips part as my breathing heightens, I roll my hips with every thrust and and I feel his strong, heavy breaths back on my skin, slowly building and mimicking my own. *So. Damn. Close.*

With one last pull of my leg toward him, I feel the plane steady as he hits a spot that sends a satisfying chill through me. The loud ambient sounds of the plane ring through my ears, my toes curl and I fall apart as my body takes over. I let out a loud moan, but quickly suppress it by covering my mouth with my hand, knowing the stewardess could be listening in. Yet, I feel immense relief as all the built-up pleasure I've been holding in releases from within me. *Finally.*

Catching my breath, we hear a clear ding above us, and we pull our foreheads apart as we glance up.

The speaker crackles slightly before hearing the Captain say, "Sorry folks! We just passed through a slight storm surge, but it should be smooth sailing from here."

I feel my cheeks tighten by the smile growing on my face, completely unbothered by the fact that we could have easily been injured during the turbulence.

Lowering my head to meet Mason's eyes, he quickly looks over his shoulder at the door. Turning back towards me, he can barely contain his widening smile, and a soft chuckle escapes my lips.

Oh, this will definitely be something to remember.

Chapter Nineteen

Lily

The warm breeze flowing through my hair is welcoming as we drive along a winding road that weaves through valleys of green hills and lush vineyards.

Closing my eyes, I lean my head back and rest it against the headrest. The sun shines over my entire face, and the blissful warmth is a stark contrast to the weather back home.

The remaining hours on the plane went by quickly, but they definitely weren't easy. I had hoped we hadn't been caught as we sat back in our seats, but when I saw the stewardess again, her face gave it all away.

My plan had been to sleep longer, but with my adrenaline remaining elevated, settling down would have been impossible. At this point, I'm honestly surprised that I'm not feeling more fatigued—either I'm lucky, or overly excited to be here.

Tilting my head to the side, I look out at the rolling hills that overlap each other as far as my eyes can see. A soft smile grows on my face and I roll my head over the top of the seat to look at Mason driving.

As far as I knew, Mason always wore suits—mirroring his brother—yet just before we arrived, I barely recognized him as he stepped out of the plane's bathroom in something far more casual. A muted green tee that hugged his chest, sculpting his muscles in a way that made me internally begging to drag him back into the plane's bathroom. He paired it with tan slacks, a brown belt and brown loafers. I shouldn't have been so caught off guard by his look, yet it confirmed to me that this man could pull off anything.

Glancing back up to his face, his short hair appears to be tangling from the wind as his forehead reaches just past the top of the windshield in the convertible. I can't see his eyes through his sunglasses, but I'm curious if he's just as captivated by the countryside as I am.

"This is just so beautiful. Isn't it?"

A subtle smile plays on his lips as he glances at me briefly, before turning his attention back to the road.

"I can think of a few things more beautiful," he smiles, as I see the dimple appear on his cheek.

"Yeah?" I ask, sitting up to look at him more directly.

He glances at me quickly, then turns back to the road as he nods.

"Yeah."

I pull my bottom lip between my teeth and turn the opposite way, feeling myself blush. Glancing at the side mirror I see how red my cheeks have become, and I quickly bring my hand up to my face. Moving my hand up and then down to my chin, I slowly tilt my head and look at him. His smile is still wide on his face as he focuses ahead and he seems to be aware of me studying his features.

With every stolen look at him, I find myself growing more and more attracted. Or maybe he's always been this attractive and I'm only realizing it now?

His jaw clenches for a moment and seeing it forces me to press my legs together once again. Feeling the heat growing, I quickly turn to face the landscape, feeling almost embarrassed by how easily he's turning me on.

I watch the needle-like trees lining the road disappear into the distance. With my eyes glued to the skyline, I ask, "Will we—"

"Don't worry," he replies, answering my incomplete question. "We'll be back in a few days for my business meeting."

"It's out here?" I ask, looking toward the skyline as I tilt my head. "In the middle of nowhere?"

He chuckles deeply and clicks his tongue.

"Yes, it'd be too difficult to grow anything on the coast's steep cliffside."

I open my mouth to speak, then quickly press my lips together, knowing that once again my mouth is prepared to beat the thoughts in my head.

"That makes sense," I nod, despite still not understanding why grapes can't grow on a cliffside—a question I'll undoubtedly ask him when we return for the meeting.

A light tickle on my arm pulls my attention between us. Resting on the center console, Mason's palm is open and his fingers are spread apart—a subtle yet clear way to show me he wants to hold my hand.

I feel a tightness in my cheeks again, and I have no doubt I'm blushing. I raise my hand slightly but immediately feel the dampness on my palm. *Oh my god, I'm nervous.* It's a small thing to feel nervous about, yet it signifies so much more.

Even though Miles may have said Mason changed, I'm still looking for the small moments where he proves that to me—giving me the assurance that it's okay for me to let my guard completely down.

I've seen a rom-com or two in my lifetime. Holding hands isn't something you do with a fling or someone you don't carry feelings for. And if that were the case, you certainly wouldn't take some random person to Italy with you either. *Could he truly care for me that way?*

I take a quick breath and rub my hand against the side of my leg, then tap my fingers together to ensure my hand is now dry. The moment I place my hand in his, he immediately begins to softly rub his thumb back and forth over the top—a small yet encouraging sign.

I rest my other arm on the door and get lost in the scenery as we wind through the hills.

Just as quickly as we drove through the countryside, we arrive at the coast. The water is blue but fades to turquoise near us, and it feels as if we are driving right over it as the road sits along the edge of the cliffs.

Passing through a small tunnel, we emerge on the other side and I see a glimpse of a coastal town. Several long docks stretch out into the water from the rocky shore, and as we pass through another tunnel, I see small cliffside homes above us that look down onto the road—each with a red or yellow shingle roof.

I expect us to drive into a quaint picturesque town that looks to be straight out of a postcard, but suddenly Mason takes a left turn, away from the town.

The narrow road winds steeply up through the cliffs, and the view of the small town behind us is quickly shadowed by the hills.

I desperately want to go back and see the town, but I bite my tongue. While this may be my first time in Italy, it's not my trip to decide where we go. After all, Mason invited me. But that doesn't mean I won't still try to pay my part.

After a few minutes, we turn another corner and pull up to a small, rocky driveway that leads to a single-story white house with a pink shingle roof. The house is surrounded by those same needle-like trees, and across the road is the continuation of the tall hill we drove halfway up.

Mason steps out of the car, and as I reach for my passenger door handle, he quickly reaches my side and pulls the door open for me.

"Thank you," I smile as I grab his hand, pulling myself out of the car. Then, I tilt my head up as I get to my feet.

"Is this where we are staying?"

"For now, yes," he nods, before shaking his head with a smile. "Come on. I want to show you something."

I follow him through the front door and down a small set of steps that lead right into the living room. The room is bright, filled with colorful furniture and a blue chandelier—something you don't see every day. The walls are decorated with scenic photos in a multitude of sizes, giving the space a museum-like feel. There's also a small fireplace that appears to be straight out of the seventeenth century.

"Oh wow," I beam, genuinely excited to just be here.

"This isn't it," he whispers, pulling me over to a large wooden door.

The door creaks as he opens it and a bright light nearly blinds me, forcing me to hold my hand up in front of my face. Stepping through the door, I blink quickly as my eyes adjust to the light and see Mason smiling in front of me.

"This is," he smiles before stepping aside.

I look around to see that we are standing outside on a terrace, with intricate tiles on the floor and shades of pink surrounding us. I take a few steps forward toward the white pillars in front of me, and suddenly I'm met with the most breathtaking view of the ocean.

Placing my hands on the short, pink wall, I look down to see a panoramic view overlooking that coastal town and my mouth drops open.

"Oh my God!"

Cascading down the cliffside are colorful homes with narrow roads weaving between them. There's thousands of them that scatter down to a large beach, with rows of bright umbrellas that line the sand. Lush green cliffs that flow into the sea sit in the distance and as my eyes glance towards the water, there's small white sailboats scattered around the small cove.

I turn to see Mason and an excited expression forms on his face.

"I had a feeling you'd like the view."

"Like it?" I cheer with wide eyes. "I can't even tell you how breathtaking it is. I've never seen anything like it."

I turn back to the view and the only thing I can see in front of me is a literal postcard of beauty, similar to a make-believe image that you can only form in your head, unless you witness it in person as I am now. I still don't believe it.

A sudden, overwhelming guilt fills my stomach. With a view like this, I can't even imagine how expensive this house must be. How much this entire trip may cost. Mason said not to worry, but this is too much. Even if I wanted to, I have nothing to contribute at this level.

"What's wrong?" he frowns, placing his hand on my shoulder and turning me towards him.

"This is too much," I mumble, taking a deep breath as I bite my cheek.

"What do you mean?" he asks, wrinkling his brow.

I look down, trying to find the right words. He said the business meeting was out in the countryside. He wasn't supposed to be here at the coast, so the only explanation I can think of is that we're here for me. To provide me with an experience I've never had before. I want to be here, but I didn't expect all of this. I didn't expect him to spend this much, to do this much for me so soon.

"Hey, tell me what's wrong," he says softly, lifting my chin up to look at him.

With his blue eyes now scanning my face, I can see he's desperate for me to speak, but what do I even tell him? He's spending too much money on someone he just met?

"If I did something wrong, please let me know," he gulps, and I see his Adam's Apple rise and fall.

"You've brought me to Italy. You've shown me this amazing place with this amazing view. I can't let you pay for all of this. It's too much."

I'm trying to look away when suddenly I feel his hand reach up to my face. Before he touches me, I slowly turn my attention back to him. As our eyes meet, I notice the new creases around his eyes, and he's no longer anxious.

"You think I didn't expect it'd be expensive?" he snickers as he raises one brow. "I knew it would be, but I didn't care."

"But—"

He shakes his head and my words quickly fall away.

"Yes, we may be planning everything around this meeting, but I wanted you to have fun as well—to actually enjoy the trip. And I might be stating the obvious here, but whether you choose to see me again after this or not, I'll be happy knowing I gave you an experience in Italy that you won't forget."

I can feel my face slowly lifting as I listen intently to his words, but then that punch in my stomach returns. *It's still too much.*

My eyes quickly break from his, and I look out at the water. His hand cups the side of my face and despite the creeping guilt, I instantly melt into it as he pulls my head back to face him. The tension in my body eases as our eyes meet again and as if he had sensed before how calming his touch was, his thumb lightly rubs across my cheek.

"It's not about the money, or how much I may or may not have spent. It's always been about you. Trust me on that."

I know I can't hold onto this. I can't continue to fight him on this, or it will only make it more difficult. I know I have to let this go, I have to in order to truly enjoy this trip. He has chosen to bring me here and I have to appreciate every moment.

"Okay," I whisper with a soft smile as I feel my cheeks tighten.

"Okay," he says, leaning forward and placing a soft kiss against my lips.

Pulling away, a yawn suddenly escapes my mouth and I immediately reach up to cover it with my hand.

"I'm so sorry," I chuckle, shaking my head as his hand falls from my face.

His mouth tightens as if he's trying to contain a silent laugh, while he grabs ahold of my hand and squeezes it.

"Tired?" he taunts as he raises a brow.

"Not even a bit," I lie, tightening my lips to suppress another yawn. "I got so much sleep on the plane."

"If you say so," he teases, tilting his head to the side.

Letting go of my hand, he says, "I'm going to grab our bags and bring them inside. Why don't you go look around?"

I nod and he walks back through the wooden door as I turn around to look out at the view. Both this house and the nearby coastal town seem asleep, because I can't hear a single sound from up on this terrace, only the faint crash of waves below.

To think that if I still had a job, I wouldn't have had the opportunity to be here—to see *this*.

I bite my lip as a wide grin of gratitude spreads across my face just before I turn around and trace Mason's steps back through the door, but a small door open to my right redirects my attention.

Leading myself inside, I see the ceiling with its exposed old wood beams. The rest of the room is bright white, and as I turn to click the switch for the overhead light, I notice the wall is smooth stucco. As the light comes on, it barely illuminates the room, leaving the two small windows on the farthest wall to provide just enough light.

In the middle of the room is a large, king-size bed with a dark wood railing headboard. Just the sight of it forces me to suppress yet another yawn, so I quickly shake my head, pushing it away.

I walk over to the bed and touch the light brown quilt covering the bed—which matches the curtains around the windows. It's soft, and despite being untouched until now, it's warm from the sun shining into the room.

I hear a quick chime and turn around, expecting Mason to walk into the room, but there's no sight of him. I listen again and this time I recognize it as a wind chime outside. It's a soothing sound that's subtly making noises through the stark silence, and it reminds me of the sounds you hear when you get a massage.

Maybe I'll just rest my eyes while I wait for him? It'll only be for a minute.

I launch myself onto the bed, releasing some of the pent up excitement I have been suppressing and instantly feel the covers hugging me in their warmth. Then, in only a matter of seconds, everything fades to black.

Chapter Twenty

Mason

Leaning against the door frame, I look out onto the terrace where the vines—intertwining between the wood slat above—are moving slightly with the breeze. The warmth from earlier fades as the sun sets just above the horizon, and the cool air from the sea moves in.

I lean back, peering slightly around the door to see a clear view of Lily lying face down on the bed, with her legs dangling off the edge.

When I came back into the house with our luggage, I called for her, but received no reply. When I stepped further into the living room and yelled out her name again, I felt my heart drop as the room remained silent. A slight panic rose inside of me as I thought of the unsettling words she had spoken. *This is too much.*

When I heard that, I didn't know what to think— whether she felt everything regarding my past was too much or if it was the trip itself. All I want is to spend more time with her and prove to her that I've changed. I was hoping she believed me and that spending time in this beautiful setting would help, but I still don't know for sure.

When she mentioned the cost of the trip being too high, I felt a huge weight fall from my shoulders. I know I should have told her from the start that all of this was already taken care of, that for a family like mine, these expenses are not something we worry about considering our wealth, but I couldn't tell her that—at least not yet.

I've experienced women who fall to their knees for money, the ones so desperate they latch onto you quickly and knowing that people like that exist feels cruel. Unfortunately, in our family, you have to keep your guard up until you know exactly how someone will react when they are given opportunities like an all-expenses-paid trip to Italy. So, is it wrong for me to keep it to myself?

Luckily, I quickly saw a humility in Lily and I continue to see it time and time again. The amount of money I have doesn't matter to her. The trip doesn't even matter to her. *Well, maybe just a little.*

And even now, she's still hoping she can contribute to the cost in some manner, and I know it's just her wanting to get her way. It's attractive as hell, but what she doesn't know is that I'd spend every penny in the world if it's on her.

When I came into the house and she didn't answer, a small bit of fear came over me. I thought she left or she had found some other reason to push me away—I didn't know. At that moment, all I wanted to do was make sure she was okay. That she was still here and that my second chance at making it all up to her hadn't ended yet.

When I walked into the bedroom and saw her like that, I couldn't help but laugh. Laugh at the ridiculousness of my thoughts, as well as how she actually fell asleep with half her body hanging off the bed. *Clearly, the jet lag got her.*

When I saw her, I quickly covered my mouth to muffle my laughter and returned to the living room. Unlike her, I wasn't tired—not even a little.

With a quiet ambiance throughout the house, I caught up on some much-needed work on my laptop. Soon, the wind whistling through the open door was tempting, and I was unable to resist, so I took my work outside to the table on the terrace.

I finally closed my laptop after hours of preparing forms and documents for the meeting with the Bombardis in a couple days. When I set it inside, I couldn't resist taking in the view.

Leaning back against the door frame, I cross my arms and look out at the setting sun. Lily desperately needed the rest judging by her position on the bed, but a part of me wishes she was awake to see this—to be by my side.

If I was asked five years ago about how I felt about the family business, I would have wished for someone else to take over, I would have wished to go down my own path. *Make my own choices.*

Now as each day passes, I am humbled by what my father has done for the company; our family has worked hard to ensure we never had to struggle to survive and for that, I'm incredibly grateful.

Maybe it's the fact that when I took over, I learned quickly that there were greater responsibilities in this business other than just caring for myself, because I started to feel like I was missing something early on. I thought it was a lack of confidence—that I would fuck something up and everything would run down the drain.

No. That wasn't it.

It was that day at the coffee shop that a lightbulb moment hit me. I realized I wasn't missing something, but rather someone.

Could Lily be that person I've been hoping to find?

Just a couple months ago, my parents had mentioned their concern with me taking over the business entirely without someone by my side. I disregarded them immediately. Why would taking on the responsibility of a business have anything to do with dating, or even marriage for that matter? It didn't. Not in my mind. *But now? How could I let her go?*

I hear a soft cough from behind me and as I turn towards it, I see Lily slowly walking over to me as she rubs her eyes.

"Hey sleepy head," I joke, turning around as I hold my hand out for her.

"What time is it?" she asks groggily as she squints her eyes toward me.

I quickly look down at my watch.

"Erm—"

"Wait!" she shouts in a panic as I look up and her eyes are now wide. "Please don't tell me I slept all day!"

"Not at all," I laugh, shaking my head.

Grabbing my hand, I pull her forward and against my chest. Caught off guard, she places her hands against my shirt, pushing my back against the door frame as she catches her balance.

I pull her tightly against me wrapping my arms around her lower back, as I look down at her. Her green eyes mirroring my reflection as the sun glistens across her cheek.

"Actually, you woke up at the perfect time."

Keeping my eyes glued to her, I gesture toward the ocean with my head. Turning her head toward the sea, the golden light beams over her and she quickly pushes herself away, mesmerized by the view. My arms fall as she turns her body to face the sunset, and I rest my hand on her lower back.

I watch as her eyes brighten, her lips part slightly and I hear her take in a breath.

"To think I almost missed this," she grins before pressing her lips together.

Her gaze stays fixed on the setting sun, and mine? Well, I can't seem to take my eyes off her.

Just as the sun drops below the horizon, she leans her head against my chest.

"Thank you," she softly says and I can tell she's smiling.

I look down at her bed head—wispy hairs sticking up all around, then I move my hand up to her side as I pull her in closely. Nuzzling her head beneath my neck, I take a deep breath in as my cheeks tighten into a smile.

"Anything for you."

Chapter Twenty-One

Lily

Death. That was the only explanation.

I never would have guessed that six hours of sleep would cure my jet lag, but it did. My only theory? I must have been dead asleep and my body went into hyperdrive because when I woke up, it felt like I had slept for days.

In fact, I thought I had. When I saw the sunset, I was relieved to find that I had only missed the remainder of the afternoon.

As darkness enveloped the sky, I watched the town below light up, illuminating the hills and brightening the streets that wove through the houses.

My stomach grumbled and I was delighted then to hear Mason say that we would be going into town for dinner.

Now, as we drive back down the steep, narrow road, we turn left at the coastline and make our way into the small, quiet town that is now vibrantly awake. We park the car on a small hill just above the beach, and walk up a small cobblestone street to a restaurant that overlooks the town.

Mason holds the door open for me and as we walk through the door, I'm suddenly met by an older man in his late forties, who has dark, slicked-back hair and is wearing glasses. He frowns momentarily, then as if he recognizes us, he holds his hands up as he walks over.

"Benvenuti!" he shouts.

He quickly turns to hold his hand up to the young man behind a small counter, who nods and smiles before looking back down at whatever is on the table in front of him.

"Bonsoir?" I hear as my attention is pulled back to the man in front of me who is raising a brow.

Confused by his swift shift in foreign languages, I raise a brow back. While I can recognize some simple words in Italian, I'm fairly positive he isn't even speaking Italian.

My forehead wrinkles and I look back at Mason as he places his hand on my lower back. I look back at the man and grit my teeth.

"Hi?" I ask nervously, hoping he'll understand.

"Ah!" he cheers, clapping his hands together. With a thick accent, he says, "Americans!"

"Yes," I smile as Mason nods.

Mason holds out his hand in a professional manner and the man quickly cups Mason's hand with both of his and shakes it.

"Welcome! Welcome!" he widely grins.

"Thank you," Mason shyly smiles while simultaneously glancing back at me out of the corner of his eye.

"What brings you in tonight?" the man asks, eyeing us back and forth.

Mason looks ahead and the man leans forward eagerly.

"To eat?" Mason asks, raising a brow. "I believe we have a reservation."

"Ah, of course you do!" he cheerfully nods despite knowing our names. "Only the finest for the lovely couple."

He looks at me and gives me a quick wink before turning on his heel and stepping next to the young man behind the small counter. They exchange a few words, then the young man steps out and walks away.

"You must be Mr. Moore!" he assumes, nodding at Mason.

His head quickly turns to me and he tilts it slightly with a raised brow.

"And you must be Mrs. Moore," he expresses as if he's impressed.

A loud chuckle escapes my lips and I quickly cover my mouth, embarrassed by the assumption.

"Oh no, we're not married," I deny, shaking my head.

I look at Mason out of the corner of my eye and he's looking up and away at the ceiling, as if he can also feel the awkwardness in the room.

I turn back forward and the man raises a brow as his eyes stay glued to mine.

"Maybe not after tonight," he jokes as he winks at me.

As the words leave his mouth, my eyes immediately widen as I feel the tightness in my cheeks. *What?*

"No, we just met," I quickly explain as I hold my hands up in front of me.

He appears doubtful as he raises a brow and looks back and forth between the two of us. He squints his eyes, as if he's secretly wondering whether we are lying or not.

Hoping to resolve the misunderstanding, I quickly say the first words that pop into my head.

"Well, not recently. We actually met before, but then we ran into each other again and this is actually our second date. Kind of a long story, but—"

I instantly stop speaking and turn my attention away as I feel myself being watched.

Looking over at Mason, his cheeks are red, but they appear to be from blushing, rather than embarrassment. My eyes drop down to his lips and they are pressed together. He's clearly holding back a laugh and I have no doubt that he thinks every part of this conversation is amusing. *Oh God, I'm rambling again.*

I quickly shake my head and look back at the man, who now has his arms crossed and his finger pressed against his chin.

"Ah!" he breathes before looking slightly down and quietly saying, "Sei qui a visitare una vecchia fiamma?"

"What?" I ask, leaning forward.

I frown as if that will help me to hear him better or somehow miraculously be able to translate his words. *Nothing.* He shakes his head, feeling my eyes heavily staring at him, and directs his attention quickly over to Mason.

"Signore, right this way."

Mason's hand falls from my back and he gestures for me to walk ahead of him. I follow as he leads us through the crowded restaurant where there isn't a single quiet table.

It's almost surprising to see so many people who genuinely look happy and delighted to be out. The amount of people I see back home at restaurants who appear to have a stick up their asses is next level. Maybe it's the Italian air? Or fresh sea breeze? I wouldn't doubt it for a second.

As we walk toward the back of the restaurant, the host stops next to a table for two that is located next to a wooden balcony. When I reach him, he grabs the chair and pulls it back, gesturing for me to sit.

"Signora," he smiles.

"Grazie," I reply confidently.

He takes a step back and as I look up at his face, his eyes are wide and his mouth hangs open. He quickly covers it with his hands, then pulls them away as a wide grin crosses his face.

"Parli Italiano?" he asks, raising his brows.

I shrug my shoulders and pinch my forefinger and thumb together leaving a small amount of space between them.

"Poco," I nod back and forth before translating, "Only a little."

He brings his pinched fingers up to his mouth and kisses them dramatically.

"Ah! Fantastico!" he says, making me cackle.

As he speaks to Mason, I look more closely at the restaurant around us. Half of the tables are situated under a terrace that has wood slats across the top—similar to a pergola. Each one covered with a bright white tablecloth and a small plant placed in the middle. Vines climb up the pillars that line the edge of the terrace balcony, and while the darkness shadows the beach below, I can hear the waves crash upon the shore. It's more than beautiful. Almost *too* beautiful.

Suddenly, I feel a tight pain in my gut and as the host walks away, I bite my lip nervously as I stare straight ahead at Mason.

"What is it?" he asks, leaning slightly forward over the small table.

My eyes grow wide and I study his expression. He doesn't appear to be nervous like I would expect someone to be, but maybe he hides it well?

I take a deep breath and whisper, "Please don't tell me you're proposing."

His eyebrows draw together as if to think and I feel my heartbeat suddenly hasten. *Why would he say yes? That's crazy.*

The silence between us grows by the second and it only heightens the anxiety growing inside of me. *Oh God, he's going to say yes.* The host knew ahead of time and that's why he made that comment at the door.

Now, I may have just met this man and I'll admit, I may be slowly falling for his charm, but definitely not that fast.

I swallow hard as the silence intensifies. I open my mouth to speak, but I feel a dryness between my lips that won't let any words escape. Shit, maybe that's why he invited me to Italy? Is this the entire plan? *This can't be happening.*

Miles said I can trust Mason, but maybe I trusted him too much? Maybe I unintentionally made him think I was all in? And now, he took it too far.

My body starts to tighten and my instincts take over. I have to find an escape before he gets down on one knee.

Out of the corner of my eye, I look down at the water below. Maybe I can jump? I may get severely injured, but at least I can avoid this entire situation. Maybe I'll still be able to swim just enough to reach the shore and then I can leave Italy without ever speaking to him again. *That'll work, right?*

I'm interrupted by the sound of deep laughter and as I quickly blink away the fear creeping in, I see Mason laughing at me from across the table. The kind of laugh where you have to hold your stomach because it hurts so bad.

"What's so funny?" I finally say in a shrill voice.

Mason tightens his lips, holding back more laughter, while pressing his fingertips against his mouth he attempts to remove the wide grin on his face.

"Do you think that's why we're here?" he laughs, raising a brow.

"You tell me," I demand, trying to confirm what his facial expression is telling me.

"If I were going to propose to you, I'd at least wait until our sixth date," he says in a sarcastic tone. He squints and then looks up as if to think, then adds, "Erm—maybe the seventh."

Laughing at his own reply, I realize he's teasing me and playing off my fear. I scowl at him, but he gives me a quick wink—just as the restaurant host did—and I shake my head. I let out a sigh of relief and now aware that I was tightly gripping the sides of my seat, I relax into it.

"Thank goodness," I chuckle as I wipe away the nonexistent sweat off my forehead.

With a brow raised, he jokes, "Did you really—"

"I don't know!" I practically shout, before lowering my voice. "I watch a lot of romance movies that had me questioning everything." Looking around, I whisper, "Sure seemed like it though!"

I tilt my head back as my eyes wander.

"Fancy restaurant—" I tilt my head in the other direction. "—Beautiful view—"

He jokingly scoffs, mimicking my movement and nods his head.

"You're right, this is a good spot."

"Oh God," I breathe as my eyes widen. "That had to be why the host assumed."

"Very likely," he chuckles. "But if it had been true, I'd have done something far more elaborate."

"What? Italy isn't good enough for you?" I scoff while also hoping he plays into my curiosity.

"Oh, it's enough," he snorts, before pausing to lick his lips. "I've been to many places and this is by far one of my favorites."

"Then?" I beg as I lean close with my brows raised.

In my romance-movie-loving mind, there isn't anywhere else that could top this location. Well, maybe except for Paris—ideally beneath the Eiffel Tower. Oh, or even in a castle in Ireland. I quickly shake my head, realizing the locations are endless and I'd never be able to make up my mind.

"Just not in this way."

I purse my lips and want to ask him what he's thinking, but the man from before arrives back at our table holding two glasses of red wine. *Wait, is he the host or our waiter?*

"Per la signora," he smiles as he places a glass down in front of me, then hands Mason a glass. "Signore. Just as requested."

I lower my head and look under the host's arm over at Mason who gives me a soft smile before looking back up at the man.

The man straightens himself up as he pulls out two menus from under his arm, then carefully presents them to each of us. As I open mine, he takes a step back from the table and claps his hands loudly, distracting me. When I look up, I see him leaning forward slightly, eagerly waiting. His eyes flick back and forth between Mason and I before a curious smile grows on his face.

"So, proposal tonight?" he whispers with his head turned.

I quickly turn to Mason wide-eyed, who appears just as confused, then I look back up at the host as my mouth drops open.

"I'm joking, I'm joking," he chuckles and then pretends to zip his mouth closed. "No more."

I let out a sigh of relief and then awkwardly laugh, hoping this will be the last time it's mentioned. As I slowly turn to look down at my menu again, I feel my stomach grumble. The sudden fear that took over me was a small distraction, but now I can focus on the important task at hand. *Eating.*

"Well, now that we've all confirmed nobody is proposing tonight," I state. "Can we order?"

"Sì, signora," he nods.

I assume he will walk away to get our waiter, but instead, he leans over us and turns his head slightly as if to wait to hear my order.

So he's definitely a waiter too?

I quickly scan the menu up and down, but with his eyes watching me, patiently awaiting my order, it's another distraction I don't need. I slowly turn to look up at him and like a dog begging for a bone, he's staring at me with a wide grin.

"Sorry," I stutter, slightly lowering my menu.

"Signora?" he asks as his brows press together.

I quickly clear my throat and repeat, "I'm sorry. I guess I didn't actually look to see what I wanted."

His frown quickly turns back into a smile as he tilts his head.

"May I suggest a meal?"

I wrinkle my forehead, surprised that I didn't think of the idea myself. *Who better to suggest a dish in Italy than a local?*

"Yes! I'd love that!" I cheer as I close my menu and carefully place it down on the table.

"That's a great idea!" Mason adds.

The host claps his hands together, startling me once again, then shakes them in the air and grins.

"Perfetto!" he shouts as he grabs the menus. "Lo adorerai! You will love it!"

"Thank you," I reply.

"Thank you," Mason nods.

"Torno subito," he smiles, nodding back to Mason before looking over at me and winking again. "I'll be right back, signora."

As he turns away, I look at Mason and raise my brows quickly with excitement.

"He's fun," I quietly say with a sarcastic tone.

I look over to see the man walking away and then purse my lips as I lean forward and glance at Mason out of the corner of my eye.

"Do you think he's the host or the waiter?"

Mason jokingly scoffs. "Seems like he's both."

"That's what I was thinking," I nod in agreement while trying to suppress my laughter.

Mason quickly grabs his glass of wine in front of him and raises it in the air between us. I follow suit, holding mine just a few inches from his.

"Salute!" he smiles.

I quickly raise both of my brows, surprised to see he knows at least one word in Italian.

"Salute!" I cheer as we clink our glasses together.

I bring the glass to my lips and my eyes widen at the flavor. Slightly fruity with a bitterness against my tongue.

I lick my lips as I pull the glass away, surprised that the wine is similar to the kind of drinks I prefer.

"What do you think?" Mason asks, raising a brow as he leans forward.

"It's really good," I nod, then lick my lips again to pull more of the flavor into my mouth. "You requested it?"

"I did. It's actually one of the products that this distributor makes."

I quickly raise my brows. "Oh, the one you're having your meeting with?"

Mason nods. "Yes, that one. I figured we could try their wine ahead of time."

"Well," I pause, taking another sip from my glass. "I might not know much about business, but I will say, this wine is delightful."

Mason playfully scoffs. "I couldn't agree more."

Chapter Twenty-Two

Lily

"This is so good," I blurt out as I take another bite of my food. "Do you remember what he called it?"

Mason tightens his lips and rubs his hand over his mouth, hiding the smile I can see behind his eyes.

Clearing his throat, he muffles, "He called it tagliatelle with ragù."

A wide grin grows on my face.

"Well, it's delicious! Everything has been so far!"

I swirl the pasta around my fork, and as I bring it to my mouth, I glance up from beneath my brow to see Mason's elbow resting on the edge of the table with his hand now gripping his chin. He's facing me, but his eyes are turned away, glancing at me every second or two.

I lower my fork slowly, studying his expression and raise my brow. *What is he up to?*

His eyes meet mine when he finally notices my undeviating scowl, and I pull my head back as he appears to struggle. He quickly tries to wipe the smile from his face, but it's too late when I hear a deep laugh from his throat.

Drawing my brows together, I tilt my head to the side. "What?"

"Nothing," he chuckles nonchalantly.

He clears his throat again, but it does little to help him as he chuckles again. *Okay, what is up with him tonight?*

I place my fork back on my plate and it dings against the glass, as I turn to look around me. *There has to be something I'm missing.*

As I turn back to him, I see him squinting as he licks his lips.

Quickly patting the side of my hair, thinking something may be in it, I ask, "What is it?"

"It's just—" he starts.

"What?" I press as I lean forward.

Lowering his hand from his chin, he pushes his chair back and partially standing, he leans over the small table. Bringing his hand up to my face, I tightly close my eyes and take a breath as my body tenses up. *Please don't be a bug.*

My eyes shoot open as I feel his thumb pressing against the corner of my mouth. He pushes down slightly at the spot and I feel a slight wetness on my face that surely wasn't there before.

Pulling his hand away, I lean my head forward, furrowing my brows as I glance at his thumb and see a small trace of the color red. Then, I squint my eyes as I lean even closer, tilting my head as I try to make out what it could possibly be.

"What is that?"

He looks down at his hand and a slight smirk grows on his face. He glances up at me shortly, licks his lips and then brings his thumb up to his mouth. Pressing his finger between his lips, his tongue clicks as he pulls his hand away and a deep chuckle escapes his throat.

Reaching for his glass of wine, he slowly turns his head back in my direction and raises both of his brows.

"Ragù," he states, holding back a laugh.

It takes me a second to comprehend, but when I do, I immediately feel my eyes bulge and my heart race.

"Oh my god," I gasp frantically, bringing my napkin up to my mouth to wipe away any remaining sauce. "Why didn't you tell me?"

He laughs and bites his lip.

"I don't know," he pauses and his eyes look up and down at me. Then, with a half smile he adds, "It was kind of cute."

I immediately look down at my lap, trying to hide the embarrassing flush of red coloring on my cheeks. After a moment, I look back up at him, and as our eyes meet, I can't help but laugh.

"That's not funny!" I shout, feeling the growing laughter in my gut.

He coughs, trying to contain himself and then shakes his head as he looks down. "No, no, it definitely wasn't funny."

Looking back up at me, he adds, "But it sure tasted good."

I quickly bite the inside of my cheek and cover my mouth with my hand as I feel the impending laughter rising from within.

There's a momentary silence between us as he presses his lips together, trying to contain himself. Soon— no longer able to hold it in—he bursts out laughing and I join him just as heartily, causing those around us to stare. But, I barely notice as my focus remains on Mason.

Walking back down the small hill to where we parked, Mason's arm rests over my shoulder and I grab his hand where it hangs. His hands are soft and warm around mine and I feel an overwhelming and joyful sense of security being in his arms. Something I haven't felt before.

In my past relationships, I always felt like I was being played. A pawn in a deceitful game. There were secrets, there was lying and worst of all, there was cheating.

When Paige experienced first-hand the pain of being cheated on, I could relate. I understood the experience fully and knew what she was going through. It's painful and even years later, you never get over it. Not even a little.

I thought Mason was just another one. Another liar full of deceit. Now, I may have to admit I was wrong. I may have jumped to conclusions when I realized who he was, but from what I know now, he isn't like that. Not at all.

Luckily, as each day passes, I feel myself slowly forgetting the old him—the one who was cruel. Because now, I can't help but picture him as I see him today: the funny, kind and handsome man I'm in Italy with.

"Thank you for dinner," I say softly. "It was delicious."

"Yeah, that little bit of sauce I spotted sure was."

"Oh God, let's never talk about that again." I quickly press my forehead into his chest, hiding my embarrassment.

He leans down and plants a kiss on the top of my head and just when I think he's pulling away, I feel his warm breath lingering over my head, as if he's trying to hide the smile on his face. After a moment, he pulls back and I silently snicker to myself, thinking of the irrational fear I had of him proposing.

"What we should talk about is that waiter," I joke. "Did you put him up to that?"

He stops momentarily on the sidewalk, glancing down at me with skepticism written on his face and my brows draw together.

"You're right," I shake my head. "That sounds absurd."

"What's absurd is that you didn't notice the sauce —"

"Nope! No!" I quickly pull my hand out from his and step in front of him as I cover his mouth. "We don't speak of that."

I glare up at him, but see a twisted hint of playfulness behind his eyes, as if he's already planning the next time he'll bring it up.

"You won't let me live this down, will you?"

I feel his smug smile forming beneath my hand and without saying a word, I know his answer.

I roll my eyes and catch a glimpse of the large beach below us, shadowed by the cliffs. Slowly releasing my hand from over his mouth, I step over to the edge of the sidewalk and glance down, discovering a small staircase in the distance that appears to lead down to the beach. The breeze from the water is cool against my face and a sudden exhilarating thought quickly pops into my head.

I quickly step back onto the small, rocky sidewalk without looking back, until I collide with Mason. Leaning my head back against his chest, I look up at him. His brows draw together in confusion, but quickly soften as a large grin spreads across my face, tightening over my cheeks.

Pulling my head forward, I immediately start removing one of my sandals, hopping on one leg as I do so.

"What are you doing?" he asks.

I glance back at him and his head is tilted.

"We—" I hop, removing the other sandal from my foot and gathering them together in my hands. "—are going swimming."

"What?" he asks in disbelief as he pulls his head back.

"You heard me," I say confidently before commanding, "Now, take off your shoes."

I glance down at his feet, then meet his eyes again, but my statement doesn't garner a reaction. I raise an eyebrow at him as I cross my arms and watch him as he tries to contemplate what I've said.

"Come on," I say, walking away without waiting for his reply.

I take a few steps down the stairs, and before he's out of my line of sight, I pop my head up until I can see him again.

"You coming?" I joke, licking my lips as I taste the salty air.

There's a burning silence and for a brief second, I wonder if he'll actually join me, but then I hear him hopping unsteadily towards me while I continue down the steps. With a quick look over my shoulder, I see him following me with his shoes in his hands.

Reaching the beach, I step onto the cold sand and it presses between my toes, sending a slight chill up my spine. A small part of me is curious about how it compares to the water temperature, but I choose to ignore that thought. I've already committed now, so there's no turning back. Besides, I did say I wanted this trip to be memorable, so if that happens to be the case, then so be it.

I hear Mason's feet trudging through the sand behind me, and as I turn around, I'm unable to see him until he is a few feet in front of me.

The houses shine brightly on the side of the hills, and only a small portion of the moon is visible in the night sky. Down here, nobody can see us, and it feels like we're in our own little world.

Mason reaches his hand out for me to hold and I grab it lightly.

"Race you!" I breathe as I raise my eyebrows and release his hand before he can grasp it.

With a turn of my heel, I'm running toward the water, feeling a rush of adrenaline pulsating through me. I pull my dress over my head and as the cool air hits my chest, I shiver slightly, but my legs continue pushing me forward.

Please let the water be warm.

Thinking this may very well be the craziest idea I've ever had, I fling my dress into the sand and stop just as I reach the shoreline. I take a deep breath as I glance at my feet, waiting for a small wave to push the water forward. When it finally does, the warm water rushes over my foot and up to my ankles, and I sigh with relief.

Thank God.

I look over my shoulder and see Mason leisurely wandering over to where I am on the beach. He doesn't appear to have taken our race seriously. Reaching me, his gaze moves slowly over my features before he looks up at me with a questionable look. *He's either turned on, or definitely judging me for this insane decision.*

"I won!" I announce proudly, holding my head up high.

"You did," he willingly agrees, wiping away the nonexistent sweat on his forehead. "You were just too quick for me."

"You weren't even trying!"

"I was," he claims, then tilts his head as he coyly adds, "You just didn't see me because it's dark out."

I playfully giggle and say, "If you say so."

"Are you really jumping in?" he asks, looking around me at the water, as if he doubts my intentions.

"You think I wouldn't?" I dare him, raising a brow.

He glances down at the little he can see of my half-naked body in the darkness.

"What if someone sees you?"

I take a step forward, tempting his words.

"What if they do?" I smirk.

I bite my lip and before he can reply, I turn around quickly and rush into the water.

As the water rises up to my thighs, I expect bath-like water, but as it reaches my waist, a momentary wave of regret washes over me. *The water is not as warm as I thought it would be.*

I hold my arms up above my head, feeling the hairs on them rise, but I continue walking further into the sea. My feet guided by my defiant proclamation I announced to

Mason, knowing my stubbornness won't let me back down from this challenge.

I swallow hard. If I'm going to commit, I might as well commit fully. I take a deep breath, and without letting another thought into my head, I dive into the darkness.

As I return to the surface, I wring the water from my hair. The cold I felt moments ago has suddenly vanished, but the breeze is now tingling slightly against my skin. I quickly lower myself until my shoulders are just below the surface of the water and turn to face the shore.

"Are you coming or not?" I shout to Mason—still standing on the shoreline with his arms crossed.

He shakes his head slowly and through a distant chuckle, I hear him yell, "You're crazy!"

"Suit yourself!" I shout back, before starting to turn back around.

"Alright! Alright!" I hear, pulling my attention back to him.

He looks around, as if checking to see if we are truly alone and invisible in the darkness, then starts to unbutton his shirt. Pulling it over his head, he throws it onto the ground before quickly removing his belt and pants. Once he's standing there in just his boxers, he crosses his arms and I imagine he is contemplating the same thoughts I had when I removed my clothes.

"I'm waiting!" I jokingly say raising my brows, but I doubt he can see them.

He takes a step into the water and slowly makes his way over to me, holding his arms above his head like I had previously. When he's within arms length, I'm able to see his face clearly with his half frown, half smile.

"I thought you may have gotten lost," I tease, biting my lip.

"You're going to give me a run for my money, aren't you?"

"What do you mean?" I ask curiously.

He moves closer to me and reaches his arms down below the water, grabbing ahold of my waist.

"You tend to get what you want often, don't you?"

"Erm, I'd like to think so," I say, moistening my lips.

I place my arms around his neck and grab my elbows, pressing my breasts tightly against his chest. In one quick swoop, he lowers his hands onto my ass, nearly dunking himself below the surface in the process, and pulls me into a straddle.

"Well, for you, I'd follow you anywhere."

Chapter Twenty-Three

Mason

We make our way down the dock and I look out at the sea. The water is calm today, but with a slight breeze in the air that promises for the perfect conditions.

Even last night, there was a slight breeze as Lily reluctantly coaxed me into the water. Her willingness to dive right in gave me a false assumption that the water was warm, yet as I stepped in and chills shot up my legs, I knew I was in over my head. The thing that kept my feet moving beneath me, slowly easing my way deeper into the water? *Her.*

I take a step down onto the stern of the boat, and as I steady my footing, I look up at Lily.

Holding my hand out for her to grab, I say, "Here, I've got you."

She appears frozen up on the dock, unaware that I've spoken a single word to her. I follow her wide eyes toward the boat, then look back at her—her mouth is slightly open in awe.

I pull my hand back and fist it against my mouth as I clear my throat. She blinks quickly before directing her attention back to me, and I extend my hand toward her once more, within her reach.

"Are you coming?" I ask, raising a brow.

She takes my hand and as she watches her steps, she climbs onto the stern. Her head lifts and she immediately looks up to the rigging, blinking slowly and meticulously.

"I thought you said we'd be going out on a boat today?"

I scratch my head.

"We are on a boat?" I question, uncertain what she means.

"No," she bluntly states. "This is not a boat. This is a house."

I can't help it as a laugh escapes my throat.

"Actually, it's a catamaran," I correct her.

"When you said boat, I expected one of those small sailboats, like the ones that can sink by a small hole." She finally turns to me gritting her teeth and her eyes are wide again. "Not this monstrosity."

Attempting to contain another laugh that's building within me, I clear my throat to brush it away.

"Would you prefer a smaller boat?"

She blinks quickly, as if she's contemplating whether that would be a better idea, but then her eyes start to relax.

"No, you planned this day out," she softly smiles before adding, "This is perfect."

"Okay then," I nod with a smile.

"Okay," she says happily. She turns her head and looks around before adding, "Where's the captain?"

I playfully scoff, "You're looking at him."

"What?" She jerks her head back towards me and her mouth falls open again. "Are you kidding? Please say you're kidding. What if something happens to us?"

I laugh deeply and shake my head as I glance at the sky.

"Nothing will happen to us, especially on a day like today." I reassure her.

Although, if something did happen, I wouldn't mind spending a few extra hours alone with her. With a boat this size, it'd be pretty difficult for that. With weather like this, the boat has no possibility of capsizing, and considering we have both an engine and sails, we'll have no issue returning.

"I promise I won't let anything happen to you," I say with what I think is a teasing grin. "But—"

She quickly cuts me off in a panic. "But what?"

I click my tongue. "But, I'll still need your help if that's alright."

She lets out a sigh of relief before saying, "I don't know anything about boating. What can I do?"

"Lucky for you, I do, and believe it or not, this one is slightly easier than one of those small sailboats you thought we'd be in."

"Seriously?" she asks in disbelief.

"Yeah," I nod confidently before gesturing with my head. "Now, can you help me with the lines?"

She turns to look and appears to understand that by lines, I mean ropes. Turning back around with a smile, she turns her hand sideways and brings it to her forehead.

"Aye, aye, captain!" she jokes, licking her lips before a smile forms.

After navigating out of the small bay, I turned the engine off and taught Lily the basics of sailing while she helped me hoist the sails. With the sails at full mast, we caught a nice lift that carried us out to sea.

Standing at the helm, with Lily between me and the wheel, she leans back against my chest. I briefly rest my head against the side of hers before directing her to steer to starboard slightly.

She glances over her shoulder with a playful grin and points out to the water.

"That way, right?"

I nod. "You got it."

"I'll be a pro in no time," she says confidently as she winks at me.

"I was wondering when that confidence would return," I chuckle.

"Just needed to ensure I had a good Captain is all," she says before turning back towards the horizon.

As she slowly starts to turn the wheel, the corner of my mouth tips up. I don't know why I expected anything less from her because within the first hour of us sailing, she was already recognizing the points of sail and telling me which direction we should go.

When I first started sailing at sixteen, that was one of the first things I was taught. Knowing which way to go is essential if you want your sail to catch a lift and propel you forward. It took nearly twenty hours at sea for me to finally have a decent understanding of it. *But her?* She's a natural.

Once I got my captain's license at nineteen, I didn't quite know what to do with it. I was in high school when I was earning my hours and I made sure I found the time to get on the water. But when I left for college, the opportunities grew slim and it was years before I went out again.

But when I cut back on drinking, I wanted a break —a way to put my mind at ease—and I found that in sailing. Whenever I find myself overwhelmed by life, or by the ongoing stress of running a business, I take every chance to escape onto the water.

Back home, there's a small private harbor near the city with a sailboat I call, "No Reins." I bought this boat as an early graduation gift for myself, with the intention of using it, but it sat in the bay for years with no name.

One day, I ran into a friend who I played polo with in college. We got to talking and when I told him about my intention to start sailing again, he joked that it couldn't be that hard. When I asked him what he meant, he said that both sports were similar.

"You have to trust that you know what you are doing," I remember him saying. "If you let go of the reins, you know you've put in the work already and you will be safe."

I had never thought of sailing in that way, but when I was out at sea, it truly was a release. I could let go of the reins, hypothetically of course, as well as the stress on my shoulders—the name fit perfectly.

When we arrived in Italy, the impending meeting quickly took over my thoughts. The doubts started to creep in and I wondered if I could truly close this deal—one that would improve the business exponentially.

I couldn't explain why the past several weeks had felt so heavy on me until last night. As we swam in the water under the night sky, I felt a sense of relief come over me. A calmness that I only feel when sailing. That moment gave me a craving for something I had long been missing and as the sun rose this morning, I found myself desperate for a taste.

As we approach a small island that appears to be uninhabited, I look out to the horizon—not a boat in sight.

I look up at the sails, and with the wind dying down, I place my hands over Lily's on the wheel.

"Ready?" I say softly in her ear.

"I'm ready."

I help her turn the wheel fast from one side to the other, letting the bow turn into the wind before returning to our center.

"Woah, what was that trick?" she gasps, turning around with wide eyes and a large grin.

"Just a little sailing technique," I whisper, releasing her hands. "Let's tighten the mainsheet and we'll anchor here."

I lick my thumb and grab the corner of my book, turning the page slowly. I read the first line of the paragraph and my focus shifts down to the water slowly rippling below us, crashing lightly against the hulls of the boat as I watch through the netting above.

With my elbows propped on each side of the book, I lean my head back feeling the sun against my forehead. If it weren't for the crisp breeze, I imagine there would be beads of sweat dripping over my eyebrows.

I look over at Lily next to me on the netting. She's lying on her back, facing the sun with her legs crossed over. She's wearing sunglasses, and hasn't moved at all while I've been looking at her, so I have to assume her eyes are shut and she's asleep.

I glance back down at the open book in front of me. Like all my other books, this one has been sitting on the shelf in my office waiting to be read—another one of my hobbies that gets pushed to the side when my mind focuses elsewhere. I packed it just in case, and I'm happy I did.

Closing my book, confident I've read enough for the day, I shut my eyes and listen to the silence around me. Out here, just the two of us, surrounded by little to nothing for miles, it seems right.

I hear a deep creaking coming from the boat's hull, soft splashes below from the water moving around us, and a distant bird cooing in the air—the perfect combination to ease my mind before I go into tomorrow's meeting.

Turning back to look at Lily, a faint smile curves my lips. Small strands of her dark, brown hair gently wisp in the breeze. As if she can feel them tickling her forehead, she reaches up and tucks them behind her ear.

She takes a deep breath and her breasts—perfectly hidden by her small bathing suit—rise with the motion. Their fullness still apparent, even though she's lying down. My thoughts wonder, and I can't help but think about what her salty skin would taste like if I placed my lips against her chest. The thought sends a slight excitement through my body and I feel myself harden under the fabric of my swim shorts.

I watch her mouth slightly part as she releases her breath and I clench my jaw, trying to push away the suggestive thoughts I'm having of what her mouth could do to me if given the chance.

Before that image can find its way to the front of my mind, she turns her head towards me and her mouth closes. Her fingers delicately grab the corner of her sunglasses, and as she pulls them down over her nose, she's staring intently at me.

"You okay?" she asks, furrowing her brows.

Realizing my jaw is still tight and I likely look like I'm in pain, I swallow hard, hoping to release the brewing tension inside of me. *Yeah, that didn't work.*

I bite my cheek, trying to find the right words—any words to say—but I'm at a loss.

Unable to control my mouth, the corners lift and I blurt out, "Fuck, Lily. I can't stop looking at you."

Did I really just say the first thing that popped into my head?

Expecting a shocked expression after my unintentional foul mouth and blunt statement, I hold my breath with anticipation. Instead, she's expressionless as she lifts her glasses back over her eyes and turns to face the sun again.

Oh God, I ruined that moment.

I feel my heartbeat quicken as I tightly close my eyes and scrunch my nose—feeling disappointed at my own words. I shake my head, and as I open them again, I watch the tip of her mouth rise in a secret smile, making me realize my words weren't too outspoken after all.

I smile softly, feeling a sense of relief wash over me, then as if she knows I'm watching, she bites her lip slowly and sensually which causes my eyes to open wide.

Fuck.

A rush of blood instantly shoots through me and now, lying on my stomach has become extremely uncomfortable.

Lifting my book and placing it just out of arm's reach, I push up against my elbows and turn my torso toward her, all while keeping my pelvis still angled toward the netting.

"What?" I ask, wondering if her mind is in the same place as mine because she damn well didn't bite her lip like that just for fun.

"For someone so reserved around others, you sure do speak your mind around me."

Okay, maybe her mind isn't in the same place?

I raise a brow. "To whom else are you referring to?"

"Paige," she says as she turns to face me.

As I hear her friend's name, the blood instantly leaves my erection as the conversation takes a turn.

Yeah, she definitely wasn't thinking what I was thinking.

"I heard you two had a brief encounter before you showed up outside of my apartment."

"That's true. We spoke a bit."

She quickly continues, "She had mentioned that you were more on the quieter side with her."

"Is that a bad thing?" I ask, wrinkling my forehead.

"No," she briefly pauses as if to think. "It's just surprising."

"Why so?"

"Well, I thought you were too," she chuckles to herself. "But then I got to know you more and realized that's definitely not the case."

I scoff quietly, knowing she is one of only a handful of people that I've been able to open up to.

"When I can be myself around someone, it's easy."

"I like that," she says with a smile.

"You do?" I ask, raising a brow and wishing I could see her eyes through her sunglasses.

"Who wouldn't?" she jokes. "Most men won't tell you how they truly feel."

"I'm not most men," I confidently state.

She smirks playfully. "You truly aren't."

"I'm not afraid to speak my mind around you, to tell you how I feel."

I pause and take a deep breath, feeling my heart pounding and another part of me hardening once more, knowing I won't be able to hide it much longer under the camouflage of my swim shorts.

"So I won't keep it in me when I tell you this—"

I grin and reach out for her face, brushing my thumb against her cheek.

"I haven't been able to keep my eyes off of you and as I've watched your chest rise and fall, my heart hasn't stopped racing, not even for one moment, because I've been incapable of looking away. And I blame myself for needing to say this—among other things—but my God, I need to tell you—"

I pause again and bite my lip as I glance down at her chest and then up to her eyes.

"Yes?" she asks curiously.

"How badly I want to taste you," I admit and my voice comes out in a lower tone.

"Taste me?" she asks me excitedly as she smirks back.

"Every part of you," I say slowly and deliberately, inhaling deeply as I shake my head.

I feel myself pulsing at the thought, and I quickly slide my hand to the back of her head, cradling her as I pull her lips to mine.

She pulls her sunglasses up and over her head, and wraps her arms around my neck, deepening our kiss as I close the distance between us. I push my hips forward as she inches closer and press the unmistakable erection I have against the side of her.

Between our lips, I hear a noise come out of her mouth, as if surprised, and I feel her body tense up against me, followed by a brief pause in our kiss. Her body eases slightly and she wraps her lips around my bottom lip, sucking it slowly. Feeling myself throb beneath my swim shorts, every part of me wants to turn her around and have my way with her right there, but I hold back.

As she pulls her lips back from mine, breaking the seal we've created, I pull my lower lip between my teeth before pressing my tongue back into her delicious mouth. I taste a fruity sweetness along with a slight saltiness, just like I imagined she would taste.

Oh, how delectable she is.

Overwhelming thoughts suddenly race back to the front of my mind, sending my restraint out the window.

But that's not really what I want to taste at this moment.

Pushing myself up with my elbow, I roll myself on top of her, triggering the netting below us to sway with the motion. With my hair tangled between her fingers, I balance myself above her and move down to meet her lips again.

Our tongues dance around, pushing me closer to the edge and my breaths are heavy against her lips as I press another part of me against her thigh. The quick brush of motion provides me momentary pleasure, and another part of me hopes she understands just how intoxicating she is to me. I know if I keep this up, all I'll want to do is shove myself deeply into her, giving her my entirety until she blissfully moans my name. However, at this moment, I have other plans.

I release her lips and move my way carefully down the side of her neck, all while tasting the saltiness of her skin that I so eagerly predicted. My lips move down to her chest, meticulously placing a kiss with every step and I can see her chest rising quickly below my mouth.

I look up at her slightly as I reach her breasts, and her head pulls back, into the bright sunlight, as if she's savoring every touch of my lips against her skin.

I lower myself onto my elbow, straddling myself over her, and with the other arm, I bring my hand down to her chest. I carefully pull the inner fabric of her bathing suit, drawing it back as her nipple pops out, instantly hardening from the breeze.

I brush my thumb over it, feeling the warmth of her skin, and I feel her quiver under my body as she is filled with excitement. Moving my thumb back over the bud once more, she trembles beneath me again as I slowly tease her.

I moisten my lips and with her head still cocked back, I watch as her brows draw together while she's anticipating my next move.

I told her I wanted to taste her, and I'll gladly savor every single part of her.

I lean down and wrap my mouth around her nipple, tightening it between my lips as I suck hard. Glancing up from beneath my brows, I see her lips tighten, and I immediately swirl my tongue around the bud again.

With her hand still tangled in my hair, her grip tightens, her lips finally part and her body twitches from my actions. I quickly suck again and she moves beneath me, curving her spine and pressing her breast deeper in my mouth.

I swirl my tongue around it again, and she emotes a faint, brisk moan that I can feel through her skin as it vibrates in my mouth. The noise forces me to curl my toes and inhale deeply, feeling a delightful, but agitating pulsation at my tip.

I eagerly position my teeth carefully around her nipple and when she lets out another moan, I sink my teeth around her, stealing her breath away.

I know it's a sharp, but pleasurable pain, and as I feel her legs tremble beneath me and her breathing growing rapidly louder, I'm sure she is enjoying it. Feeling myself throbbing again, I release my teeth, pausing over her radiant chest.

"More," she begs softly and I give her a muted chuckle in response.

Not yet, Beautiful. I'm not done devouring you.

I lightly squeeze her breast before slowly inching myself down her body peppering her with kisses as I search for every freckle on her that I can find. Reaching her waistline, I push myself up onto my knees, staring down at the way the fabric hugs her hips beneath my fingertips. She's unaware that I'm looking down at her as she tilts her head to the side, basking in my touch.

My fingers dance across her waistline and I finally grab onto her bathing suit bottom. As I start to pull at it, I feel her legs immediately clench together, and she cocks her head slightly, glaring at me wide-eyed. I tilt my head in confusion and she quickly pushes herself up from the netting, and reaches for my hands, stopping me.

"What are you doing? We can't do that," she anxiously gasps, and I feel her abs shaking beneath my fingers as she attempts to hold herself up.

She then warns, "Someone will see us."

I pull my shoulders back as I straighten myself, confidently knowing she's wrong, but I try to hide the cock-eyed smile I have on my face by tightening my lips together.

I lean back slowly, leisurely looking left and right, then glance back down at her with a raised brow.

"I don't see anyone," I reply, tempting her.

She pushes herself up onto her arms and her chin tips up as she attempts to get a better view around us. Confirming to herself that there is no one as far as she can see, she looks back at me, rolling her eyes.

"What? Afraid a bird might see?" I joke.

"No," she frowns, almost embarrassed.

"I thought you weren't afraid of someone watching?" I raise my brows. "Just last night, you said on that beach that—"

"I know, I know," she interrupts. "But that was different."

"How so?"

"Well, for one, it was dark out and two—"

I lean close to her, keeping one hand against her waist, until our faces are only inches apart, and I can see the bright green in her eyes.

"You always get what you want," I taunt as a playful smirk forms on my face. "Now it's my turn."

She brings her hand up to her lips, pressing her nail between her teeth as if to think. As she inhales slowly, she licks her lips, and a soft smile forms on her face.

I take a deep breath and I know then that she's willing to listen and doesn't care if anyone is watching. I don't care either, as long as I can give her the satisfaction she unquestionably deserves.

"Perfect, now be a good girl and lean back."

Surprised by my words, her brows rise and she opens her mouth to reply, but quickly closes it. I lean in and press a soft kiss against her lips before she pulls away and lies on her back, willingly following my request.

I shift my weight back onto my knees and curl my finger beneath the fabric as she relaxes her head against the netting while closing her eyes. Slowly pulling her bathing suit bottoms down, my hands slide down the sides of her thighs and I pull the material down past her ankles.

With her legs still clenched together, I move my hands up, feeling the hairs raise above her skin as I reach between her pressed knees. Parting them slowly, I position myself between her thighs as she widens for me like the good girl I know she is.

Leaning down, I kiss the inside of her leg, slowly kissing every inch of her warm, sun-kissed skin as my head gets closer to the intense heat I imagine is radiating from within her. My hand wraps below her leg and I lift it carefully over my shoulder, followed by the other. With my head low, I place a gentle kiss against her wet center and her body clenches around my head, overwhelmed by the sensation against her bundle of nerves.

I pull up slightly, as I comfortably position myself and glance up at her beautiful body looming in front of me one last time from between her legs. Her hands are tightly gripping the netting below, anticipating when I'll begin, and her eyes are closed as she faces the sky, completely oblivious to the delighted smirk on my face.

Anything for you.

Turning my attention back downward, I moisten my lips then quickly thrust my tongue into her, instantly tasting the parts of her I craved. She cries out in pleasure, and I instantly feel her body start to shake around me once again.

Lapping my tongue attentively, I reach up to cup her breast and she arches her back again, filling my hand. My tongue dances inside of her and my erection—that had diminished slightly—quickly returns. I ignore it, focusing on the movement of my tongue swirling around. Her legs tremble from every small motion and all I can think about is how delighted I am to be giving her what I had hoped she wanted.

Every part of her I crave. Her beauty, her heart and especially her taste, like that of a fine bourbon—sweet, a bit spicy and addictive as ever.

I had a dependency once, but I found discipline and kept my ground. Yet with her I have no need to hold back or to bury my compulsion because she satisfies my every need as I satisfy hers.

Chapter Twenty-Four

Lily

Two full days I've spent with him and I can feel a part of me slowly igniting. As the old memories of him steadily burn away and I'm consumed by flashes of his current self, I feel the strings between us tightening with each trickling moment.

I can't get past the overwhelming feelings that grow inside of me—the feelings I'm having for him.

But the worst part of it all? I am fearful that this entire trip will feel like a fever dream when I return home —something I made up in my head that I wish were true. Because truly, is it possible that a single trip can change the course of a relationship?

As we drive back inland through the picturesque rolling hills, I can't help but wonder what it will be like when we return home. Will this relationship still feel new, or will we have reached a point where we've already silently confirmed where we stand? Will the past be forgotten for both of us? Either way, one thing's for sure—I don't want to let go.

Turning down a small pebble stone road, I spot the same pointed trees I saw a few days ago. I watch as we pass each row of grapevines and through quick, momentary glimpses, I'm able to see for miles as the rows flow over the hills.

After a few short minutes, we ride up a small hill, and as we reach the top, there's a large group of houses surrounded by a short old brick wall at the end of the road.

The buildings are huge, built with tan hand-hew blocks and reddish-brown roofs, and every window has black shutters. Each building sits close to the next with the gaps between them filled by massive trees or vines that climb along the sides.

Pulling up to the small enclosed courtyard near the closest building, an older woman with short black hair and plump cheeks stands near the entrance. She removes the small apron around her waist and drapes it over her arm just as we roll to a stop.

Mason places the car in park and turns toward the back seat, reaching into a small briefcase-style bag. He pulls out a small stack of papers, and brings them to the front, looks down at them, then smiles up at me.

"Can't forget these," he says, raising the stack slightly into the air.

Tucking them under his arm, he turns to get out of the car, then quickly makes his way around and opens my door.

I don't know if I'll ever get used to this.

He holds his hand out and I grab ahold of it, steadying myself as I climb out of the low passenger's seat. He closes the door behind me, then places his arm behind my back, and we walk over to the woman standing near the entrance.

"Ciao! Benvenuto in Italia!" she beams as she extends her arm for Mason.

I look up at him and see his brows raise slightly before he steps forward and removes the papers from beneath his arm.

She quickly makes her way over to Mason and cups his face with her hands, looking at him with a large grin. Then, she clicks her tongue and leans forward, kissing him on both cheeks. As she pulls away, her hands move from his face and down the side of him, stopping at his biceps. His shoulders appear to tense up and he anxiously smiles at her, likely caught off guard by the gracious welcome.

"Hello, Flora!"

"No," she sternly asserts as she brings her eyebrows together. Her expression quickly disappears and the smile on her face returns. "You can call me Mamma."

"Okay," he agrees with a nod.

She leans forward scowling as if she's waiting for him to say it to her.

"Mamma," he adds with an anxious chuckle.

As the words leave his mouth, she takes a deep breath and smiles widely, as if relieved to hear him say it.

Turning her head slightly, she looks out of the corner of her eye and appears to finally notice me.

"Chi sei?" she asks, taking a step toward me.

I tilt my head, unsure of what she asked, but she doesn't appear as happy to see me as she did with Mason. *Maybe she wasn't expecting me?*

"I'm sorry," I anxiously say, trying not to offend her in any way. "What did you say?"

She squints her eyes and turns back to Mason before asking, "Who is this?"

"This is Lily," he assures before turning to look at me. A wide grin grows on his face as our eyes meet.

As he turns back to her, his Adam's apple rises and falls as he notices her facial expression shift.

"She's a close friend of mine," he adds.

Friend? I mean, I'd say we are definitely more than that at this point. But this is a business meeting and he has to be professional, so I'll let it slide. I mean, we don't even have a label for what this is yet anyways.

I am determined to make a good impression though. She didn't expect me here with Mason, and probably assumed he would be coming alone, so I need to convince her I'm not going to be a nuisance in any way during their meetings.

"Hello!" I cheer. "You must be Mrs. Bombardi?"

She glances over in my direction and scowls at me for no apparent reason. *Maybe she didn't understand me?*

Quickly trying to pull the easiest Italian word from my brain, I spit out, "Ciao!"

I have no doubt she understood that. I always strived for the perfect accent when I was learning Italian, even if I wasn't very good at remembering words or phrases. This one's an easy one.

She raises a brow as she looks up and down at me, then hums shortly before shaking off whatever thought she had. I politely smile, waiting for her reply, but she quickly turns back to Mason and I immediately frown. As she smiles at him, I can see deceitfulness behind it, like she's swallowing any thoughts she has of me while trying to stay calm in front of him.

Well shit. Can't say it was my fault if something goes awry with the deal.

"Well—" she shouts happily, switching up her demeanor as if nothing is wrong. "Come in! Come in!"

She takes a step between Mason and I, gives me a smug smile that is hidden from Mason, then places a hand behind his back, practically hugging him from the side. As she walks him toward the entrance, I follow closely behind and through the front door.

She leads us, or should I say *leads Mason*, through a dark, narrow hallway illuminated only by the light coming through the door. I nearly run into them as they suddenly stop in front of me, then she guides Mason into the large living room.

The room has wood beams across the ceiling, similar to the place by the sea, and the walls are a tan— almost mustard color. The large floor-to-ceiling windows brighten the room, making it appear more spacious while the furniture is in shades of red and green.

Stepping further into the room and down another narrow hallway, I hear the laughter of several different people echoing through the walls. The sound grows louder as we reach another small living area where there's a wooden doorway that's open, leading to a small courtyard outside.

Flora pushes Mason through the door and before I can follow, her loud voice immediately silences the laughter from outside.

"Eccolo! Tutti, date il benvenuto a Mason!"

I don't understand what she says, but as I make my way outside, everyone cheers as they stand up from their seats. *The cheering is definitely not for me.*

Several women, in their mid-sixties to seventies, quickly walk over to Mason and take turns kissing him on the cheeks and hugging him. It's like an unknown dance routine as each person follows on cue, the kind where you don't recognize the song, so you just stand there awkwardly. *Except I always danced anyway.*

Honestly, I didn't expect them to be so welcoming to Mason just because of a business deal. I've always heard that Italians treat you like family, and Mason is clearly experiencing that firsthand—a truly warm welcome.

Since nobody appears to be acknowledging me yet, I'm not too disappointed. Mason hasn't been able to take his thoughts off of this deal and for him, he's probably relieved that it's finally nearing its end. Clearly, this family is happy about it too.

I walk down a set of small steps and step beneath a large pergola that's wrapped in vines where everyone is standing. There is a long wooden table, which appears to be able to fit at least 30 people, and it's filled with an assortment of food and drinks. There are platters of various meats and different kinds of cheeses, as well as some pasta dishes.

I look over at Mason, who seems slightly overwhelmed by the amount of people giving him attention, and I can't help but quietly chuckle.

This is definitely more than he bargained for, considering the kind of person he is, but according to him, it's necessary. I'm beginning to believe that his business is quite large, and if he is doing business in Italy, it must be even bigger than he made it out to be. So, he'll have to do whatever it takes to win them over, even if it means getting out of his reserved-personality bubble.

Stepping over to the table, an older woman sitting down—who appears older than the rest of them—gestures for me to take the seat next to her.

As I sit down, I say, "Grazie."

She gives me a soft smile and I return the gesture, but she stares at me as if she's waiting for me to speak. Her eyes study my face happily before she quietly says a few words in Italian to me.

I wrinkle my forehead anxiously. "Sorry, what did you say?"

As if she is oblivious to my words, she continues speaking quietly to me and her eyes softly gaze into mine, but I'm still unable to understand any word out of her mouth.

Licking my lips, I nod politely as I pretend to listen, wondering if she even realizes that I don't actually speak Italian, except for a few seldom words. Despite my nervous expression, she continues talking with long Italian sentences to me, rambling on about something regarding a girl and a sun—or at least that's what I think.

Suddenly, I feel a hand rest on my shoulder and as I turn around to look up, I see Mason standing over me.

I politely hold my hand out for the woman to shake, then offer her a soft smile until she finally stops speaking and takes it. Standing up quickly, I walk with Mason over to a tree that's just far enough for us to momentarily be alone.

"Thank you," I chuckle, scratching my temple.

"I figured you needed an escape," he says.

"I had no idea what she was saying, but I wasn't going to just walk away. That would have been rude."

"Don't worry," he chuckles. "You don't have to explain."

"I appreciate that," I smile.

I gesture with my head toward the table.

"So, you're popular, aren't you?" I tease.

"It appears so," he laughs as he turns to look behind him, then back to me.

"You definitely got quite the welcome compared to me."

He frowns. "Yeah, sorry about that. I have no idea what was going on."

I shrug my shoulders. "It's alright. They probably just didn't expect someone else to be joining them for the meeting."

"Yeah—" Mason says nervously. "—about that."

"What?" I ask, frowning.

"So, they want to wait until their entire family is here for us to sign the paperwork."

"Isn't this everyone?" I say, peering around his body to look over at the table filled with people.

He tightens his jaw then snickers, "Apparently not."

"Damn," I say with a slight shock, wondering why they aren't as prepared for the meeting as Mason is.

"Apparently their daughter isn't here and Flora wants her here for the meeting."

"Careful," I joke, biting my lip. "She may get upset at you for not calling her 'mamma.'"

"Well, we'll keep it between us, okay?" he says with a wink.

I quietly chuckle as I nod my head.

"So, when is the meeting?" I ask with my tongue in my cheek.

"Tomorrow," he says bluntly.

"Tomorrow?" I ask, slightly disappointed.

Earlier, Mason had mentioned us checking out the countryside once everything from today was handled. Apparently, that's no longer the case.

"I thought we were going to—"

He takes a quick breath in then sighs, "I know."

He glances down at his foot and shuffles it across the ground, before looking back at me quickly with a grin.

"But I have an idea for what you can do in the meantime."

"What is that?" I ask curiously, raising a brow.

"Mason!" I hear from behind him and I recognize the loud voice immediately.

Mason turns around and I peer around him to see Flora standing at the end of the table with a wide grin.

"Vieni qui!" she shouts, waving for us to come over. "Come!"

Mason turns back to me with a smile and gestures with his head. As we reach her, Flora places her hand on his back, and as he stands at the end of the table, she starts speaking to everyone in Italian and gesturing to him. I can only imagine it has something to do with their businesses merging and them being happy he's here. Mason glances at me and shrugs his shoulders—as if to confirm our mutual confusion.

Flora grabs the wine glass on the table and holds it up in front of her, and I raise my brows, noticing everyone else is doing the same.

"Is the speech over?" I ask under my breath, turning around slightly to the person next to me.

"Cin cin! Mangiamo!" Flora announces loudly before taking a sip from her glass.

"Oh, okay," I chuckle quietly, having no idea what is going on.

She moves her hand up to Mason's shoulder and appears to press down on it as she gestures for him to sit at the head of the table. I smile as I notice an empty seat next to him and take a step over to it, however, Flora takes a step in front of me.

"No," she shakes her head, holding her finger up between us. I pull my head back and scowl.

Excuse me?

A feigned smile forms on her lips, and she takes a step around me, placing her hand on my back as she moves me forward. We walk past Mason, then several other people as my feet practically drag against the ground.

"Sit," she commands when we finally stop.

She holds her arm out toward an empty seat and I glance back over to Mason, realizing this seat is halfway down the table.

"But—" I say, but fake a smile as I sit down.

This trip is not about me. It's about Mason, I remind myself.

I look over at the woman to my right, who appears to be in her mid-to-late forties with long, curly dark hair. Turning to my left, there's a man with dark tanned skin and gray hair, who is focused solely on the food in front of him. And honestly, I don't blame him because the food looks delicious.

I glance up at Mason at the end of the table, and his brows draw together as the corner of his mouth rises. His expression shows he's displeased with our circumstances, but I smile at him, showing him he shouldn't worry. I understand it's about business, so there's no reason to fret.

Making light of the situation, I quickly look around for a glass of wine, which I do not see. However, there is plenty of food.

Leaning over so Mason can get a clear view of me, I raise a brow as I hold up a slice of bread. He quickly follows suit and with a smirk, I mouth the words, "Cin cin."

"If you look, you can see these clusters. We will eventually choose the best one to keep on the vine, which will help it to ripen the most."

Antonio, the "vignaiolo" or wine expert as he explained to us earlier, reaches into the vine and shows us the grape clusters he speaks of.

I lean slightly to the side, attempting to peer around him to look. I may not be familiar with plants or how the process actually works—taking grapes and turning it into wine—but it's worth listening to. I mean, who doesn't love a tall glass of wine?

I imagined that a winery in Italy would have plenty of wine readily available, but apparently that isn't the case because I was the only person without a glass earlier—well, apart from a child who appeared to be four years old. Even

Mason had a glass handed to him once Flora sat down. Honestly after that, I wouldn't put it past her that she had a hand in that. I'm just hoping that by the end of this tour, I'll finally get a taste.

I didn't expect a tour to begin with. After lunch, Flora insisted that Mason get a glimpse into their production, starting with the most vital ingredient: grapes. She introduced us to Antonio, who spoke flawless English, and we made our way out to the vineyards.

Leaving the grape vines, Antonio leads us up a small hill, where a large, single-story rectangular building sits at the top. It's similar in color to the small villas where we had lunch, but this one is much taller, with a large round wooden entrance. I'm not an architect by any means, but it's surprising to see a brick building that can reach such a height.

As we make our way inside, there's rows of pillars with large arches connecting them at the top. *Well, that explains the height.*

Nestled in neat rows along the wall and between the pillars are large wooden barrels, almost as tall as me. A small table, probably made from an older, smaller barrel holds several glasses of wine. *Finally!*

As Antonio grabs a glass from the table, he turns around and looks at Mason with a smile, holding it out.

"Here you are," he says, handing Mason a glass. "I imagine you are familiar with our wine already, yes?"

"Yes I am," he nods agreeably.

He glances down at his watch and then turns to me and says, "Can't go wrong with wine for dinner."

I sigh, knowing he's teasing me about my enthusiasm for the wine samples, especially since I was shocked by the delicious flavor earlier on this trip when we had a glass during our seaside dinner.

Before turning back to Antonio, my eyes land on Flora, who is wide-eyed and she joyfully says, "Divertente e bello!"

Her words push a subtle memory—one which I had almost forgotten—back into the front of my mind. A reminder of the words that were texted to Mason by an Italian woman when he had left his phone behind. *Handsome.*

I look down and away from Flora as I recall the conversation with Miles in the park. The woman who texted Mason was the daughter of the Italian distributor. *Flora's daughter.*

Before any sort of jealousy regarding their meeting tomorrow can unfold within me, my thoughts are interrupted by the sight of Antonio's hand holding a glass of wine out in front of me. I look up to see him smiling at me and quickly shake my head.

"Per la bella signora," he winks and I immediately understand his words. *For the beautiful lady.*

I raise my eyebrows in excitement as I take a sip, and when the delicious flavor hits my tongue, I don't know why it surprises me every time. First at dinner, and now again—*Of course, they make delicious wine.*

As I pull the glass away from my mouth, I bite my lip. *Antonio called me beautiful.* I may not know much about Italian culture, but maybe that's common to say? Calling someone beautiful or handsome?

I direct my attention to Mason, who's quietly taking small sips of his wine as he looks around the room. After another sip, he turns to me and smiles. He may not have said anything to me, but this smile gives me a sense of relief. *It's just a business meeting. Nothing more.*

I look back over at Flora, who is looking at Mason with a slight glower. *I wonder if she has any doubts about the deal?*

Mason said it was the spirits industry, so I imagine that entails all kinds of liquor, including his favorite— bourbon. *Oh wait, no.* Whiskey. Bourbon is made in the United States only, and whiskey is everywhere else, so they must make whiskey. *Shit, is that right?* I didn't think I'd have to remember facts about liquor until now.

Realizing I'm still staring at Flora, she turns her attention to me and of course, she's glaring. *Yet again.*

Maybe it's just her expression? I know plenty of people in the city with R.B.F.—resting bitch face. That must be it. I mean, it's not like I did anything to her except show up with Mason, and that didn't seem to make a difference during lunch, considering the amount of food they served.

I shake away any unanswered questions forming in my mind, and decide to fake kindness.

"Where is the whiskey made?" I ask, trying to shift her attention away from me, knowing that Mason is likely curious himself.

"Scusa?" she asks, leaning forward as if she didn't hear my question.

I grit my teeth through my smile, trying to contain the urge to roll my eyes as I ask her the question again.

"The whiskey. Where is that made?"

She leans back and looks over at Mason, who turns to her and says, "I'd love to know."

As if his smile is a consolation for my question, she happily says, "Sicily!"

I pull my head back slightly as I raise my brows, not expecting the answer. *An island?*

"How does that work?" I ask, tightening my brows.

"Mio figlio," she proudly says, looking directly at Mason as she places her hand on his shoulder and smiles softly at him.

"My son," she continues. "He lives in Sicily and handles it all. But, we serve many liquors, and soon, we'll be able to produce yours," she pauses to turn back to me. "And then, ours will be in America."

"And you handle the wine. Got it." I confirm, nodding my head as I glance around the room. "This is definitely a lot of wine."

Flora sneers aggressively and crosses her arms. "Lei non sa niente."

"What does that mean?" I tauntingly ask with brows raised, sensing that I've likely hit a nerve.

Antonio takes a quick step in front of me, blocking my view of Flora. As I look up at him, he chuckles anxiously, then raises his brows in question.

"Would you like to see the cellars?" he offers with excitement.

"Sure," I say hesitantly, knowing he's trying to redirect my attention.

"Right this way!" he insists, and I reluctantly follow.

We make our way through a small hallway near the back of the building, and as Antonio leads us down a small set of stairs, tiny bumps rise up and down my arms. The sudden change in temperature is surprising.

"I didn't expect it to be so cold," I chuckle, crossing my arms to contain my warmth.

Mason takes a step closer to me, placing his hand on my lower back and whispers, "Sorry, I wish I had a jacket to give you."

"It's okay," I smile at him. "Not as cold as the day we left."

"Very true," he chuckles.

"And if you take a step through here, this is the cellar room," Antonio explains, holding a door open for us to walk through.

Flora takes a step around us, and walks into the room. Then, Mason holds his arm out, gesturing for me to go in after her.

As we enter the room, I'm taken back by what's in front of me. The room is dark with small ceiling lights, hanging between familiar brick arches and a muted red tile runs across the floor. The room itself is as wide as a bus and on each side, there are large barrels, similar—if not larger—than the ones I saw just moments ago. And the most surprising part? The room appears to stretch at least 2,000 feet long, similar to a basement, but I'm shocked that it's this big.

Flora takes a step down further into the room and places her hand against a barrel. She takes a deep breath and smiles softly, as if she has her hand placed against someone's heart, feeling the warmth. And honestly, it's the first time I've seen a different side to her.

"Tomorrow will be a new start," she announces as she turns to us, and her voice echoes throughout the room.

The reminder of the meeting scheduled for tomorrow brings me back to Mason's suggestion earlier regarding an idea he had for me to pass the time.

"Yes it will," Mason nods and hearing his voice echo, he chuckles, "Oh!"

Straightening himself up, he adds, "I'm looking forward to us making it official."

"As am I," she replies.

Flora smiles and walks over to Antonio, their voices echoing in the room as they speak.

"So, what did you have in mind for me to do tomorrow while you have your meeting?" I whisper to Mason, eyes raised out of curiosity.

He smiles and says softly, "You know that town Scappa that we passed on the way here?

"Yeah?"

Flora quickly takes a step over to us and cheerfully confirms, "Scappa? Are you going to Scappa tomorrow?"

How did she—oh, the echoes.

"Actually, you might know," Mason says, turning toward her. "Is Scappa a good place for shopping?"

Shopping? *Yes please!*

The excitement on Flora's face grows as her eyes grow wide.

"Sì! That's the best place to shop!"

"Well then!" Mason beams, raising a brow as he looks back at me.

I press my hands flat against one another as if I'm praying and I bring my hands to my lips, trying to hide my wide grin.

Lowering them slightly, I cheerfully say, "I love shopping, and I've always wanted a genuine Italian handbag!"

"You'll love it!" she cheers with a smile on her face as I turn back to her.

Woah. Is she genuinely being kind to me? And not acting fake?

"There's plenty to buy to fit your American style!"

Not sure if I should take that as a compliment or an insult. But from her, it's likely the latter.

I choose to ignore her comment and turn to Mason.

"Well then, it's settled."

"Perfect," he smiles. "I'll drive you into Scappa as I head back here tomorrow."

"No, no, no!" Flora insists, grabbing Mason's shoulders and turning him toward her. "You will stay here tonight—" she appears to grind her teeth and then quietly adds, "—both of you."

"Oh, thank you so much for the offer, but—" Mason pauses, looking at me for support as his eyes scan my face for a reason to say no.

I don't blame Mason for not wanting to stay. I mean, who wants to get the death stare from this random woman for the rest of the night? *Definitely not me.*

I bite my cheek and look down at the ground, searching for a valid excuse—any reason—why we can't stay.

I look up at her and I sigh, "We didn't bring any extra clothes or belongings, if we did, we would absolutely stay."

I scrunch my nose as I click my tongue, trying to appear saddened by the words coming out of my mouth.

"Sorry about that," I say, tilting my head.

Flora looks down and mutters some words quietly to herself in Italian, then looks back up at Mason.

"Capisco. I understand," she nods, before smiling, "We will give you something to wear and wash your clothes tonight. You can stay."

Well, shit.

My eyes widen at the same time as Mason's, and I feel we have no way of digging ourselves out of this hole. His anxious expression makes me think he's worried she may be upset with him if we do not stay—or if we make up another excuse—so I give in for him.

"Are you sure?" I ask. "We don't want to intrude."

"Sì! Sì!" she says, placing a hand on his forearm. "Anything for you, mio figlio."

Chapter Twenty-Five

Mason

If I considered the list of things to expect on this trip, sleeping separately from Lily would not have been included. I couldn't argue about it though. It wasn't my house, and I wasn't going to put up a fight over something so small, when it truly was my fault for introducing Lily as just a friend. Besides, I don't know if I'd have it in me to raise my voice at anyone either.

Did I ever think I'd sleep in someone else's silk pajama set? *No.* Did Flora assure me that they were brand new and were specifically for me? Yes, but I don't believe it —even if they are my size.

Luckily, I am back in my own clothes today, and looking down at them, they appear to be freshly pressed as well. By who? That's another question, but considering the Bombardis' wealth, they probably have staff who take care of things like that.

As I drive us to Scappa, one hand is on the wheel, while the other rests in Lily's—who is sitting next to me in the passenger's seat.

Last night I wasn't aware of how distant I felt from her until I saw her this morning. Her face glowing with happiness as she hugged me in the kitchen before breakfast, followed by a quick kiss before anyone joined us in the room.

Until that moment, I hadn't kissed her since the morning before. We had already created a routine of sorts here in Italy, and we both had recognized this was out of the norm.

Unfortunately, the kiss was cut short all too soon as Flora walked into the kitchen. She was already dressed for the day, and was holding my suit on a hanger in one hand, while Lily's dress was slung over her arm. She stared at us with an unpleasant look on her face as we pulled back from one another. It was as if we had been caught kissing under the bleachers at a high school football field.

Who can blame her though? We're her guests, and we're kissing in the kitchen. I imagine it would make anyone uncomfortable.

So, in that moment, all I could do was try to act as if it didn't happen, but in actuality, my heart was racing from that kiss. Like I had been missing out on something for God knows how long, then, everything was right again as I felt her lips against mine.

I'm just lucky the rest of the morning flew by. An awkward breakfast and a shrugged, "See you soon" as Lily left the kitchen. Flora was beaming with delight, and I just hoped it was because of the meeting planned for later.

Out of the corner of my eye, I catch a glimpse of my hand resting on Lily's thigh as we drive. She gives it a gentle squeeze, and I wonder if this is what comfort truly feels like. I bite my lip and quickly turn my focus back to the road, hoping it's not too good to be true.

Just as it did this morning, the physical touch between us brings me another sense of relief. A small indication to me that even while parading with me through Italy, and dealing with my jumbled schedule, she's happy to be here. Still next to me and still going to be here even after all of this—a reassuring sign that I've succeeded in my second chance with her.

As we drive down the narrow, cobblestone streets of Scappa, through the bright houses in every shade of yellow, it's surprising to see a town so quiet. A motorcyclist quickly passes us here and there in the small gaps between our car and the houses around us, but the town lacks what it should have: people. There is only the occasional person in a window or at a doorway as we drive through.

Then, as we reach the town square, I begin to see the town liven up. A market of goods being sold under small tents around a fountain with people walking around in every direction. A stark difference from the other areas of the town, as this one is both energetic and lively.

There are barriers at the end of the road, preventing me from going further, so I pull the car to the side and park it. Releasing Lily's hand, I step out of the car, and walk around to open the door, but before I can reach it, she's already out.

Next time.

Walking around to the front of the car where she's standing, her eyes are wide and I see the excitement taking over—like a kid in a candy shop.

She takes a few steps forward, and I realize she has honed in on a particular tent. As she heads in that direction, I quickly reach out and grab her wrist, stopping her in her tracks.

"Where do you think you're going?" I chuckle.

"I already have my eye on something!" she insists, grinning widely.

"Well, come here for a moment."

With a slight tug, I pull her into my arms, and her hands rest against my chest.

"Was I even able to say no?" she jokes, as she looks up at me.

"Not this time," I playfully scoff.

The morning sun gleams over her face, making her green eyes shine brightly, while her facial expressions soften. I take a deep breath in, admiring her as our eyes lock. I lift my hand to her face, and tuck a loose strand of her hair behind her ear.

It feels like there's been no time for just the two of us in the past 24 hours. No time for swift glances, soft smiles, or the occasional kisses—except the one this morning. Once again, it feels like those will be placed on hold as I leave to go to this meeting. *But only for a short time.*

I feel the invisible bond between us, pulling me forward, convincing me to stay with her and not leave. I want to confirm our connection and understand whether we are thinking the same thing, to know if she wants to be with me just as badly as I want it.

I smile softly to her, taking in her beautiful face, and thinking about the hours that will separate us—even shortly, then I finally open my mouth.

"The meeting shouldn't last too long, so once everything is finalized, we'll have time for just the two of us, and then we can explore the rest of the town," I confirm, then add, "Together."

"I'd like that," she says softly.

"And later, I have another idea in mind."

"And what would that be?" she asks curiously.

I look up slightly, then raise my brows in a light-hearted manner.

"It involves cooking."

Her eyes grow wide and she bares her teeth.

"What?" I frown, caught off guard by her response.

"Nothing," she chuckles. "You'll just get to see my terrible cooking skills!"

I scoff through a slight chuckle. "You can't be that bad."

"Oh—" she laughs. "—I'm bad."

"Well, we'll have to see about that," I joke, then gesture with my head towards the market. "Well, at least you'll have one activity you'll love today."

She peers over her shoulder at the tents behind her and then turns back to me.

"Oh, don't you worry," she says with a smirk. "I think I'll keep myself busy."

With my voice low, I say, "With you, I never need to worry," before adding, "Come here."

I wrap my arms around her waist and slide them down to the lower part of her back, pulling her tightly against my chest. I glance down at her breasts pressed against me, slightly lifted beneath the fabric of her light purple dress. I lick my lips, blocking out my unruly thoughts, and look back up at her. As I meet her eyes, a thought resurfaces in my mind.

Taking a deep breath, I lean close to her head, my lips grazing her ear. My anxiety is rising and my lip quivers against her skin, and doubts creep in as I hesitate.

Do I tell her? Will she immediately know what it means? She took Italian in college, but as far as I can tell, she seems to have forgotten a lot of it.

I choose to risk it all, wanting to leave a small memento for her to ponder on, while she waits for my return.

I take a quick breath and then whisper, "Penso che mi sto innamorando di te."

As I pull back, she has an unclear expression on her face, but her gaze moves slowly over my features. Did she understand it? Or did I just horribly butcher my own words?

I tilt my head, waiting for her response, but she immediately looks off to her side, squinting as if to think.

When her eyes meet mine again, she excitedly asks, "What does that mean?"

Last night, after looking up the sentence online, I took the time to practice alone in my room—preparing for this moment.

I know I could easily tell her—at least in English—how I'm starting to feel about her, but I have a slight fear it could possibly scare her away. I don't want to make any mistakes, especially after she's seen a past version of me, so I made sure it wouldn't be easy to translate—or at least I tried.

I barely know Italian, so for all I know, I may have said something completely different than what I had practiced. But I'll eventually tell her what it means. I just couldn't keep it to myself, and had to find a loophole. This was it.

I shake my head, then joke, "Can't tell you."

She frowns, then raises an eyebrow.

"And why not?" she argues playfully.

"Just can't. You'll have to figure it out on your own."

"Well, now you have to tell me," she insists, biting her lip.

"Nope," I say, holding my ground as I shake my head.

"You know I generally get what I want, right?" she smirks.

I chuckle and reply, "Well, not this time."

She quickly wraps her hand around the back of my neck, and pulls my lips to hers. It's forceful, but I love every part of it. Her mouth tastes sweet, and I can still slightly taste the wine from yesterday, and I don't mind one bit.

As the seconds pass, our kiss deepens as I slide my tongue into the back of her mouth, and she hooks her arm around the back of my neck, keeping me in place. She tightens our lips against one another, and I wrap my hand into her hair.

A part of me starts to wonder if she truly did understand my sentence, because now she's succeeded in showing me her answer with a feverish kiss—one that will be in my mind for the remainder of the day.

She bites my lip slowly and sensually, and our lips pop from one another as she pulls away. She tilts her head to the side, and with a smug grin on her face, her eyes wander back and forth across my face.

"Did that convince you at all?" she pleads, battering her eyes.

"Convince me to do what?"

She purses her lips and begs, "To tell me what you said."

I was so distracted that I had almost forgotten our conversation from moments ago.

"Nope," I clarify confidently.

Despite her tempting look and well-thought-out plan of winning me over by kissing me, my apprehension causes me to keep the words to myself—at least for the time being.

She appears disappointed that she cannot get what she wants this time, but then she lets out a soft sigh, acknowledging defeat. I chuckle, and with my hand still wrapped behind her neck, I pull her in for a peck. As I pull away, I wrinkle my nose, trying to hide the satisfied expression showing on my face, knowing I won this round. Shaking my head, I refocus on her bright green eyes.

"You'll know what it means eventually," I state with a grin. "I promise."

Taking a step back, my hands slide down her arms and into hers. I look down at them, and then take another step back, watching them fall away and down to the side of her body.

As I walk to the car and rest my hand on the windowsill of the car door, I look back at her and she's smiling through pressed lips.

"Now don't miss me too much," I joke.

"Don't you worry," she says with a wink before eagerly turning around toward the tents.

When I walk back into the bright yellow room that I slept in the night before, I head straight to the nightstand. Sitting on the small table are the papers I still neatly stacked from when I had left them.

When I began this trip to Italy, I originally had one goal—finish the deal with the Bombardis. As things changed, I had another goal in mind—give Lily a trip she wouldn't forget.

I had already decided this long before we arrived here—even if she insisted on paying her share. She was very adamant, but this was the right thing for me to do. I am fortunate to have the life I do and hadn't thought about sharing it with someone until Lily came along. I want to be the person to give her what she wants and to make this trip unforgettable.

As far as the meeting goes, I can't imagine it'll take long, or at least I hope it won't. I may be the CEO, and my parents may be relying on me to get everything for this deal, but my social skills are definitely not the best. I guess that's the one downside of being introverted, and I can only blame myself for that. Hopefully, I'll be happy to push through with some small talk, sign the paperwork, then be on my way.

Stepping out of the bedroom, I grab the lapels of my suit jacket as I glance down and take a deep breath. I'm feeling my best and I'm ready for the whirling stress I've been enduring to finally be gone—for it all to be over.

Entering the room, Flora walks quickly over to me with an excited grin on her face. *She must be happy about the meeting as well.*

"Perfetto!" she says, placing her hand on my chest and looking up. She's nearly half my size, so when she lifts her arm to my chest, it's fully extended.

"I've got the paperwork now, so where would you like to sit?" I ask, raising a brow.

She pulls her hand away, then without replying, she turns around and walks over to the kitchen. I raise a brow as I watch her grab a small bag on the table and retrieve her car keys from within it. With a smile on her face, she walks back over to me, and I frown. *What is she doing?*

Pointing out the window, she says, "Head down to the old cellar right there, and there will be a small table near the vineyard."

"Okay," I hesitantly reply. "Is that where the meeting will be?"

"Sì, sì," she confirms, patting my arm before turning around and heading toward the door.

"Wait, where are you going?" I ask, tilting my head as I take a step forward. "Aren't you coming to the meeting?"

"Torno presto," she shouts without turning around.

"Come again?" I holler, furrowing my brows. "What did you say?"

Reaching the door, she looks over her shoulder.

"I will be back soon," she says with a smile as if she's keeping a secret, and as she walks out the door, she adds, "Vai a divertirti!"

What does that even mean?

I grimace towards the door. Is she kidding right now? Did she really just leave?

I scratch my head as I glance around the empty room. Maybe she forgot something in her car and has to go get it? Or her leaving means the deal is already over? I quietly scoff, wishing it were that easy.

I turn to look out the window in the direction she was pointing to. She said the meeting was that way, so am I expected to still go? Will her daughter be there waiting?

The entire reason we pushed back the meeting to today was because her daughter hadn't arrived yet. Am I to presume everything is still on, and Flora will join us later?

I lift the pile of paperwork and stare down at it. All this hard work for nothing—or at least it's starting to feel that way.

I clench my jaw, feeling the frustration growing within me. *Well, there goes that perfectly simple plan.*

I close my eyes, concentrating on my breathing as I drop my head down. I place a hand over my forehead and as I pull it down, I open my eyes and look up at the ceiling, releasing my breath.

If Flora said to head outside, there has to be a reason for it. I need to accomplish my main goal, and this deal has to be sealed one way or another, so it might as well be now. Worried that standing here will inadvertently delay the deal longer, my legs push me forward.

I walk down the small hallway, out through the wooden doors leading to the backyard, and head toward the old cellar. Once I reach the cellar—about 1000 feet from the main house—I look around for the table Flora mentioned. There isn't a table in sight. I do a small loop around the cellar, but once again, nothing—just rows of vineyards for what feels like miles.

I scratch my head, confused by her insistence that I come here. Was it just a distraction while she did God knows what? Am I being played a fool for listening to her in the first place? I really hope not.

Having no choice, I take a step away from the cellar, and make my way back toward the main house. After less than a minute of walking, I stop as I hear a voice call out, "Ciao!"

My head cocks back, surprised by the unfamiliar voice, and I slowly take a step backwards. Turning on my heel, I make my way once again toward the cellar, carefully looking in both directions for this voice that called out.

Between two rows of grape vines, I spot a small table, nicely decorated with a white tablecloth and a small vase of long, pink rose stems. There's also two chairs and sitting on one is a woman, with long, straight dark hair, whom I've never met before.

Surely, this has to be the table Flora implied? If that's the case, this is definitely the most informal meeting I've ever had, and that's saying something, considering most of my meetings involve a glass of our spirits.

"Mason?" she asks as I move closer to the table.

I notice she's shorter than Lily as she stands up and I raise a brow at her as our eyes meet. I wonder if there's a chance I could have met her and forgotten, but her face isn't even vaguely familiar.

She tilts her head to the side and smiles, like I'm an old friend playing a joke on her, but at this point, I'm feeling like the joke is being played on me.

"Yes?" I hesitantly reply, slowly taking another step toward her. *As to why? Who knows.*

A wide grin suddenly grazes her face, and she quickly steps around the table and rushes over to me. My eyes bulge out, shocked by her sudden pace. Without a moment to comprehend what is happening, she practically jumps at me, as she wraps her arms around my neck, and pulls my body down to her level. My body goes stiff, and I blink rapidly as she tightens her hug around my neck. All I can do is remain calm, hoping she'll release me soon.

She knew my name so she must know me. There's no other explanation. But, should I know her?

When her grip around me loosens, I feel the tension in me ease as the numbness leaves my neck. As she pulls back, she looks straight at me, as if she's been eagerly anticipating this moment.

I wrinkle my forehead as I look down at her and pull my head back, feeling the uncomfortable lack of space between our faces. She has green eyes, similar to Lily's, but her dark eyebrows and the wide smile on her face make it impossible to ignore her giddiness. *What is she so damn happy about?*

She rubs her lips together intentionally, as if she's just applied lipstick to them, as she stares up at me in what appears to be her most seductive look.

"Mia madre diceva che eri bello," she says in a soft, sultry tone. "Aveva ragione."

I have no clue why the hell she said it like that, but it's enough to make anyone uncomfortable—especially a stranger.

Trying to pull my head away, I glance around for any reason to escape from her embrace. Even though I don't have the slightest idea what she said, I could tell by the tone of her voice that it was a compliment, and with the way she's looking at me, I'm now afraid to ask.

I know Flora hugged me when I arrived, and I thought maybe it was a friendly gesture, but nothing like this. This is different.

As I open my mouth to try to ask her to explain this overzealous physical touch, she tightens her grip around my neck, pulls me forward, and her lips are suddenly on mine.

What the fuck?

I'm wide-eyed with shock at her unexpected actions, and I'm caught in the middle, unable to escape. My arms hang stiffly at my side, while I try my best to hold onto the papers in one hand, as the rest of my body remains frozen by her lips pressed against mine.

Understanding that this painfully inappropriate gesture is not ending, I blink rapidly until my body finally acknowledges what the fuck is happening, and the feeling returns to my arms. I forcefully pull my head back, breaking her unyielding grip at the back of my neck and with that, our lips finally part as well.

With my eyes still wide, I take a few steps back, catching my balance, as I press my index finger up to my lips. I wipe my mouth and I can see the red smudges have transferred from her lipstick. I rub my lips together, trying to remove it from my mouth, but instead I taste a stale cherry flavor, and I'm unsure if it was her lipstick, or if it was just from the taste of her mouth.

I rub the back of my hand over my lips, take a deep breath as I stare down at the grass, and beneath my brows, I look up at her with a wrinkled nose.

"What the hell was that about?" I snap, hearing my voice crack slightly.

She looks down, and appears shocked as she lightly strokes her finger over her smudged lips. Then, as she looks up at me slowly, she appears complacent as a smirk forms on the corner of her mouth.

"È quello che fanno le coppie," she chuckles, biting her lip.

She takes a step toward me and with a playful look in her eyes, she bats her eyelashes.

"We'll have plenty of time to practice."

Alright, at least I know I can speak to her in English, but what does she mean by practice?

Oh god.

Please don't tell me this is just another welcome gesture I'm unfamiliar with. I'd rather this not happen again if I can help it.

"Practice what?" I hesitantly ask.

She purses her lips as if to think, but remains quiet. I know she can understand me, but I need answers now and I'm not willing to wait.

"Why did you kiss me?" I stammer, holding my hands out in front of me.

"Volevo baciare mio marito," she responds, batting her eyes.

"English please," I demand.

"Because you're my husband," she states with confidence and a smug look on her face.

"Husband?" I snicker. *She has to be confused.*

I shake my head quickly and argue, "You've got the wrong guy."

She *definitely* has the wrong guy.

"Scusa," she giggles quietly as she holds her hand up to her mouth. Then, with a brow raised, she slowly says, "Fidanzato."

"Fidanz–what?" I stutter as I lean forward. That's got to be either an insult or a compliment.

"You are my fiancé," she cheers. Her eyes then proudly inspect me up and down, as if I'm a shiny trophy she's won.

She's hit her head. That has to be it. By now, she'd realize I'm not her husba—*no*—fiancé.

Cautiously keeping my eyes on her to ensure she doesn't run off, or possibly injure herself more, I glance around, searching for a rock. Or possibly a large boulder. Maybe even a sharp stick. Really anything that she could have hit her head on, that caused her momentary and unexpected memory loss.

Nothing. I can't find anything that could have caused it.

I clench my jaw as I turn back to her, and her eyes glide back up to my face.

"I think you are confused," I cautiously advise, then clarify, "No, I *know* I'm not confused. I am not your fiancé."

"Of course you are," she beams, biting her lip seductively.

Oh, God. Please don't try to kiss me again.

I chuckle nervously, quickly trying to think of a way to convince her otherwise as I rub the back of my neck. Noticing the expression on my face, she releases her lip between her teeth, frowns, and tilts her head. Then she straightens herself up as if to realize her mistake.

"You're Mason Moore, no?" she asks, raising a brow.

Oh good. She's thinking clearer now.

"Yes, I am," I confirm.

"Then, I am not wrong," she beams.

But she is wrong.

I press my tongue into my cheek as I scowl at her, then ask, "And who are you again?"

She opens her mouth and before she can respond, I quickly add, "And don't say your fiancé."

She closes her mouth and then takes a few steps forward as she purses her lips.

"Scusa, ho dimenticato," she states, shaking her head before joking, "Where are my manners?"

She holds her hand straight out in front of her, straightens her shoulders back and says, "I'm Elisa. It's nice to officially meet you."

Elisa Bombardi. Well that answers one question.

"I think we may be past courtesy greetings," I grumble as I clench my jaw.

She frowns slightly as if she's disappointed, and I blink suddenly, realizing I've not only raised my voice at her, but now I'm being rude. *Even if she did kiss me.*

Taking a deep breath, I scratch my head and then reach out to shake her hand.

"But it's nice to meet you," I mutter through a pressed smile.

I step back as she releases my hand, still anxious she'll come to kiss me again. *Considering how this started, I can't put it past her to try again.*

But it's time to move on and forget the friendly welcome—a little too friendly in my opinion, but I have to be professional as there's business to attend to. Seeing that Elisa is here, I look over my shoulder and I recognize that Flora still hasn't arrived. As I look back at Elisa, I click my tongue.

"Your mother told me the meeting was rescheduled to today since you couldn't make it yesterday, but she's still not here."

Elisa chuckles. "Sei divertente."

"Huh?"

"Scusa," she says, softly smiling. "My mamma said you were funny. She was right."

"What's so funny about that?" I ask, frowning.

"Because she isn't coming."

"You're joking, right?" I huff as I cross my arms.

"No. Why would I be?"

She tucks her hair behind her ear as she tilts her head, and a confused expression clouds her face. I hold my hand into the air and twist my wrist so the pile of papers I'm holding crackles.

"We are supposed to be signing paperwork right now. Please tell me that is still happening."

"What gave you that idea?" she playfully giggles.

She turns on her heel and walks back over to the table, pulls the chair out slightly and sits down. She grabs a glass of wine resting in front of her, and places her other arm on the table before leaning back into the chair, crossing her legs as she does so. Once she is comfortable, she presses her lips together as our eyes meet again.

I scratch my head as I furrow my brows in her direction, trying to make sense of whatever is happening right now. Every sentence is absurdly vague, and I need answers. *Now.*

She squints as she leans forward in her chair, studying the expression on my face. Trying to avoid her sharp eye contact, I glance around, feeling the silence weighing heavily on me. Then, she pulls back and quietly chuckles, thinking that my expression will change, and I will finally understand her joke, but when it doesn't, she bites her cheek.

"If you want to call our date a meeting, then yes. It's a meeting."

Date? No, she's definitely mistaken.

"This isn't a date," I argue, snickering as I shake my head.

She places her wine glass back on the table, then slowly stands up from her seat.

"Of course it is," she loudly insists.

She waves her arms over the table, as if she's conjuring some sort of spell, then adds, "What do you think all of this is for?"

I look down at the table. White tablecloth, a small vase of flowers, and two glasses of wine. As my eyes trail down to the ground, and onto the small grassy patch that runs between the two rows of vines, my eyes widen as I see them—white rose petals scattered across the ground.

What. The. Actual. Fuck. How did I not notice those when I first saw her? Was I really that oblivious?

"We are not on a date," I insist, trying to understand the circumstances that I clearly did not register.

"Call it what you want," she says with a smirk. "A meeting. A date. The start of our marriage."

The word immediately brings a pungent taste to my mouth.

Marriage? Is she serious right now?

"Excuse my language, but what the fuck do you mean by marriage?"

This is a joke. A cruel, awful joke. Please say it's a joke right now.

"Our marriage. You and me," she declares happily.

I scowl at her, trying to understand where she plans to go with this, and she raises her brow in response.

"The one our parents arranged for us?" she hesitantly challenges. Then tilting her head, she frowns and adds, "Why else would you have come to Italy?"

No. They wouldn't do that to me. She's lying.

"You're mistaken," I cautiously reply through an anxious chuckle.

I look down at the ground, trying to collect my thoughts, before meeting her eyes again. Now, a serious expression forms on her face, which shakes me to my core, and I immediately look away. *Please don't let this be true.*

I inhale deeply, closing my eyes as I lower my voice. "I came here to finish the agreement between our companies."

I nod slightly, confirming my own statement, then I take another deep breath.

"Only that."

After telling her what I know is true, I clench my hands, feeling the moisture between my fingers. Then, I feel a bead of sweat just above my lip, and another one forming above my brow. I quickly press my hand against my forehead and wipe it away, ignoring the signs that I know exist.

"This wasn't part of the deal," I say in a shrill voice, blinking quickly.

"The entire deal was contingent on our marriage," she explains, taking a step forward. "You knew that."

No I didn't. Not at all.

I find the strength to look up at her once more and her eyes say it all. Not a single lie behind them.

Although she sounded absurd before, I can see that she believes what she is saying is the truth. The most unthinkable and shocking truth that has come at the worst time.

My eyes widen, and once again I feel my body tighten, freezing in place, and I can't move, no matter how hard I try.

My mind races, and my eyes blink, as I think back to the meeting last week. The one my parents had without me in attendance. That had to be it. The time when they added this contingency to the deal.

Of all the people that could wrong me, I didn't expect it to come from my own parents—the ones that know me best. I never imagined they would be the ones who would betray me, and go behind my back to add this component to the deal.

They mentioned only a few months ago that I should have someone by my side, and I somewhat agreed, but this is not what I meant by that. *Not one fucking bit.*

Just when I thought I was handling everything on my own and doing well, my father found a way back in—a way to continue to puppet the business, to puppet his son and be certain everything went his way.

"Are you okay?"

Her voice causes me to flinch. All I want to do is run, scream, but when I try to open my mouth, only a stifled whimper escapes, and my knees are locked in place.

As I realize my heart is pounding out of my chest, Elisa's bright yellow dress fades and when my eyes drop down, the greens of the vines turn gray. My vision begins to blur, and despite the absence of her grip around my neck like before, it might as well be there, but around my throat instead. Choking me until I can no longer see straight.

When I look up at Elisa again, I don't see her black hair and yellow dress, but instead I see Lily. Her brown hair, her beautiful green eyes and that smile that could melt anyone's heart.

Fuck. Lily.

My chest tightens as I imagine the expression on her face when she finds out about this arrangement. This marriage that I had no part in planning and had no clue I was a part of. This fucking mess of a business deal, if I can even call it that now.

But no, instead all I can see is the fear in her eyes. Fear that I've—yet again—betrayed her. Gotten close to her, just to break her apart again.

It happened to us just after our first date and it'll happen to us again. It'll be the only way Lily sees it. And it'll be a confirmation in her mind that I have never changed.

But in actuality, I have. Every part of me has changed. I know in my mind that I am not the person she knew six years ago. And I know she sees it too, but now she won't believe me. Who would? I wouldn't believe me either if I were in her shoes.

As the invisible grip around my throat tightens to the point of no return, there's a shakiness in my legs, and I feel them give out. I try to breathe, but the air in my lungs is completely absent. And, before I know it, everything is black.

Chapter Twenty-Six

Lily

Did I expect to be shopping in Italy a week ago? *No.* Did I have the money? *Also no.* Did Mason surprise me by not making me pay for anything on this trip? Yes, but I'll continue to offer to pay every night until he finally gives in.

Once the house quieted down last night, and I assumed everyone was asleep, I tiptoed across the house and down the narrow hallway. I reached Mason's room and tapped my finger against the door, it inadvertently caused me to flinch, afraid that Flora would run out, and tell me to return to bed like I was a prisoner. I mean, I kind of felt like a prisoner when she gave me her snarled death stare throughout the day. Luckily for me, Mason opened the door after only a moment.

As I slid through the small crack in the door, I carefully grabbed the knob and closed the door behind me. It creaked in every way possible and I squeezed my eyes shut, hoping no one else heard the sound. Once the door was closed, I turned around, pressed my ass against the back of it, and smiled at Mason standing between the door and the bed.

"I don't think you're supposed to be in here," he teased as he raised his brows.

"Who says I can't?" I asked playfully.

Pressing his tongue to his cheek, he shook his head with a smirk, confirming he understood my nod to his own words he spoke on the plane. Then, I took in a quick breath as I looked up and down at him standing in front of me, dressed only in his boxers.

He turned his head and whispered quietly, "Well, Flora maybe."

"She may make the rules, but that doesn't mean I have to follow them."

"So, you decided to come to my room?" he chuckled with a raised brow.

"Should I leave?" I joked as I bit my lip.

He shook his head as his pupils dilated and took a step toward me. As he stood just inches away, he pressed his hand against the door, just above my shoulder and leaned forward. Looking down at me, I saw his Adam's apple rise and fall.

"I didn't say that," he dared.

With his other hand, he placed his fingers around my ear, wrapping his palm beneath my jaw. His thumb caressed my cheek, causing me to close my eyes as I pressed my face against it. Then, he leaned down, holding his lips just in front of mine before quickly pulling his head away. When I realized he wasn't going to kiss me, I opened my eyes and looked up at him.

"I just meant that you are impulsive," he jests.

One of the many ways I get what I want is by impulse. I consider it a strong suit of mine. And this time wasn't any different.

"But I like that you are," he smiled.

"I don't know if I like it when you are," I joked.

"Me?" he disagreed as he pulled his arm away and shook his head. "I wouldn't say I'm impulsive at all."

I bit my lip and chuckled. Placing my hands against the door beside my hips, I pushed myself forward, carefully stepping toward Mason. With every step forward, he took a step back until he was wedged against the bed.

"Okay then," I clarified quickly. "Explain the private jet."

He laughed and confidently replied, "That was pre-planned."

"Fine, I'll give you that, but what about when you asked me to go on this trip?"

He looked up at the ceiling, then back down to me. "That was not planned."

A wide smile grew on my face, knowing I found one thing he had done on impulse, which proved my point.

"But, I wouldn't say that was impulsive."

"Okay," I playfully noted. "What would you call it then?"

"Me—" he tilted his head to the left, "—You—" he tilted his head to the right, "—I wanted us both here. As soon as I found out I was going, I made that decision."

The corner of his mouth tipped down and he frowned slightly.

"Well, I had hoped you would go," he smiled and wrapped his hands around my lower back. "And I'm glad you said yes."

Glancing up, my eyes rolled back to meet his, and I said, "You know, I have to ask again."

"Okay, have at it."

"You have to let me pay for my portion of this trip. Please."

He pretended to think as he looked around the room, then looked back at me as he shook his head.

"No can do," he said, deciding firmly.

I rolled my eyes at him.

"I can't let you pay for everything. It's way too much money," I pleaded.

"I can't let you pay for anything. It's my treat," he claimed.

I repeated my sentence again but with more emphasis. "I *won't* let you pay for it."

"Erm, still no."

I dropped my head and looked down at our feet, then I looked up at him with the best puppy-dog look I could make.

"You're cute when you make that face."

I couldn't help but smile at his remark, as I sensed he could be the first person that I couldn't get my way with. I brought my head back up and sighed, admitting defeat, but as my eyes met his, a quick thought came into my head.

"Okay," I said, taking a deep breath. "I know you planned to join me tomorrow in Scappa, but how about letting me pay for myself, okay? Anything I buy, I buy it with my own money. Deal?"

He raised a brow, then quickly tugged my back, pulling me against his chest. As I looked up at him, he smiled.

"Deal."

While I was exploring the open market in Scappa, Mason kept his promise. He had a meeting that I had no doubt would take up all of his time, and I was on my own to explore what Scappa had to offer.

With only two bags in tow—one on each arm—I now feel a high sense of self-discipline, knowing I didn't throw all my money away. Two dresses, a jacket, a brown leather bag that was non-negotiable in my mind, and a small blue glass-blown sailboat that the woman said was from Venice. If Mason wasn't going to let me pay for anything on the trip, the least I could do was buy him something in return.

I hand the woman behind the booth a €2 coin, then grab the bag on top of the stand and thank her before turning away. Reaching into the bag, I grab onto a singular grape and tug on it, ripping it from the vine. Bringing it up to my mouth, I look down at it and think to myself—Is it socially acceptable to eat grapes from a bag here? I mean, Italians drink wine with their breakfast. Does that mean grapes can be eaten in any way?

I pop the grape into my mouth, and as I bite down, the juice shoots against the inside of my cheeks, and I can only compare the flavor to cotton candy. Sweet and delicious. *I wonder how it would taste chocolate-covered.*

I pop another grape into my mouth and as I turn around to head toward the market square, I spot *her*— *s*tanding in front of a vegetable booth, and luckily, she's distracted.

I quickly turn around, but my eyes widen as the grape glides to the back of my throat and lodges itself there. I quickly press my hand against my neck, and begin coughing profusely, trying to dislodge it.

Oh my God, I'm going to die from choking on a grape.

With some effort, the grape finally pops back into the front of my mouth. A sense of relief washes over me as I'm able to breathe again, and as I look up, a small crowd has formed around me. Several people are nervously staring at me, but with some nodding reassurance, I'm able to ease their worry.

I quickly look around and turn my attention back to Flora, hoping she didn't notice me or the commotion. Unfortunately, I should have guessed it because she's looking directly at me and once again, her smile is obsolete.

I quickly look around me, trying to find an escape from her joyless eyes, but there's nowhere to hide. The people near me have returned to their activities and I'm now standing in the middle of a relatively quieter market street. As I turn to face her, she's already making her way toward me as our eyes meet.

Her scowl quickly diminishes with each step she takes toward me, and once she's within arms reach, a cock-eyed smile has formed on her face.

She's wearing a long, dark green dress, has a tote slung over her arm, and in the opposite arm, she is carrying a white bouquet of flowers wrapped in brown paper.

As she raises a brow, she says in an unusually cheerful voice, "Ciao Lily!"

She holds onto one of my shoulders, and leaning forward—careful not to damage the flowers—she plants an air kiss on each side of my cheek before pulling away.

"Ciao Flora," I say with a less than enthusiastic manner as my brows draw together.

"Che cosa stai—" she gasps, then pauses as she shakes her head. "What are you doing here?"

I scratch my head. *Is she joking?*

"Remember? Yesterday I mentioned that I would be in Scappa."

She tilts her head to the side as if this is the first time she's heard about it. I raise both of my brows. *Does she seriously not remember?*

I lower my head and add, "You suggested I shop at the market?"

She looks down at the bouquet and as she looks back up at me, her eyes widen.

"Ah, sì!" she nods, then her attention turns to the bags I'm carrying. "You bought something, no?"

"Yeah, I did."

I look down as I hold my bags slightly up, then raise my eyebrows politely as I point out the bouquet.

"I see you did as well."

I tilt my head slightly forward, trying to get a better look at the florals in her bouquet. With wide eyes questioning, she angles the bouquet towards me and I begin to smile with excitement. *White lilies.*

"Lilies!" I cheer. "Those are my favorite."

I raise myself slightly up onto my tiptoes, as my body fills with delight. I might be the only person that gets excited when someone buys lilies. I mean, why wouldn't I? They share my name, and have such a rich smell to them.

I nod my head back and forth as I try to hold my joy.

"For obvious reasons," I playfully add.

As the words come out of my mouth, her once fake smile is gone, and her entire body seems to react to the fact that the flowers she just purchased happen to be my favorite and my namesake.

"Fiore nazionale," she grumbles with a stern face.

Wrinkling my forehead as I look down, I try to interpret her words, but they aren't familiar to me. Biting my cheek, I give up with a sigh as I glance back up at her.

"The lily," she reiterates slowly. "Italia's national flower."

"Oh!" I cheer, surprised to hear something I definitely should have known. "I had no idea!"

At that point, I lean forward to try to get a slight whiff of the smell as I add, "Well they look lovely."

I see her chest rise as she inhales and exhales a breath, and it seems as though she is trying to make me aware that she is uninterested in our conversation, and definitely doesn't want to continue.

"Who are they for?" I curiously ask, leaning back to create distance between us.

"Mia figlia—my daughter—to celebrate," she beams.

"Oh yeah!" I quickly reply. "Mason said she will be here today for the meeting."

My words fade as they leave my mouth, and my mind begins to race with a million questions. I quickly glance at Flora and notice what is out of place, or better yet *who*.

"Wait, shouldn't you be at the meeting?"

Her cheerful demeanor quickly vanishes, and a crooked grin grows on her face. By the look in her dark eyes, she appears to know something that I don't, and as usual, I want to know what that is.

"The meeting is still happening, right?" I ask with a suspicious scowl.

Flora doesn't reply, but rather lifts her head proudly, trying to show me that she won't budge, but then it's like she can't hold it in.

"Well, I wouldn't call it a meeting," she clarifies.

I tilt my head to the side, wondering if there could be a different term for a business meeting that I'm not aware of.

"What does that mean?" I inquire as I scratch my head.

"Oh!" she beams with a sarcastically amusing look on her face. "You don't know?"

"Know what?" I hesitantly ask.

She glares down at me, appearing to fight her internal monologue for an answer. A moment passes and I frown, wondering if she's just trying to waste my time at this point, but then, she inhales deeply through her nose and as she exhales, a wicked smile forms on her face.

"They are together."

Together? Obviously.

I let out a huff as I roll my eyes, seeing how she was just playing a game. I cross my arms in front of me, and my bags rustle against one another, still hanging from the inside of my elbows.

"I knew that already," I groan. "They are discussing business. I just don't understand why you aren't a part of it."

Surely, there's some sort of language barrier.

Flora tries to contain the smile on her face as she shakes her head.

When she stops, she hisses, "*You* do not understand. My daughter Elisa and Mason are to be wed."

Wed? Okay, now I know she doesn't understand me.

I let out a laugh as I glance around, then look back at her.

"Wed?" I snicker. "As in marriage?"

"Sì," she says as she nods her head proudly. "Mason sarà un vero Italiano—he will be a true Italian in no time."

I uncross my arms as I reach to scratch the back of my neck, feeling a nagging itch as I collect my thoughts.

The moment we arrived at the vineyard, Flora disliked me, and this is surely just another tactic she's employed to get under my skin. Mason isn't engaged—I know that—and if he were, I surely would have known about it. There would have been some sort of sign at least.

I lick my lips and place my bags on the ground, feeling like I need both arms free to convey how crazy she sounds. I tilt my head to the side as I cross my arms in front of me, and give Flora a skeptical look.

"You want me to believe that the man I'm dating—Mason—is engaged to your daughter?" I clarify, then through a chuckle, I add, "Elisa?"

"Americano sciocco," she snorts.

She holds her head high, looking down at me with a smug grin. As her eyes drop back to me, she shakes her head and speaks in perfectly clear, legible English.

"This is not just a business deal. They are the deal, and both of our families couldn't be happier."

I feel a small tapping in my chest as my heartbeat quickens.

No, that can't be true.

Once again she scoffs, and I quickly shake my head, realizing I am now looking at the ground with a million questions running through my mind. As I look back at her, she pulls her shoulders back with arrogance.

"Did you really think *you* were with *him?*" she taunts. "You never were. He even said it himself, you are just a friend."

Blinking rapidly, I shake my head. "You're lying. He wouldn't do that."

As I reach up to quickly scratch the annoying spot of my neck once again, she chuckles in response, as she slowly leans forward.

"Do you really think he came all this way to Italy just for us to sign paperwork that he could have emailed us?"

My eyes quickly grow wide, and my mouth drops open.

No. I don't want to believe it.

She clicks her tongue, and as she leans back with her shoulders straightened, she suddenly appears taller than she did before, and I feel myself slowly shrinking into the cobblestone road below my feet.

"Whatever you had with him, it's over now," she cautions, tilting her head down at me as I feel her eyes glaring through me.

No. I need to talk to him.

I open my mouth to reply, but my tongue feels numb, making me choke on any words I attempt to say. I swallow hard in an strive to fire back, but I'm incapable, as I feel the muscles slowly tightening up in my legs.

This can't be true.

My heart starts to pound out of my chest, and I quickly jerk my head around, searching for help—anyone who can get me out of this nightmare. But there is nobody around, as the market continues to ring with sounds from down the street—people who are oblivious to my internal fight. Unfortunately, the only thing my eyes land on is Flora, looking at me with her glaring eyes and vicious smile.

As her eyes pierce through my body, my lips start to quiver, and tears well in the corners of my eyes. I press my hands together and start twisting them, trying to keep any further emotions from escaping, but I feel the tightness reach my arms, wrapping around me.

Afraid that my entire body will stiffen up next, and I'll truly be unable to hide, I swallow hard—which stops my lips from trembling, and I finally find the words to speak.

"He wouldn't do this to me," I explain frantically. "Not after everything."

She clicks her tongue several times as she shakes her head.

"He probably just wanted to spare you the pain my dear."

Could that be true?

Suddenly, I feel my legs buckle beneath me, and I lose my balance as I fall to the ground.

"I have to see him," I say in a panic as my eyes search beside me. "This can't be happening."

Before I can look up, Flora slowly kneels down in front of me, and once she reaches my level, she places her hand under my chin. Tilting my chin up so I can see her face, she scowls at me and shakes her head.

"He doesn't want to see you. Do you understand?" she exclaims and I blink rapidly, trying to comprehend what she's saying. "You need to disappear."

I swallow hard and tightly close my eyes as I find the words.

"Disappear? What do you mean?"

"If you do anything to ruin this between our families, you will be sorry," she snarls. "You need to leave Italia. Now."

She releases my chin with a flick of her wrist, and I suddenly feel my stomach churning. A wave of heat passes through my head, and then it begins to spin.

She stands up quickly and begins to fidget with her handbag as my vision blurs at her feet. Then, she reaches down in front of my face and appears to be holding something. I blink rapidly as I try to focus on her hand, and I see then that she is holding a stack of cash.

"You need to take this and leave," she orders, dropping it to my feet.

I watch as the paper bills slightly disperse across the cobblestone street beneath my knees. I shut my eyes tightly, trying to ignore it, and immediately shake my head.

"I can't," I say in a shrill voice, squinting up at her as my eyes begin to sting.

She curses something in Italian, then bends down in front of me once more. I can't look her in the eyes any longer, but I feel her breath against my forehead, and I know she's close to me.

"I've met women like you before. This is all you want, so take it and leave," she scolds.

She slowly stands up, and out of the corner of my nearly swollen eyes, I see her brushing down the side of her dress.

"Think of it as Mason's parting gift," she sneers.

My head feels heavy, but I force myself to slowly look up once more. I need to look her in the eyes. I need to see if there is any truth behind what she says. Maybe her eyes will tell me a different story? Maybe she'll even tell me how good of a joke this is, and how she really got me? Unfortunately, just as I'm about to look up, she turns around and walks away, leaving me on my own.

A tight pain runs through my head, and I feel my body tighten once more. On the outside, my body starts to tremble uncontrollably, and on the inside, I just feel numb.

I close my eyes and the thoughts I had when I first arrived in Italy with Mason come rolling back. I imagined this trip might be the dream of my lifetime, yet here I am. Down on my knees on the cobblestone streets of Italy, and all I can think about is when will this nightmare end?

Chapter Twenty-Seven

Mason

I wish I could say that when I regained consciousness, I went to Scappa and found her—that she was clueless about the details of the conversation I had just had, and ran into my arms like nothing had happened, that I was able to explain the misunderstanding with Elisa and how I had nothing to do with it. But, that didn't happen.

Instead, I ran into Flora—who appeared delighted as ever when she excitedly explained to me that Lily was gone. She had found out about the marriage, no less from her I gathered, and had decided to head back without me.

If only I had raced back to the house we were staying in just in time to catch her before she left. But I was too late. Every item of hers was gone. The bed was still made just like we had left it, and even though I hoped she would have left a note, there weren't any to be found. She left as quickly as she could, leaving no trace of her even being in Italy, and all I had were my memories of our time together.

When I returned home, all I cared about was Lily. I wanted to make it right between us as soon as I could. I called several times, but it always went straight to voicemail. I should have known when I dialed her number that she wouldn't answer, but I wanted to try. *I needed to try.*

Even though I knew where she lived, I resisted the urge to just show up. I played out that conversation in my head over and over again, but every scenario brought me to the conclusion that she would never speak to me again.

Despite my best efforts, I knew there was still a pressing matter at hand: my marriage. Until that was handled and entirely in the past, I wouldn't be able to get Lily back, and I especially wouldn't be able to win her trust again.

I feel my phone buzz in my pocket and when I pull it out, there's a text:

Senior Citizen: You can't put off this conversation any longer. You need to let us explain it all to you. Please come to the house tonight.

I squeeze the sides of the phone with my hand, and clench my jaw as I grind my teeth together. With a deep breath, my grip loosens, and I sigh, placing it face down on the table.

It's been five days since I returned, and I've been avoiding every text and call from my parents. I don't know what they expected when they hid this from me, but whatever their explanation is, it better be good.

Not only did they ruin a business deal that was already perfectly arranged, but they ruined my relationship —or what would have been—with Lily. The only thing I truly care about. The only thing I care about now. I got a second chance before, but how likely would it be to get a third?

But if there is going to be any resolution, I have to speak with my parents—even if resentment has been brewing inside me since that day in Italy. It's unusual for me to hold onto these kinds of feelings, especially towards family, so I know I can't avoid them forever.

As I pull into the circular driveway, my body starts to shake slightly. I'm not sure if it's because of my anger towards them for going behind my back, or the hatred for their reason why they would do this in the first place. All I know is I fear there will be no out and no way to escape this plan that has been in place for God knows how long—I fear that when I left Lily that day in Scappa, that will be the last happy memory I'll have of her.

When the feeling returns to my legs, I get out of the car and look up at the large, gray brick house as I close the door. The bright lights shine through the windows from inside, illuminating the driveway as I walk up the steps to the curved wood door.

I step inside and my shoulders tense up as an eerily tense sensation runs through me—like I'm a stranger in my own home. Like I'm intruding.

Even though I grew up in this house, it has been almost a year since I last stepped foot in it—on the day of Miles' wedding. Cars lined the streets, the home was decorated with flowers on the steps of the entrance as well as at every table in the house, and it was filled with bustling people coming in and out. In the backyard, there were lights strung across the trees and surprisingly, it looked like an actual wedding venue—our house was barely recognizable.

Tonight, the house is just as I remember it growing up, quiet, calm, and exceptionally tidy—like my mother prefers. Regrettably though, it no longer feels like a home to me. It no longer feels like a place I am welcomed and happy to be standing in. Maybe it's the looming conversation, or just the time that's made a difference.

Walking into the living room, my feet echo across the tile floor, and it isn't long before I hear another set of footsteps heading my direction. I listen intently, waiting to hear the soft, relaxed steps of my mother, but instead, I hear a heavy thudding echo from down the hall.

"Mason," my father says sternly as he enters the room. "Can you please join us in the office?"

I nod, but he turns around to walk back down the hall before seeing it. I take a deep breath like I'm the one in trouble—something only my father can make me feel—and drag my feet as I follow him.

Despite being the highest ranked person in the Moore Corporation, I might as well be at the bottom when the business involves my parents—specifically my father.

Passing the doorway to my childhood bedroom, I feel the pit in my stomach sink deeper. I know I should be yelling already, but I imagine it wasn't his idea alone, no matter how much he strives for successful business relations.

Following my father into the office, I spot my mother sitting on the leather armchair in the corner near the fireplace. I look around the room for a moment, before stepping through the doorway, noticing how every light is on, brightly illuminating the room. My father walks over to her and she smiles softly at him before he sits down on the loveseat couch across from her.

"Hi honey," she says quietly.

I turn away and stare at the unlit fireplace, knowing I need to watch my words carefully when given the chance.

I see her slowly frown, then gesturing over to the empty cushion next to my father, she asks, "Would you like to sit down so we can talk?

I look down at the empty spot and feel a sharp pain in my chest, just as my father's eyes glare through me.

"I'd rather not."

I look over at the large desk in front of me, take a step towards it, and check the height before leaning my full weight against it while I cross my arms.

"I'll be fine right here."

My mother looks over at my father and nods her head towards me. He coughs, but remains silent as he sinks deeper into the couch, crossing his arms as well. *Stubborn as always.*

My mother turns to look at me, and her brows draw together. I close my mouth tightly, waiting for her to speak, knowing my father has already decided to keep whatever he has to say to himself. But the silence is deafening.

I take a deep breath and push myself up from the desk.

"Alright, clearly neither of you will start, so I will," I declare sharply as my nostrils flare, then I snap, "Does someone want to tell me what the fuck is going on?"

My mother's eyes grow wide as she lifts her brows like she's shocked by my words, but I press on when they remain silent.

"I was under the impression I was going to Italy to complete the deal with the Bombardis."

I hear the agitation in my voice slowly forming when I know I should hide it, but at this point, I don't care. I'm pissed, and they need to know it.

"And by the way, when the fuck were you going to tell me I was supposedly engaged to their daughter?" I scowl, then snicker, "On my wedding night?"

I see my mother's eyes flash up to mine. Placing her hand upon her cheek, she looks over to my father on the couch as if to wait for his permission to speak.

"You asked me to come talk. So talk," I demand, gritting my teeth at my father, whose silence is burning.

"This is your business—" he erupts harshly, uncrossing his arms to stand. "—and to be successful, you will need a strong partner by your side if you're going to be able to manage it all."

Clenching my jaw, I quickly shake my head in disagreement. Is he seriously that ignorant that he'd disregard his son's own choices?

He ignores my reaction and walks over to my mother, placing a hand on her shoulder. He looks down at her and then back at me, then asserts, "So we found you one."

"You had no right," I snap, pounding my fist on the table—wishing the fire were ablaze so I could throw a glass of bourbon into it instead.

I close my eyes and take a deep breath before turning to look back at him with my teeth bared.

"You had no business going behind my back and arranging this," I scold. "Especially with the Bombardis, who are supposed to be our partners strictly in business, not whatever—" I sweep my arms out in front of me and add, "—this is."

My father straightens himself with his head high, and crosses his arms once again.

"You should be grateful," he sneers—his gaze piercing. "You're engaged to a strong, independent woman —one who is like your mother to me."

He takes a step forward, pointing at me, and it feels like a stab into my chest, then scolds, "And if you know what's good for you and the business, you'll follow through with this."

I can't help but let out a loud laugh as I shake my head at his words. His utterly absurd idea that this "relationship" will actually be moving forward.

"This marriage is not happening," I growl. "Not now. Not ever."

"Yes it is," he commands. *Your outdated ways are the reason for your contact name in my phone.*

"Was this your idea?" I sneer as I keep my eyes directly on my father.

"Actually, it was the Bombardis. They came to us with the proposal."

I chuckle and sarcastically mimic his words under my breath, "Proposal."

Then, loud enough for him to hear, I say, "So that's what that meeting you had last week was about. Is that right?"

"Yes," he confirms, taking a deep breath and checking to make sure he is still standing up straight. "We added an amendment to the deal. The Bombardis—like us—wanted to ensure this deal went through. It would benefit both of our companies, strengthening it both financially and socially. They wanted a guarantee that the deal would happen," he pauses, then adds, "and the proposal was it."

I feel my nostrils flare once more and I ball my hands into fists on the side of my body. *How dare he.* Suddenly, an overwhelming rage rushes through my entire body, and I can no longer hold it back.

"This is my company now. Not yours," I shout.

I bring my fist up to my mouth and close my eyes as I take a deep breath, trying to keep myself under control.

As I slowly open my hands, I say in a stern, but less aggressive tone, "And I'm handling it perfectly well without anyone by my side."

"We were just trying to help, honey," my mother's brittle voice forces me to look towards her. "You haven't dated anyone in years, and when they suggested the new terms, we felt we were doing the right thing."

I hear the truth in her words as my gaze drops to the floor. My mother is always the one to do something with only the best intentions. She wouldn't have done this out of spite, nor solely for the business. Despite not knowing about Lily and I, she likely just wants me to be happy and not be loaded down in work, like I know my father has always been.

"Well, I'm telling you right now, it's not happening," I assert, before scowling at my father once again. "If this deal falls through, it won't be because I refused this sham of a marriage. It'll be because you caused it to fail."

My father clenches his jaw and gives me a pinched, unhappy expression as he frowns at me, likely in disappointment. Unlike my mother, he only cares about what will push the business into the next chapter, what will ensure it stays its solid, thriving self. Yet, his silence is daunting.

For the first time, I don't see his eyes ready to fight back, he opens his mouth to speak, but no words come out. He glances down at my mother, places his hand back on her shoulder, and she softly smiles at him. He turns to face me, and his anger fades away with little awareness before he lets out a decisive huff.

"Fine," he grumbles, and I raise my brows in surprise. "It's your company, your business, your life. You can tell the Bombardis it's over."

I frown at him, waiting quietly to see if he'll take back his words, but when he doesn't, I pull my shoulders back.

"I will," I say confidently, despite the heaviness still in the room. I can feel my veins pressing against my temple, and I quickly declare, "Are we done here?"

"Yes, if—" he starts, but before he can finish, I turn on my heel, and leave the room. He said what I wanted to hear, and now, I need to leave to cool off.

As I make my way down the hall, it finally registers that this is the first time I've heard him call it *my* company —he's always referred to it as *our* company. But knowing my father, he doesn't mean it. He probably just wants to prove a point, to prove that if I'm going to open my mouth and say I'll do something, I'd better do it. *And I will.*

I know that if I had stayed in that room one more second, I would have argued with him more and definitely said something I would have regretted.

All I've wanted was for him to recognize that I've been handling everything for months now. Handling every aspect, and fixing all the issues that he put in place. *Why does it feel so unnerving though?*

Now, I'll have yet another issue to deal with—this marriage they've arranged. God knows why they even thought it was a good idea, but the Bombardis must have been pretty convincing for my parents to agree to it. But still, they made this decision without my consent. Even though he may have set up the original deal before I took over, I can only see my parent's actions being the one to end it all—not mine.

I quickly grab my phone from my pocket and call my secretary.

"Hello Mr. Moore. How are you tonight?"

"Hi Marissa, please remember to call me Mason, okay? Mr. Moore is my father," then I sternly add, "We are nothing alike."

"My apologies Mason. What can I do for you?"

"Sorry for calling this late, but with the time difference, it may be best," I pause, knowing this cannot wait. "I need you to contact Flora Bombardi and ask her to meet me."

"Okay, I can do that. Would you like me to set up a meeting at your office?"

"Yes, that would be great."

"And what should I tell them the meeting is about?"

"Let them know I'd like to discuss the marriage."

"Marriage?" she confirms.

"Yes, marriage," I clarify. "They'll understand."

"Okay, I can definitely do that for you. Is there anything else?"

"No. Thank you, Marissa. Have a good night."

"You as well Mason."

When the call ends, I tuck my phone back into my jacket pocket just as I reach the foyer. Glancing towards the living room, a foggy memory replays in my head.

I've made mistakes—everyone has. But the one I made six years ago? That's the mistake I can never undo.

She didn't know it then, but I saw her—truly saw her; the devotion she had for her friend—my brother, her quick replies, witty remarks, and the beauty she carried. And if I had been in the right state of mind at the time, I would have seen the beauty within her—the personality that I'd eventually fall for. But, I can't change the past, so I will focus on the future.

I finally got her to forgive me—or at least I thought I had, but despite my best efforts, I messed it up again. But it doesn't have to stay that way.

Once I meet with the Bombardis, I can sort everything out. I'll tell them that the marriage they arranged with my parents was just that—an arrangement, not a contract. I was handling the deal and nothing was signed, so it is not binding. And when that's cleared up, we'll find a way to move forward as previously established. No marriage, just a solid, permanent business deal as originally planned.

Then, I can turn my attention to what truly matters. The one that's been tearing at my heart since I returned home. The one that I truly care about, and no business deal can stand between. But, will I be able to prove myself again? Prove myself to her? I can only hope.

Chapter Twenty-Eight

Lily

If I could hate Mason Moore, I would. He's nothing but a liar. I gave him a second chance, and he ruined it. I let him prove he had changed, but I should have known better than to trust someone like him.

I wish I could stop caring. I wish I could tell myself that he isn't worth thinking about, but that's not possible. He's dug himself too deeply into my heart, but he doesn't need to know that.

All he needs to know is that I'm done with him. I'm done playing his games. I'm done making excuses for someone that doesn't deserve them.

I've thought about it, and keeping this money only shows him that I'm still involved. Still clinging to something that justifies my decision to leave. And I can't allow that.

When Flora threw the money at my feet, I had a gut feeling that the money was from him. That it was his way of telling me to leave, and decided to spare me the pain by having her do it instead of looking me in the eyes.

My gut feeling has been wrong before, but I had to trust it. I have to believe that he was the one to do this, and I was the fool to believe we would be anything more than friends—that we *were* anything more.

As soon as Flora was out of sight, I gathered the money at my feet, scooped it into my bag, and ran to the nearest busy street to find a ride to the airport.

I should have left the money there. I know that, but I couldn't. I barely had money at the beginning of the trip—which I mostly spent at the market, and I knew I needed to get home first before anything. I would use what I needed and recoup the difference once I got back. Then, I would be done with it.

Even after a week, I still haven't unpacked my bags from the trip. I think a small part of me is afraid of what might come out—whether it be the memories that travelled with me, or the decisions that I've yet to make.

The one thing that has been opened is the shopping bag filled with cash. I haven't counted exactly how much it is, and to be honest, I couldn't care less, but I did keep track of what I spent and can account for it. Now, all that's left is to get it out of my life.

I pick up my phone and type in Miles' name into my phone. Returning the money to him will be simple, and it'll be one less reminder that I'll have of Mason. Miles won't ask questions either, which will make the parting so much easier.

I type out a text to him, something quick that conveys to him that I have something to give him, but I quickly delete it as my thoughts spiral. Curiosity takes the best of me as I type out a different message, and quickly press send before I can regret it.

Me: Is it true? Is he engaged?

My heart races as I place my phone down on the armrest of the couch, but before I can lean back, I hear it ding.

Miles: I'm so sorry Lily.

Lily. His sympathy, as well as his use of my real name, is enough for me to know it's true. That it wasn't a nightmare, and that what happened is that much more real.

Me: Did you know?

I hold my breath as I stare down at the screen, watching the three dots pop up and disappear as he replies.

Miles: I had no idea. If I had known, I would have told you. You know that. I just found out about it when he got back.

I close my eyes and clench my jaw, feeling my heart pounding out of my chest. From anger? *Definitely.* From sadness? *I really hope not.*

From the living room couch, I look over at the shopping bag sitting beneath my bed, then quickly look back at my phone.

It needs to be gone. He needs to be gone from my head once and for all.

I quickly hit send.

> **Me:** I have something for you. Well, for him actually, but can I just give it to you?
> **Miles:** Of course you can. When would you like to meet?

I huff acknowledging that any day would work as far as I'm concerned. I still don't have a job, despite my efforts after returning home. *God knows I've been trying.*

I look back over at the bag, and tilt my head. It's not the greatest hiding spot for that amount of cash, but it's the only place I can think of. At least it'll be safe where it's at until I meet up with Miles.

Although I'm across the room from the bag, I feel it inching closer and closer to me, staring at me from beneath the darkness of my bed.

While others may feel obligated to count how much there truly is, I—on the other hand—feel a burden holding onto it. If someone came into our apartment and saw it, they'd think I'm about to flee the country. I guess in retrospect, I did sort of flee a country, just not the current one I'm in.

What's worse is that the cash is in denominations of twenty, rather than hundreds. *Who does that?* So unfortunately, if anyone finds it, it'll appear as though I have three times the amount than what's actually there.

My eyes grow wide as I remember Paige pointing out Mason's tie under the bed. *Shit.* That's definitely not a good spot. If she spotted that before, she'll easily spot this bag at some point, and then I'll have to admit what actually happened in Italy—a conversation I'm clearly not in the right mental state to have at the moment. Some things are just better left unsaid—at least for now.

I frantically lift my phone to my face.

Me: Tomorrow! Let's meet tomorrow.

The sooner I get this over with, the better. If I meet him tomorrow, this money will be gone.

Miles: Okay, that works. Where do you want to meet?
Me: Somewhere private if that's okay?

Typing that out definitely sounds suspicious, but I can't hand him a bag full of cash at the park or in a place it could possibly get stolen.

Miles: Alcord! Need I remind you I'm married?

I chuckle and roll my eyes at his response as I look down at the screen. *I knew that wouldn't come across the way I wanted to.*

Me: Miles, don't be weird! We both know if I wanted to, I would have in college!

Miles: Good point. I'll think of a place and let you know. Okay?

Me: Thank you.

I lock my phone and walk over to my room. Once I reach the end of my bed, I carefully press the side of my foot up against the shopping bag, and slowly slide the bag further back. I take a quick glance to check if it's out of sight, and then fling myself onto the bed.

As I stare up at the ceiling, watching my fan circle, I let out a premature sigh of relief.

Tomorrow the money will be gone. The weight I've been bearing will lift from my shoulder as I hand it over to Miles. I'll be letting go of something that I brought back with me from Italy. And with that, I'll be letting go of Mason as well.

Chapter Twenty-Nine

Lily

A ringing sound drags me out of a deep sleep. With my eyes still closed, I sit straight in my bed and place my hand on the nightstand, smacking the wood until I find my phone that continues its annoying chime. When I feel the rubber from my phone case in my hand, I quickly pull it toward me, and without looking, I click the alarm button to stop it. When the sound is no longer ringing in my ears, I open one eye, and through blurred vision, I read the almost illegible time on the screen. *5:02.*

Lowering my phone onto the covers draped over my legs, I pull myself backward, falling onto my pillow. As the pillow engulfs my head, I feel small strands of hair fly onto my face, tickling my nose. I bring my hands up to my forehead, and drag my hands until my hair is tucked behind my ears. As I let out a sigh, I place my hands over my face.

I've almost forgotten the feeling of exhaustion—or at least the pain of being woken by an alarm. How can something so simple—such as the time you wake up—feel so vastly different in only a few short months?

Pulling my hands slowly down my face, I stop when I reach my eyes, and carefully rub the top of my eyelids to wipe away the eye boogers. Then, I fling my hands down to my side, aggravated by waking up so early.

Opening one eye and then the other, my vision starts to come into focus. The light peeking in from behind the curtains is barely enough to illuminate the room, and it's a stark reminder that at one point, I woke up every day at this time for work.

Inhaling deeply, I let out an elongated sigh as I release my breath. *But that doesn't mean I'm used to it now.*

When I had asked Miles to meet the following day, I had hoped he would tell me a time in the afternoon—or at least later in the morning. Maybe even after nine o'clock? But I've clearly been unemployed for too long, that I've forgotten Thursdays generally fall under the category of "work days."

I pull my legs to the side of the bed and let them dangle over the edge as I take another deep breath, hoping to bring myself into full consciousness soon. I shake my head, and when I finally feel awake, I walk over to my closet to get dressed.

By the time I check my phone again, it's 5:34 and I'm heading out the door of my apartment complex. I quickly throw my hand up in the air as I reach the edge of the sidewalk and a taxi glides to a halt in front of me.

The driver rolls down the window, and as he leans over the passenger seat, he asks, "Where to?"

Leaning forward, I place my hand on the windowsill and open my mouth, but quickly realize I don't have the slightest clue as to where I'm going.

"One moment," I pause, pulling away from the window.

I quickly scramble, looking for where I put my phone that I had in my hand just moments ago and find it in my jacket pocket. Pulling it out, I see a text from Miles that likely just came in.

As I lean in to read it, I just as quickly pull my head back when I recognize the address. I shake my head and lean back down into the taxi window.

"Sorry, it's not as far as I thought," I say.

The driver leans back into his seat and holds his hand up.

"Not a problem."

I tightly hold the shopping bag against my chest and quickly turn on my heel to start walking. Less than ten minutes later, I arrive at the corner of Lancing Avenue and 86th Street—an intersection that over the years has become all too familiar.

As I stand in front of Hanley's, I look up at the numbers on the buildings around me, but the combination I'm searching for is nowhere to be found. I scratch my head and type the address into my phone, but the pin pops up almost right where I'm standing. *Well that was pointless.*

I turn to peer through the window of Hanley's, and when I catch a glimpse of Sophie behind the counter, I quickly head inside.

The bell above the door chimes, and as I walk inside, I stop in place. What is usually a packed coffee shop is now the complete opposite. Almost every table is vacant, the room is unusually quiet and apart from me, there's a dark-haired man in a suit sitting at the small booth that looks out towards the street. He turns suddenly to look at me and I lower the shopping bag slightly from my chest as I notice his piercing green eyes.

"Lily?" I hear, turning my head away.

Sophie steps over to the open counter separating us looking confused.

"Hi Sophie!" I beam as I step over to her. Her expression quickly turns to a smile. "How are you?"

"I'm good," she nods, wiping the surface of the counter. "You know, I don't think I've ever seen you here this early."

"Definitely not, and I don't plan to make a habit of it either," I declare.

She laughs and asks, "Shall I get you your usual then?"

I scratch my head and peer over my shoulder, wondering if there's enough time before I meet with Miles. He's the one doing this favor for me, and despite how exhausted I am, I shouldn't keep him waiting, especially when I can grab a coffee afterwards.

"Not right now, but thank you."

My eyes fall down to my phone in my hand and I quickly shake my head as I look back up at her.

"Actually, I'm trying to get to this address, but I can't find it. Can you help me?"

I show her my phone screen and she presses her lips together, trying to hide her smile.

"White building," she states as if she's been asked this question all day, then she points out the window. "It's brand new. You can't miss it."

Looking back at her, I smile, "Thank you Sophie. I appreciate it."

She smiles back, and as the bell above me chimes once more as I open the door, I turn to look back at her.

With a short wave, I add, "I'll be back in a bit, then I'll take my usual!"

When I reach the white building—which can't be more than 1,000 feet from Hanley's, I quickly pull the handle on the glass door, but I'm jolted forward because the door won't budge. At the same moment, my shopping bag drops to the ground, and my eyes immediately grow large. I quickly pull the bag back up to my chest and look around at the people walking past me on the sidewalk. Luckily, they appear oblivious to its contents, or the fact that I appear lost.

Staring at the door handle, I look up at the building towering over me. It's exactly as Sophie described, but the top appears to still be under construction. *Is this even open?*

I take a step back and notice a small sign stuck to the window with the numbers 1268. *Nope, this is definitely it.*

Taking a step forward again, I cup my hand around my eyes and peer into the window. At first all I see is a large, desolate lobby, but suddenly I spot a dark-haired woman behind the front desk. She quickly notices me and motions for me to come in. Pulling away, I grab the handle of the door, but this time, it opens.

"Lily?" she asks as I step inside.

"Yes?" I confirm.

"He's waiting for you. Floor three," she says.

"Thanks!" I beam, just as she turns her attention back down to her computer.

I quickly make my way over to the elevator, and when I reach the floor, the doors open up to the middle of a wide office space. As I step out, there's several tables with rolling chairs on each side of me, and just across the way is a sitting area divided by black-trimmed glass.

I take a step to the right and peer further down the hallway, where the rows of tables continue.

"Miles?" I holler, the sound echoing throughout the floor.

"Alcord!" I hear his voice from behind me, nearly making me jump.

I turn around and let out a sigh of relief as I see Miles walking over to me. I loosen my grip on the shopping bag and lower it to the floor as Miles pulls me in for a hug.

As he pulls back, I tease, "You know, when I said private, I didn't expect an empty office building."

Miles laughs and says, "Well, it was either this or a dark alleyway, so I went with the safer option."

"Much appreciated," I chuckle. I look over my shoulder, then back to Miles. "How'd you find this place anyways?"

Miles' brows draw together as his smile fades and he quickly glares at the floor.

"I—" he starts, but he's suddenly interrupted.

"Lily."

Immediately recognizing the voice behind me, I quickly take in a deep breath of air and prepare myself. *Please let this be my imagination.*

I anxiously wait until Miles looks up and meets my eyes again.

"I'm sorry," Miles mutters, and I watch his Adam's apple fall. "He begged me to let him come."

I take a deep breath and slowly shake my head, but my vision blurs when I redirect my focus on the windows behind Miles.

"You wouldn't answer any of my calls," Mason pleads from behind me, and then in a low voice that sounds closer, he adds, "Please let me explain."

I squeeze my eyes shut as I hear him grow closer behind me.

"I didn't plan for this to happen. Any of it." he confesses, taking a deep breath. "It all started out as just a business deal. That's all I ever wanted. They would supply our products in Europe, and we would supply theirs here. But then it got out of hand and the marriage was added to the deal."

As he says the word "marriage," I feel a tight pain in my chest, holding my breath as I hear him take another step forward.

"You have to believe me when I say it was done without my knowledge," he continues. "I didn't find out until we were in Italy when Elisa told me. That was the first time I heard about it. About any of it."

I feel my breathing increase with every word that comes out of his mouth. I can't believe he's lying to me yet again. Does he honestly think that I'd believe this story of his? That he—the CEO—had no knowledge that marriage was part of what he said was one of the most important deals.

I slowly lower my head and open my eyes intending to move my feet, but they are glued to the floor. I can't run. I can't hide from all these feelings I've been bottling up inside of me. Luckily for me, this may be the best thing for me right now because I don't know how I'd feel if I turned around and looked him in the eyes.

I glance down at my hand, trembling as it holds the strap of the shopping bag laying on the floor. I clench it tightly, stopping the motion, but my legs are starting to shake.

I open my mouth to speak, but my tongue is numb, muting any argument that I could make. It feels like the same constraining reaction I experienced back in Italy.

"You have to believe me," he begs. "I wouldn't have done this to you. I wouldn't have hurt you again."

Suddenly, I feel his hand on my shoulder, sending a spark throughout my body that releases me from the floor. I quickly turn myself around to face him, and as I hoped, his hand falls from my shoulder.

Staring down at his feet, I take a deep breath, clench my jaw, and find the strength to look up at him. As our eyes meet, my body stiffens again, pained by the betrayal. His eyes soften, sensing it, and for a brief moment, I feel my heart skip a beat—a subtle reminder of the person I once thought I knew. I quickly shake my head and push the thought deeply into the back of my head.

Swallowing hard, I woefully whisper, "How can I?"

Inhaling deeply, I grit my teeth as I forcefully release the shopping bag while pushing it toward his feet. Breaking our eye contact, he glances down at the spilled euro banknotes lying against the floor. I keep my eyes focused in front of me, trying to avoid showing him any mercy.

Looking back up at me, his eyebrows draw together. "What is this?" he asks.

I bite my tongue and scowl at him as I shake my head. *I can't believe he's still putting on this act.*

"Don't act dumb," I hiss, straightening myself up as I slowly try to find the words. "Of all the ways you could have told me to leave, this may have been the worst."

"I didn't—" he desperately explains, but I quickly cut him off.

"This is low, even for you," I scold. "I never understood what you meant before when you said I would never be with someone like Miles—like you—but I understand it all now."

He quickly shakes his head and reaches out, gently brushing his hand against my forearm, but I immediately pull my arm out of his reach. He takes a slight step away from me, puzzled by my reaction, and I hear the cash move around his feet.

"You have it all wrong," he assures. "The marriage isn't happening. I'm calling it off."

Marriage. That word once again painfully hits me. Then, I quickly scoff at the ridiculousness of his words.

"Calling it off?" I shake my head and look at him intently as I continue, "So, what? You try to apologize, but yet you're still engaged? You're unbelievable."

I step away from Mason and look over my shoulder at Miles. His shoulders immediately droop as his attention narrows, and he appears saddened by the conversation.

I turn back to Mason and attempt to scowl at him while fighting back the tears that have now fully formed in the corners of my eyes.

"Keep your money," I snap. "I want nothing to do with it."

I pause and take a step back as I glance down at the cash on the floor.

One thing.

With a distasteful tone, I add, "Or you."

Two things.

Pulling his head back, Mason raises his brows in shock, then his shoulders quickly fall. Before he can say another word, I turn away and look back at Miles, standing behind me. I bite my lip as a tear falls from my eye, hoping I can hold back the rest of them.

"I'm so sorry," Miles mouths the words silently.

I slowly shake my head as I sniffle, then mouth, "It's okay."

I truly mean it too. While Mason did everything wrong, I can't blame Miles for being in the middle of it. I imagine he just wanted me to find closure—to feel some comfort after speaking to Mason and hearing his side.

Before I let him reach me again, I quickly push my feet forward and walk over to the elevator. Miraculously, the doors open immediately and I step inside and into a corner where he can no longer see me. As the doors close, I let out a sigh of relief, feeling unexpectedly lighter than when I had arrived, but it doesn't stop the tears from running down my cheeks.

And with that, I can finally move on from Mason Moore.

Chapter Thirty

Mason

I can deny it all I want, but she's right. Of course she is. And if I had known better, I would have waited to talk to her in person when everything was over, but I couldn't help myself. I couldn't wait.

I'm the moth attracted to the flame. The light is burning brightly, and all I want is to be near it. To touch it. For it to be the one thing that I can focus my attention wholeheartedly on. But the light suddenly went out. I'm lost, searching for a way to find it. I'm being pulled back deeply into the darkness, and while I want to find the light, I can't. I can't find my way—at least not yet. I'm stuck dealing with the consequences before I can search for the light again. Dealing with this out-of-hand business deal that has already become more than I bargained for.

I had every intention of moving forward with the Bombardis as we had originally planned—a simple deal and a straightforward cross-country distribution. Including our proposed special edition spirit we would create together to publicize it all. Yet, that's no longer possible.

When I saw that cash, alarm bells went off in my head. Maybe it was because I felt protective over Lily, or maybe it was the businessman in me spotting a shady deal. But deep down I knew that money was given with ill intent. Who pays someone to disappear unless they need to make sure the marriage will go as planned?

I couldn't go into the meeting with only accusations. I needed proof because if this multi-million dollar deal is going to fail on my account, I'm not going to go with a hunch.

When I knew the Bombardis were arriving soon, I spoke to my accountant, Alice, to have her dive deeper into their business ventures.

Time was not on our side. She had less than twenty hours to get as much dirt on the company as she could— otherwise I would be walking into this meeting with measly accusations, instead of solid facts.

As the hours finally trickle into minutes and I stand outside of my office door, I fear I'll have no choice but to go in blind. Just as I'm about to give up, I feel my phone buzz in the inside pocket of my suit jacket. My eyes grow wide as I see Alice's name on my screen, and I can't answer quick enough.

I listen intently as she gives me every detail she's found on their company, their family, and every deal they've done in the past. Then, after only several minutes, all I need is a confirmation.

"Are you sure?" I ask, swallowing hard.

"Yes, I'm positive."

"Thank you Alice," I say, before quickly hanging up the phone.

I straighten myself, grip the handle of my office door, take a deep breath, and push it open.

Chapter Thirty-One

Mason

I choked.

I was capsized into the unknown, sinking deeper and deeper with every hour. I gasped for air, feeling myself slowly descend as my lungs filled. My chest caved in, and I could no longer breathe.

Well, I could have. At least that was how it felt.

Every hour leading up to the meeting, I could feel the words I rehearsed bury deeper in my mind. While it could have been as simple as telling them I'm no longer doing business with their company, the overpowering pressure of my father's words shadowed over me. *Your business*. I knew I couldn't just turn them down.

Yet, I couldn't ignore the gaping sign that they weren't who they said they were, and it weighed heavily on me. If in the end, it was just a hunch that I had, and not the facts, then I had to be prepared, which scared the living shit out of me. I had to be the one to propose a new contract, but one that couldn't be changed, and definitely without a marriage amendment.

My only beacon of hope was Alice, and my God, she deserves all the credit for helping me out of this unbelievable situation.

The entire meeting was a blur after I walked into that room, but as far as I remember, it didn't last long. I'm not the one to be the center of attention, but at that moment, I had to be, and as soon as I opened my mouth, it all came crumbling down.

On paper, they appeared to be a successful, thriving distributor throughout Europe—which drew us to them in the first place. My father always did his due diligence when planning a deal—and this one was no different. Except, they found a way around it.

Their numbers showed they were spending more than they were actually bringing in, which was slowly sending them into debt. From what I gathered, they scrambled to try to find a solution, and unfortunately made bad financial investments that sent them reeling. All of this was long before we came into the picture however.

With the impending collapse of their company, which had been in the family for over 100 years—like ours —they needed an out, and they needed it fast.

When we reached out to them looking to establish our own distribution in Europe, they quickly jumped at the opportunity. We had the finances and—unbeknownst to us at the time—they didn't.

Later, when they saw the slightest inkling that I may be interested in their daughter, they thought they found an even better solution. If somehow we discovered their financial crisis—which eventually would come to light—having a solid partnership through marriage would keep their funds afloat, and with it, their business.

The Bombardi Family took it upon themselves to reach out to my parents, thinking my father was still the head of the company, and pushed for that security blanket. I'm not sure they considered the fact that I could say no, or if maybe it was worth the risk in order to save their business.

I quickly learned why they were willing to pay off Lily with the cash. To them, she was an adversary. The only limitation that might stop me from moving forward with the contract my parents created with them. The obstacle to a guaranteed marriage.

So, as expected, I terminated it all. And boy were they unhappy.

Surprisingly even my father—selfish in his ways—acknowledged his mistakes. One could say he was proud that my subtle observation led to the end of a deal bound to bring us down with it, but as I saw it, I only proved how capable I was in my role.

Yesterday, I didn't realize how heavy the air was suffocating me. Today, I feel as though I can breathe for the first time in over a week.

I take a deep breath and quickly pull on the halyard line, hoisting up the mast on my boat. As I set the sails with the wind, I'm hit with a small droplet of water in the corner of my mouth. Pressing my tongue against it, I taste its saltiness momentarily before the cool breeze dries it away.

I look around the large sail and out to the horizon. Closing my eyes, I can feel the fogginess in my head already shifting, and a lightness breathing through me.

When I open my eyes, I look over my shoulder at the city behind me. A white haze shadows it, but it appears to be slowly drifting away as the wind carries it out to sea.

It's been four months since I've stepped into this position, but it feels as though I'm taking control of the company. *Finally.* All I can hope is that I can take control of my relationship, if there's still one to be made.

I lick my lips, tasting the saltiness against them once more and turn back towards the horizon. Running my hand through my messy, damp hair, I slowly grab the line, but quickly ease up my grip as my attention turns to the top of my mast. I watch as my small, red flag at the top slowly lowers, indicating the wind has momentarily let up around me.

I tie back the line, understanding there is no predicting when the wind will pick back up, and I lean back in my seat against the helm. Crossing my arms, I direct my attention to the sky, where the wind is much more active blowing the clouds quickly past me.

While new sailors might agonize over when they'll be picked up again, a seasoned one knows that all you can do is wait patiently until that momentary breeze returns— one that is just enough to catch in your sail and push you forward. But until then, I'm happy to have what I came out here for—time to think. It's what I do best when I'm out here alone on the open water.

Pushing myself forward and away from the helm, I uncurl my arms and rest my hand on the top of the wheel. The wood on the wheel is rougher than I remember, likely due to the boat sitting on the dock for so long, or maybe my hands have grown softer, since I've dived into work and strayed away from the ocean. No matter the reason, it's a stark reminder of how long it's been since I've been out on ole' "No Reins."

My friend's words always find their way back into my head when I need them most.

"You have to trust you know what you are doing," he said.

I chuckle at the thought as I lean back once more and place my leg over the opposite knee to rest.

These days, I feel as though I can't trust anything I'm doing. Just when I begin to think I'm doing everything right, something comes back to bite me; my arrogance, my past, my parents, my business. What's next?

I focus on the boat slowly rocking from the water below. The wind may be calm, but the ocean always has a mind of its own. Always moving even when everything around it is still. And just like us, when I believed it was calm, it was actually drifting away. A slow, yet chaotic storm quickly brewing below, that can suddenly carry you out to sea. It feels as though nothing will stay still, but just like nature, there's always a calm after the storm. And hopefully for us, the storm will be over soon.

I was drawn to her, in every way I can imagine. In the past, in the present and even now, I'm still utterly drawn to her.

All I've ever wanted in a relationship was something sincere and genuine, and now it's finally clear to me. She is and has always been what I wanted—maybe even what I needed too.

Whether it was luck or not, I found her and although our previous encounter was entirely my fault, she gave me a chance. It was in that chance that I fell—quickly and hard. There's no denying that.

I didn't deserve that chance by any means, and even now, I still don't know if I deserve another, but I have to try.

"If you let go of the reins, you know you've put the work in already, and you will be safe," I hear his words playing in my head.

Now I can only hope that the foundation we created will be enough, that even after it all, I'll be able to show her I'm there for her, that she'll feel secure—safe—in everything I do moving forward. I'll never need to ask for another chance again, because there will be trust between us, and another storm will not return. She will be forever the person I choose, the only one I want, the one that nobody will take away from me again like they tried to do before. But, she holds the reins, and if she chooses to let go, I have to let her.

Realizing my gaze has fallen and my focus has blurred as I stare at my feet, I blink quickly to adjust my vision.

As I straighten myself back into my seat, a slight movement shifts my focus. I quickly look up at the small flag at the top of the mast, but it appears to be still, just as before. *Not yet.* Then, just when I'm about to turn away, I catch the end lifting, sending me a glimmer of hope that the breeze may return.

I reach out to touch the line, hoping to feel the vibrations of the shifting movement, but a slight tickle across my forehead pulls my hand away. Reaching up to my head, I brush away a strand of my unkempt hair and as the tickle disappears, I chuckle quietly at the distraction.

I reach out to touch the line in front of me again, and suddenly I hear a loud flutter from above. The red flag is now fully straight, indicating the wind has picked up, and without pause, the rest of my hair falls across my face from the now brisk breeze.

Seeing my sail beat back and forth, I quickly dig my fingers through my hair, pull it back from my face, and grab a hold of the line. Pulling the line with one hand and rotating the wheel with another, I turn the boat and the wind forcefully fills the sails. Pushed back into my seat as the boat propels itself forward, I fasten my line and when I find my balance, I place both hands back on the wheel.

Quickly, my face becomes soaked by the ocean spray from the boat powerfully gliding forward. As I wipe it away, I feel the water fall from my cheeks, and a wide, gleaming smile appears in its place.

I'll be waiting.

Chapter Thirty—Two

Lily

After returning the money to Mason, I moved on—
or at least I'm trying to, even a month later.

It sucks to be deceived once again by someone I
thought I knew, someone I was falling for. I guess it was
another game played on me.

So what better way to distract myself than to occupy
my time?

I found myself engaging in my hobbies, trying to
convince Paige to watch a little too many rom-coms, and
continuing my job search. Still no luck on the last one.

Even though I no longer work at The Harper
School, I still find time to volunteer at the afterschool
program. It's one success of mine that I will never forget,
and I don't plan to put in the past.

About a week ago, I ran into a friend of my
mother's whose children attended the school. She was
disheartened to hear I was no longer working there, but she

couldn't stop talking about how impressed she was by the program I developed. Both of her children were involved in it and were thriving. Fortunately for me, she knew someone that may be able to help me get back into doing what I love, and today, I may get that chance.

Walking up a large staircase that rises above the street below, I enter the Mayfair College campus. Quickly sniffing myself to check that I still smell like the rose-scented perfume I put on this morning, I feel a sense of relief. I just walked five minutes from the train station up to the campus and unfortunately, the steep incline caused me to break out in a light sweat. Yet, it appears that the cool breeze, and my perfume have saved the day.

As I reach the top step, I straighten my lavender blazer and take a deep breath as I continue to walk through the campus. The long brick sidewalk is wide, but the bustling students—walking and riding their bikes—fill every available space around me.

As I reach a crossroad where the sidewalk branches out in several different directions, I look around for any sign or indication that I'm heading in the right direction. Unfortunately for me, nothing is popping out.

I'll admit, I didn't consider how big an elite college truly would be. When I was searching for my own college courses in the city, everything had signs—streets, buildings, classrooms—and if I couldn't find something, there were maps taped inside of every building window, making it simple and easy to navigate.

Here, however, I don't have the slightest clue where to go, and there isn't a map in sight. So, my best bet is asking around.

As students race past me, I quickly hold my hand up to try to stop someone on a bike, but they ignore me and continue on their way. *My first mistake.*

I step off of the path and onto the grass, hoping to flag down a student walking. Soon, a blonde-haired girl acknowledges me with a smile.

Lowering my hand, I step over to her, meeting her halfway.

"Hi!" I smile, glancing around me to show I've tried. "I'm a little lost."

She smiles back and nods her head in agreement.

"I figured as much. How can I help?"

Tilting my head, I mumble, "I'm looking for the Childhood Development Building. Do you know where that is?"

"Yeah, you were so close," she nods.

"Was I?" I scoff.

"Yeah, it's actually just over there."

She points behind me, and I quickly look over my shoulder, not sure where she's pointing. As I turn back around, I wrinkle my forehead.

"The red brick building over there is Moore Hall, the one you're looking for is right behind it."

The name immediately brings Mason to my forethoughts. A harsh reminder that I don't want nor need. I shake away the thought and focus back on the girl.

"Thank you!"

"You're welcome! Good luck with the interview!"

I furrow my brows, taken back by the statement.

"How'd you—"

"It may be Mayfair, but even the professors don't dress up that nicely," she taunts, then looks down at my top. "So I just assumed."

I look down at my outfit—a lavender blazer, loose white button down top and black slacks with heels. I blink my eyes, then glance back up at her.

"I thought I was underdressed," I chuckle.

"Not at all," she says with a smile. "But you've definitely got that fun yet professional look. Good luck!"

"Thank you—" I say, taking a step back. "—for your help and advice!"

"Anytime!" she says, before continuing down the path.

I look back down at my outfit one more time, and if she's right, I'm relieved I didn't add a briefcase like I had planned to.

As I reach the red brick building, I see a small, almost unrecognizable sign near the entrance that reads "Moore Hall" and I scoff quietly to myself. *Well, that explains my lack of direction.* They couldn't make the signs any bigger?

Glancing over to where I was standing with the girl, I take a step back from the building to confirm the direction I need to head. As I walk further backward, my feet reach the brick path again, and I nearly run into someone.

"Watch out!" I hear a man on a bike yell, and he quickly veers around me.

"Sorry!" I shout, turning myself around.

Just then, I faintly hear a familiar voice calling out from behind me. I quickly dismiss it thinking it's my imagination getting the best of me, until I hear it once again.

"Alcord!"

I look over my shoulder and to my surprise, Miles is lightly jogging down the front steps of Moore Hall and heading in my direction. I turn around to face him just as he reaches me, and he pulls me in for a hug.

"Hi!" he gasps, pulling away, but still holding onto my shoulder. "I never expected you to be here."

"Neither did I," I chuckle.

"Don't you remember I told you I worked here?" he asks, releasing his hand from my shoulder and crossing his arms.

As soon as he says it, I remember why Mayfair had sounded so familiar when my mother's friend mentioned it. When I had met up with Miles to return Mason's phone, he told me he worked there as a professor, but I must have been too preoccupied to remember it until now.

"My bad! I must have forgotten," I say, shaking my head.

I quickly look down at his outfit and he's wearing dark blue jeans, dress shoes and a gray polo. Seeing his clothes confirms what the girl just mentioned.

"You know, I don't think I've ever seen you dressed so casual," I joke, pressing my finger on his arm.

He laughs and glances down. "That's right. You probably remember all of the suits I wore when we went out."

"Yes!" I beam. "It didn't matter what day, you were always dressed to the nines."

When he looks back up at me, he seems surprised by what I said.

"You should have told me I was overly dressed back then!"

"What?" I blurt out sarcastically. "You can never go wrong with a three-piece suit."

He laughs, then says, "Nowadays, I'm wearing jeans—much more comfortable."

"That's true," I nod, looking down at my own outfit, wishing now that I had worn jeans. "I never would have guessed that though since you were wearing a suit the last time I saw you."

"I had a meeting later that day, so you caught me in my formal wear," he chuckles, then furrows his brows. "So, what are you doing here?"

"I actually have an interview," I proudly say.

"What!" he shouts excitedly. "That's awesome! What's the position?"

"Early Childhood Education Lecturer," I say anxiously. "But I have no idea if I'll get it."

"Pff! Why wouldn't you?"

I sigh through a slight chuckle. "I think I'm a little under-qualified."

"That's nonsense," he insists, shaking his head. "I'll put a good word in for you."

I raise my brows in surprise. "Oh, well thank you! I appreciate that."

"Anything for a friend," he smiles. "Let me walk you to that building."

Gesturing for me to step back onto the brick path, he joins me. I look over at him, and while I hadn't noticed it before, I can see the resemblance between him and Mason; the same dirty blonde hair, square jawline, and matching dimple.

I don't want to ask. Actually, I know I shouldn't ask, but I can't help it. My curiosity always gets the best of me and this time won't be any different.

I bite my lip as I look down at the ground, then look back up at him. Taking a breath to push the words out of my mouth, I whisper, "How's Mason?"

Miles is silent for a moment contemplating my question. Then, out of the corner of his eye, he glances over at me and proclaims, "I had a feeling you'd ask me about him."

I quickly glance down and shake my head. "You're right. I shouldn't have—"

Miles quickly adds, "He's doing well."

I know I shouldn't have asked, but I'm glad I did. Mason may not be in my life, but I still care, even if I don't want to.

There's another moment of silence between us as we continue walking, and while I try not to ask, another question about Mason slips out.

"The wedding must be coming up, huh?" I inquire, keeping my eyes on the ground and kicking my foot.

Then I realize that Miles is no longer walking next to me. Lifting up my head to check, I turn around and see him standing in place with a frown on his face.

"What?" I ask puzzled.

"There is no wedding," he admits, taking a step closer to me as he shakes his head. "There never was."

"What do you mean?" I cautiously ask as Miles reaches me and we continue walking.

"Mason was telling the truth when you saw him the last time. He didn't know about the marriage and it was set up by our parents, thinking they were doing the right thing."

My thoughts start racing and a glimmer of hope ignites in me, causing my heart to start beating rapidly.

Miles continues, "He ended it as soon as he found out. That was the truth. The entire deal fell through because of it."

"Wait, what?" I gasp, grabbing ahold of his shoulder to turn him toward me.

Miles lowers his head slightly and looks back at me smiling.

"You didn't know?"

I shake my head slowly and swallow hard, feeling overwhelmed by this new information.

"He knew that if he was still doing business with them, any chance of winning you back would be ruined."

I look down at the ground and my eyes race back and forth, until they meet Miles' again.

"It's been almost a month," I argue. "Why hasn't he reached out?"

Miles shrugs his shoulders. "You gave him a chance once. He didn't think he had another."

I open my mouth, but I can't think of anything else to say. If this is true, then I've had it all wrong, and Mason didn't lie to me—even when I thought he did.

"Well, here we are," Miles says, looking up at the building next to us.

I turn my head and read the small sign at the top of the stairway near the entrance. *Early Childhood Development.*

"Oh," I frown, wishing this conversation wasn't about to end.

I take a deep breath, then look at Miles with a grin and quickly thank him.

"No problem," he smiles, patting the back of my shoulder.

He brings his hand up to his head and scratches his temple, then adds, "Hey, I'm not sure if you are busy on Saturday, but the company is throwing a cocktail event to celebrate their new drink. You should come."

I purse my lips and anxiously ask, "Mason will be there?"

He answers my question with a nod.

"That may not be the best," I admit.

He frowns, but as if a thought pops into his head, he looks up at me with a smile.

"Yeah, but you may not even see him," he says, but I know it's a lie. "If anything, it'll be a fun event with free drinks! Who doesn't love free drinks?" he winks before clarifying, "For you, not me."

I consider it for a moment and think, there's never a good excuse to turn down free drinks. When I look back up at him, I give him a soft smile.

"Plus, you can meet my wife Alice! I think you two would get along well!"

It's hard to contain the grin that spreads over my face, as Miles is now making puppy dog eyes at me. What he doesn't know is that I've already decided.

I chuckle with a nod and nonchalantly say, "I'll think about it."

"Perfect," he smiles, as if he can read my mind. "I'll send you the details."

I turn to walk up the steps of the building and before I can make it all the way up, I hear Miles clear his throat behind me. Turning around, I look at him and pause momentarily waiting for him to speak.

"Good luck in the interview!" he shouts before smiling. "And I'll be seeing you soon."

Chapter Thirty-Three

Lily

As I stepped back into the lobby of the place where we had our first date, the flood of memories caught up with me. The dark, vibrant bar full of people, the memories of our first date when I knew nothing about Mason, and the conversations where I found myself smiling harder than I could help. I never would have imagined what would happen between us. It was clear that Mason had connections at this hotel before, and I suppose that is why this cocktail event is here—but I am surprised.

After taking the elevator alone to the private lounge area, the sound of people mingling rushes in as the doors open.

A man quickly rushes forward. "Welcome miss. Can I get your coat?"

"Oh, yes. Thank you," I answer.

"May I?" he asks, holding out his arms.

I politely nod and turn away from him as he holds the collar of my coat and slides it down past my arms. As I turn to face him again, he's holding a small ticket and I take it.

"Enjoy," he nods.

I smile politely before he turns around and hands my jacket to a woman behind a small counter with coats hung up. I place the ticket securely inside my small clutch before turning away.

Taking a step out from the small hallway adjacent to the elevator, I turn a corner and the room suddenly expands in length and height. The tall windows that wrap around the room are slightly hidden behind long, floor-length curtains, and the ceiling is intricately detailed with an ornate design. It's a dimly lit room, but I can easily see the faces of those near me, standing closely around tall tables draped in black tablecloths.

I glance down at my violet—almost black—silk dress. It hugs my hips and hits just past my ankles to my black high heels. Looking back up at the other guests around me, I'm relieved that I dressed properly when I assumed it was a black tie event.

Looking through the crowd of people, I spot Mason across the room talking to someone. His hair is neatly pushed back, a stark difference from his more relaxed style he had in Italy, and he's wearing a black tuxedo.

He brings a small glass up to his lips, taking a sip, and as he pulls it away, he appears to laugh and a wide grin spreads across his face. I spot his small dimple on his cheek indent and I can't help but recognize how handsome he looks tonight. Something I must have forgotten. *And to think at one point he wasn't my typical type.*

As his eyes scan the room, my heart races and I quickly turn away, searching for the bar, and an escape. *I don't know if I'm ready to face him. Or if I'll ever be.*

Making my way through the cluster of people near the bar, I place my hands on the counter, setting down my clutch as well. The bartender is cleaning a glass at the opposite end, but quickly spots me and walks over.

"Hello, what can I get you?"

I hesitate for a second as I consider my options. I click my tongue and think back to the drink Mason recommended on our first date, but the name is on the tip of my tongue.

"Something smooth, but with a slight fruitiness. Do you have something like that?"

The man chuckles and quickly grabs a glass in front of him that's facing upside down.

"You've just described the drink of the night."

"Oh?" I question, raising my brows. "What's it called?"

He keeps his focus turned down and grins as he pours the drink. I watch as a purple liquid forms in the glass and I can't help but think how similar it is to the drink I had on that first date.

"We all have to wait to find out," he says, garnishing the top with a thin orange slice.

He places a napkin down on the counter in front of me as I pull my clutch away to make room and he places the drink on top of it.

With a quick nod, he smiles, "Enjoy."

I pull my lips in with curiosity, then reply, "Thank you."

I grab the drink and as I turn around, I spot Miles, also dressed in a tuxedo, walking toward me.

"You came!" he cheers wide-eyed with a grin.

I roll my eyes as I joke, "Well, I figured it was better than sitting on the couch."

"Well, I'm glad you came," he nods, before stepping aside.

A woman, whose hand Miles is holding, steps up beside him. She has long, blonde hair, blue eyes and is wearing a navy strapless gown that flows closely down her body in a mermaid style.

"Lily," he says with a smile, trying to contain the joy on his face. "This is my wife, Alice."

"Oh! It's so nice to meet you!" I grin, quickly tucking my clutch under my arm.

I take a step forward and she gives me a sideways hug as I hold my drink away, careful not to spill it.

"I've heard so much about you, Lily," she says with a kind smile.

She turns to Miles then looks back at me and adds, "It's nice to finally put a face to a name."

"Same for you," I agree, smiling back.

"Oh, I see you've got the drink of the night?" Miles points out as he raises his brows questionably towards my glass.

"Yeah, I did," I say, holding it up slightly.

"How do you like it?" Alice asks.

I hold the glass up as if to study it intently. "I actually haven't tried—"

Before I can finish my sentence, the tapping of a microphone redirects my attention forward. Miles, stepping off to the side, turns to face that direction as well, allowing me to see the speaker.

My eyes scan the crowd as several people around me turn toward the front of the room, I hear a deep voice quietly chuckle, "Is this thing on?"

The guests begin to leave their places at the cocktail tables and form a small crowd towards the front of the room near the speaker. Miles and Alice also step closer towards the back, and I slowly follow behind.

"Hello everyone," I hear Mason announce over the speaker. There's a slight pause and then he clears his throat. "Thank you so much for joining me tonight."

I'm unable to see him, but I carefully try to peer in between the heads of the guests in front of me.

"I'm not one for talking, so I'll keep this short," he jokes, just as I find a clear viewing point from the back of the crowd.

"Recently we had planned to release a new drink celebrating a new business deal, but as you know, things can change in an instant, and unfortunately that fell through."

"Yeah, it did," I whisper quietly under my breath, then I quickly glance over at Miles, hoping he didn't hear me.

As I look back at Mason, he continues, "But there's no reason to waste a perfectly good party, so I've decided to move forward with the release, which is why I've brought you all here tonight."

He takes a step out of view and when he returns, he's holding an identical drink to mine. *Purple liquid garnished with an orange slice.* Holding the drink up in the air slightly, he looks at it sideways, as if he's proudly admiring it.

"Persuasive. That may be one word to describe it," he confesses as he turns back to face the crowd. "If a drink can convince you to like it, it's this one."

The corner of his lip tips up as he glances down at the ground, then back up. His eyes search the front of the crowd before landing on someone.

With a playful scoff, he adds, "Well, convince you to go with our products at least."

As the crowd laughs, he looks back at the drink in his hand and as the noise fades, he continues.

"It has just the correct balance of sweetness," he states, and after a quick breath, he says softly, "And it's beautiful too."

Quickly raising his voice as he turns back towards the crowd, he utters, "Am I right?"

I see several people nod their heads in agreement as they look around the room at one another and a few people chuckle.

"Made with our brand new blackberry vodka, sweetened with honey, and a few extra ingredients that make it irresistible."

Looking down at my drink I consider what he says. *Irresistible, huh?* Realizing I haven't tried it yet, I bring it up to my lips as Mason begins talking again.

"So, without further adieu, I would like to introduce you all to—"

I take a sip and as the fruity, yet pleasant flavor hits my tongue, I hear, "The Lily Drop."

What?

Suddenly, I feel myself gasping for air while I'm holding the small amount of liquid in my mouth. Drowned by the noise of the crowd clapping, my eyes tighten as I choke silently on the drink before I finally swallow hard to relieve myself. As I pull the drink away from my face, I cough again several times until I find my breath.

What did he just say?

Inhaling deeply, I shake my head and glance down at my drink with its bright purple hue.

Wait a minute.

From the start, I understood that Mason's company was creating a drink with the Italian distributor. This was in play long before its release tonight. Of course. I remember Mason talking about it when we were in Italy, so it makes sense that he used this name. Flora told me it was the national flower, how could I forget?

I'm delusional. Of course I am. Did I really think for even a second that he would name a drink after me?

I laugh at myself and shake my head as I start to turn around to walk away with the crowd—thinking that I may be crazy to even consider the name had anything to do with me. As I turn, my attention is drawn to where Miles is standing a few feet away. I stop in my place and look in his direction, waiting for him to notice that I'm looking at him. I realize he does not have his usual happy expression, and it makes me frown trying to understand what's going on.

When he finally sees me looking at him, his eyes grow wide and he presses his lips together, as if he's hiding a secret. I raise a brow at him, suspicious now, and quickly walk towards him. Suddenly as someone walks between us, Miles turns away, clearly trying to lose himself through the moving crowd.

Oh. My. God. He is trying to hide from me.

I quicken my pace and try to catch up with him, but my heels slow me down, and he's able to escape into the swarm of people. Shaking my head, I chuckle quietly to myself, finding humor in a grown adult running away. Suddenly, my eyes grow wide as my suspicion about Miles' behavior is confirmed. *There's no way. It can't be.*

As everyone around me slowly disperses, returning to their cocktail tables or back to the bar, I'm no longer hidden like I was before. I glance around, feeling as though

I'm being watched, and carefully check out of the corner of my eye. *Am I imagining it?*

I turn my head and quickly spot Mason, who hasn't moved since his speech. A soft smile appears at the corner of his lips, and for the first time in a month, his eyes are directly on me.

My heart starts to race and my head feels light. A tumbling emotion that I thought had drifted away with him. Carried deeply out to sea after everything happened. *But, there it is.* Fluttering inside me, fast and steadily. Swept back in as quickly as a wave.

Mason's eyes raise slightly, his smile shifts before he takes a step forward, making his way over to me. I realize my mouth is dry, and I quickly swallow while glancing downward, anxiously waiting for him to come over. When I begin to lift my eyes slowly, I see his polished shoes standing before me and my cheeks suddenly tighten.

"Hi," he whispers.

I take a breath and as our eyes meet, I see a thousand thoughts race across his face, but they quickly settle as I smile up at him.

"Hi," I whisper back, feeling my cheeks tingling as I recognize I am blushing.

After a moment, Mason clears his throat, straightening himself up, and I snap back to reality as I hear the noises around me again, just as the first night we met. He rubs the back of his neck as he glances at his shoes, and as his Adam's apple drops, I recognize he is nervous.

Looking back up at me, he mutters, "I didn't know you were going to be here."

"Miles invited me," I confess.

He looks around the crowded room as if to search for Miles, and then looks back at me and smiles again.

"Well, I'm glad he did."

His smile quickly fades as he takes a deep breath, then he exhales and adds, "You have to know that none of it was—"

"I know," I reassure him as I slowly lower my head. "You told me once, but I just didn't believe you then."

"And now?"

His forehead creases as he lowers his head slightly, meeting my eyes again. I take a deep breath and nod slightly.

"I was wrong. I'll admit that," I say.

He takes a moment to acknowledge my statement as I quietly wait, feeling vulnerable for admitting I was wrong. *At least I've said it.*

Feeling a stark chill biting at my fingers, I glance down at my hand, then look back up at him with a smile.

I quickly raise my drink between us and lightening the mood, I joke, "What is this?"

He tosses his head back, like he's been caught, then squints down at the drink, observing it carefully as if he's never seen it before.

He clears his throat, trying to act serious, scratches his temple and states the obvious, "That's The Lily Drop."

"Interesting name choice," I say, holding the glass up to my face, and peering intently through the liquid.

"I thought it sounded nice," he exclaims, nodding his head confidently.

I move my head back and forth as if I'm examining every inch of it, then peering around the glass, I add, "And purple. Bold color choice."

He laughs softly, before a smirk forms in the corner of his lips.

"Yeah, actually, did you know the national flower of Italy is the Lily?" he stutters, trying to hold himself together. "Because I didn't."

"Actually, I did," I brag.

I quickly bring the glass back up to my lips and take a large sip from it, trying to playfully act as if it isn't anything special. Smacking my lips as I swallow the liquid, I hold my drink out to my side as if I'm carrying a dinner platter. I glance over at the nearly empty glass, then look back at him.

"But I don't think that's where the name came from," I playfully sneer.

Looking directly at me without losing eye contact, he grabs the top of my glass and lifts it out of my hand.

"Taste good?" he asks in a husky voice.

"Delicious," I say sensually.

He licks his lips, trying unsuccessfully to hide his pleasure, then glances away until he spots a waiter walking by. After a quick head nod, the waiter walks over and

Mason politely smiles at the man as he places my glass on the waiter's tray.

"I guess you'll never know," he teases, as he turns back towards me pressing his tongue against the inside of his cheek.

I stare at him intently, waiting to see what he has to say. *If it's true, he's definitely not telling me that easily.*

He catches me off guard when his face lights up with a very big grin, he leans towards me and reaches his hand out to lightly grab my chin. My demeanor instantly softens as I feel his fingertips lightly stroke my skin.

"You've been the only thing on my mind—the only one," he says softly as his attention focuses on his fingertips against my chin. He takes a deep breath, and as his eyes shift back to mine, he adds, "Who else would I have named it after?"

I swallow hard as I feel my forehead wrinkle, then quickly pull away, forcing his hand to fall from my chin. Then, after a moment, I bite my lip.

"I knew it," I tease, feeling justified.

He scoffs quietly then he suddenly becomes serious.

"It was my last shot," he woefully admits.

I consider his words carefully. "Last shot for what?"

"For another chance," he sighs. "I didn't think you'd give me another."

Suddenly, I realize he doesn't understand. Even though I'm standing right here in front of him at his event, he doesn't know that the only reason I came here tonight was to fix it all, to fix the misunderstanding, fix this silence between us that has gone on for nearly a month. I'm here for us, and to fix what we had.

I glance up at him and see the sorrow in his eyes, and I know that what I'm about to say will help to quickly fade that away. But suddenly I'm nervous and I can't get my words out. My cheeks tighten, in anticipation, and I laugh softly at myself.

Swinging my foot a little, I look up at him and tease, "Erm, that doesn't sound like something I'd do."

He immediately recognizes the lighthearted humor and begins to chuckle softly.

"No?" he jokes.

"No," I playfully say, shaking my head as I crinkle my nose.

"Well, what would you do then?" he asks, carefully placing his hand on the side of my arm.

I playfully purse my lips as if to think and chuckle, "Well, I'm a sucker for a good fruity drink, so I'd say that would have reeled me in immediately."

"Yeah?" he confirms, closing the distance between us as he places his other hand around my lower back.

I tip my head back and forth, and scrunch my nose again as I joke, "Yeah, I'd say so."

He slowly brings his hand up my arm and to the side of my face. Taking a deep breath, his smile fades as his eyes move to my cheek and his thumb brushes over it.

Looking back into my eyes, he slowly shakes his head and sighs, "I didn't know any of this would happen.

All of it. I'm not that kind of person—I never have been, and never will be. All I ever wanted was you."

"I know you aren't that person," I say softly, looking deeply into his vivid ocean eyes. "But I'll admit, I haven't been able to get you off my mind."

He thinks about my words, then slowly asks, "So what does this mean?"

I look away briefly, then turn back and open my mouth slightly, but I can't find the words. The words to tell him how I truly feel, that I've been unable to stop thinking about him since the moment I left Italy, even though I tried. How I planned a small speech in my head for this very moment, but I've somehow forgotten every word.

His eyes search my face, waiting for me to speak, and then he glances down at my lips, still partially open. I quickly look up at him from beneath my brows and his caress against my cheek pauses as he studies my face.

"I think you may have run out of chances," I admit.

His finger lifts cautiously and his hand begins to pull away, but I quickly reach up and grab his wrist to stop him. He glances over at my hand holding his wrist, and as he looks back up at me, his expression shifts. *It's now or never.*

I quickly shake my head and confess, "But that no longer matters," he waits for me to continue, and I say, "Because you've already won me over."

As soon as the words are spoken, his face lights up, and before I can catch my breath his soft lips are on mine once again.

Epilogue

Lily

"Don't peek," he whispers as he leans over my shoulder from behind.

Holding my arm at the elbow with one hand, and covering my eyes with the other, I cautiously take another step as he carefully leads me forward.

I can feel the wind tickling my face through his hand, but nothing else I hear sounds familiar. I can't hear any cars rushing past me, or the bustling noise of people walking by. It's nearly silent. The only sounds that fill the air are leaves bristling, and a bird cooing from far away.

I don't know what Mason is up to, but he's been awfully suspicious lately. He's not subtle, and can't keep a secret for the life of him, yet somehow he managed to keep this on lockdown. Lately, he started dropping hints, and I figured out that he had planned a trip for us—which was confirmed when he suggested I finally use some of my vacation hours.

When I put in the request, it was quickly approved like I thought it would be. It isn't hard to take time off—especially when your boyfriend's family makes generous donations to the school you work at.

After putting in eight months of hard work at Mayfair, my coworkers were also begging me to take time off. I was beat, so a vacation was definitely needed.

I take another step forward and almost trip over a small groove in the floor, but I laugh it off.

"Sorry!" he says anxiously. "I didn't see that."

"It's okay," I reply with a soft smile, knowing he didn't see it.

I take one more step forward and keep my eyes tightly closed as requested, then he removes his hand from my face.

"Wait!" he gasps. "Not yet."

Placing a hand on each side of my arm, he directs me into position and turns me slightly to the side.

"Alright, open your eyes," he whispers in my ear as he slides his hands up to the top of my shoulders.

When I open my eyes, the light is nearly blinding. I blink rapidly, trying to adjust to the sun shining through the awning above me. Slowly I'm able to focus on the green vines weaving through the wooden beams overhead.

I turn my head to the left to see a sunshade flapping in the wind in front of a dark-bricked house. It's older and unrecognizable, but with my little knowledge of architecture, I'd say we're definitely not in the United

States anymore. The 12-hour flight was a big hint. *Did he really think I wouldn't guess?*

Turning to look in the opposite direction, I lean backward, pressing my back against Mason's chest, as he reaches out to steady me. I'm awestruck by the beautiful view of green hills and forests that stretch for miles. Vaguely familiar, but still unrecognizable. Squinting my eyes, I can even see what appears to be a small town in the distance. *Could this be France?* As I continue to turn my gaze, I suddenly see a man with a dark beard wearing a white apron standing behind a small table, who nods a friendly smile at me.

"Where are we?" I hesitate, glancing up at Mason, while watching the man out of the corner of my eye.

"What?" he beams. "You don't recognize it?"

"Recognize?" I ask, before quickly turning back to face the greenery.

I squint my eyes, as if it will help me to see farther into the distance, and I come to the realization—*I do recognize this place.*

I quickly turn back to Mason, whose hands fall from my shoulders and swallowing hard, I frown at him.

"Why are we here?" I ask cautiously.

"I wanted to bring us back," he smiles softly, but when my eyes drop as I'm considering his words, he quickly responds, "You're disappointed. I know I shouldn't have brought—"

"No, I just didn't expect this, that's all," I interrupt.

I give him a short reassuring smile, but I can tell by his expression that he doesn't believe me.

He takes a deep breath as he furrows his brows and says, "If you truly don't want to be here, we can go."

"Okay, let's go!" I joke, raising my brows sarcastically before attempting to pivot and walk away.

"Just wait one minute Lily," he replies, turning me to face him, before joking, "I never expected a place to waver your confidence so easily."

"It's not that, it's just—"

I swallow hard and quickly glance at the ground.

When I said I didn't expect this to be the vacation destination we were flying to, I wasn't lying, but I'm not disappointed—at least not entirely. If anything, I'm just a little anxious. I had both joyful and heartbreaking memories in this place. The final ones being the most prominent—the ones that stand out when I think of Italy. But, maybe that can change.

When I look at him again, our eyes meet and he studies my expression, as if trying to read my mind.

"You are what I want. What I choose," he whispers, then, in a firmer tone, he adds, "Got it? What I choose. And nobody else will take that away."

My expression softens, and I nod, "I know. I just didn't think we'd be back here."

He places his hand on my cheek and gently rubs his thumb back and forth, prompting me to close my eyes.

"That was the past—a distant memory now. Okay? And you are my future."

I smile gently as he leans closer and kisses the top of my forehead. When he pulls back, his hand glides down my cheek until he's holding onto my chin. Raising my face upward, I open my eyes to his boyish laughter.

"Besides," he jokes, "They're out of business now, so they won't get anywhere close to you—" he pauses, then corrects himself, "—us."

I quietly chuckle to myself. I'm still not used to feeling safe and secure, but I have confidence that he truly is the man for me. His continued reassurance shows me that I've made the right choice once and for all.

"Okay," I whisper, trying to hide my relief.

Then, he confidently says, "If they do show up, I'll just tell them that I'm in love with you—only you. That our love is deeper than the oceans, and we can withstand even the most intense storms."

"That's very poetic of you," I joke.

"Only for amore mio," he winks.

He leans down and kisses me on the lips slowly, and as he pulls away, his eyes grow wide. He quickly steps back and brings his hand down to the side of my arm. Then, looking up and down at me, his expression changes, and his mouth falls open.

"Sorry, one moment while I pick up my jaw from the floor," he says, pushing his mouth closed.

I press my lips together, hiding my smile and shake my head.

"Not this again," I say, rolling my eyes as his hand glides down my arm and grabs my hand.

Stepping further away, he extends my arm and with a wide smile, he continues, "I'm sorry, you are just too beautiful! I look at you and I still don't believe how lucky of a man I am."

"Oh my God," I laugh, smacking my hand against my forehead.

I quickly take a step forward and reach out to him, pushing my hand against his chest playfully, forcing him to take a slight step backward.

"You're such a dork," I jest.

But at least he's mine.

He quickly takes a step back to me and wraps his hands around my lower back while looking down at me with a grin.

"Shall we get started?" he asks.

I grow stiff, quickly remembering that we aren't alone as I peer around Mason and see the man in the apron. The man leans to his side and raises his brow, which causes me to anxiously chuckle as I straighten myself up.

"Who is that?" I whisper, leaning closer to Mason.

"Lily—my love," he says, taking a step to the side and holding his hand out as if he's presenting. "I thought this would be the perfect opportunity to take a cooking class together."

"A what?" I anxiously chuckle as I take a step back, but it's too late as Mason wraps his arm around my waist and pushes me slowly forward.

"A cooking class," he states, looking down at the table where several ingredients are laid out. "It was my mom's suggestion since we never had the chance before—we're going to make homemade pasta."

"I mean, that sounds delicious, but I'm the worst cook," I argue, looking over my shoulder and trying to nudge myself backward. "Maybe I shouldn't have admitted that to your mom after your parents were so welcoming to me. Hopefully, they don't hold it against me."

He nods his head back and forth, while joking, "Eh, you're bad, but definitely not the worst, and you know they love you now as much as I do."

He grabs both of my shoulders from behind—like when we arrived—and squeezes them as I anxiously step forward.

"It's not my fault if our dinner turns out horribly," I warn as I glance at him over my shoulder.

I hear his deep chuckle as if he doesn't believe me, but I know that as soon as I touch the food, it'll somehow end up being a plate of disaster. He just doesn't realize it yet.

Suddenly, his warm breath is against my ear as he leans in close to me, and teasingly whispers, "That's okay, I like a little chaos."

He moves his face into my neck and places a slow, yet sensual kiss against it.

"Mmm," he moans against my throat.

I quickly sip in a breath as my eyes widen. *The audacity of this man.* Did I somehow let the animal out of the cage when we met? Because he hasn't held himself back since.

My eyes quickly shoot up to the man in the apron in front of us, and I'm relieved to see him focused on preparing the ingredients rather than watching us.

As Mason's lips pull away from my neck, I feel his lips move back up to my ear.

"Well—" he playfully whispers. "—at least I know the dessert will taste good."

"I'm impressed with myself," I say proudly as I take a bite of the homemade pasta.

Mason takes a bite, then looks up and away while making a long, steady humming sound.

"Eh, it's alright," he jests, tilting his head to the side as a smirk grows in the corner of his mouth.

I scowl at him as I place my fork back into my bowl.

"Hey! It could have turned out way worse."

He chuckles and says, "You're right, it could have, but luckily it's delicious."

I straighten myself in my seat, hold my head high, and proudly brag, "You're welcome."

I feel his eyes roll at me as he quietly laughs to himself while looking down at his bowl, pushing the noodles around with his fork.

I take another bite, and as I bring it to my mouth, I look out over the balcony at the setting sun. The orange hues slowly spreading throughout the sky, while the sun fades behind the rolling hills.

I smile, thinking back to the last time we were in Italy, and we watched the sunset on the coastline together from the large house. It feels like so long ago, but the memories of the trip are still so vivid in my head.

I turn my head back to Mason and find him staring at me intently.

"What's wrong?" I cautiously ask.

He takes a deep breath, and his soft smile returns.

"Remember when you thought I was going to propose to you at that restaurant here in Italy?" he recalls, raising a brow slightly.

"Yeah, I do actually," I chuckle. "I'm not sure why our waiter thought you were proposing."

"Neither do I," he admits. "But, do you remember what I said to you?"

I squint at him, as if he doubts my memory and I say, "Of course. You said you knew exactly how you'd propose, and it wouldn't be that way."

"That's right. It wouldn't," he mumbles with a straight face.

Pushing against the table, he pushes his chair back and stands up.

"Where are you going?" I frown up at him as I slowly lower my fork.

He quickly grabs his wine glass, takes a quick sip, and then licks his lips. He glances down at me and takes a deep breath, before lowering himself onto a knee.

"What are you doing?" I demand, as I push myself back into my seat wide-eyed.

"What does it look like I'm doing?" he jokes, tilting his head to the side. "I'm prop—"

"Wait, no," I interrupt. "You said you didn't have a plan. You've been telling me for weeks that it wouldn't be happening any time soon."

He chuckles as he rests his elbow against his knee and leans forward, looking up at me from beneath his brows.

"Lily, did you really think I wouldn't have a plan?" he questions with a raised brow, then confidently adds, "I've had a plan since the moment you asked me that question back at that Italian restaurant."

I quickly lean forward as I place my hands on his shoulders.

Trying to push him up from the ground, I shake my head and say, "Well wait, you need to get up. It can't be right now."

Mason straightens himself up and my arms fall from his shoulders.

"No?" he dares.

"No. I'm not ready," I assert, hearing the slight panic in my voice.

A wide grin comes across Mason's face, and as he presses his lips, I can tell he's trying not to laugh.

"You've been practically begging me to propose to you for weeks now," he playfully scoffs.

"That may be true, but not now," I answer, shaking my head as I feel my forehead wrinkle. "There's no photographer, I don't have my nails done—"

Quickly searching for something else that isn't perfect, I look down at my white sundress with small purple flowers on it, then start frantically looking around.

"Babe?" he asks calmly.

"—I'm not even dressed in the outfit I had picked out, and I don't even have it with me! You've got to—"

"Lily?" he asks again, placing his hand on my knee.

I suddenly pause and focus on him, staring at his bright blue eyes, then glancing down at my favorite—well only—dimple on his cheek.

"I know you have your way of doing things, but you're going to have to trust me on this, okay?" he says in a slow and reassuring manner.

"But I—" I press, raising my brows.

"Nope."

He smiles softly, and as I look back into his eyes, I feel myself willingly take a deep breath to calm my nerves.

"Okay," I agree slowly, placing my hand over his resting on my knee.

He squeezes my hand and swallows hard before pulling his hand away to reach into his pocket.

"I know you pictured this perfect proposal in your mind, but all I ever wanted was for it to just be the two of us. Just you and me. Nobody else."

He carefully reaches into his pocket, retrieves a red ring box with gold writing on it, and looks intently back at me.

"And I definitely didn't want a crowd like at that restaurant," he says with a nervous chuckle.

I bite my lip as he straightens himself up while still kneeling and clears his throat.

I bring my knees together as I place my hands in my lap, and lean slightly forward so that our eyes are at the same level.

With a wide grin, he holds out the box in front of him and places his fingertips over the top of it. I lean forward and tilt my head, anticipating him opening it right away, but when he doesn't, I glance back up at him with raised brows.

"Not just yet," he teases.

I quickly lean back into my seat, anticipating the speech he has prepared, but his expression turns serious. He searches my face, our gazes intertwining, he clears his throat once more, then begins to speak calmly and confidently.

"Lily, I never expected to meet someone like you. Well…meet you again. Our paths crossed long ago, and we didn't get to know each other then—for good reason. You didn't realize it, but you saw me at my darkest. When I didn't care for others as I do now. I found a way back from that shadow of myself. I didn't know it then, but you came back into my life exactly at the right time—when I was ready to find someone. When I was ready to be with someone who truly made me feel whole again."

He takes a deep breath and continues, "I fell in love fast. There's no denying that. How could I not?"

He pauses and purses his lips to the side, trying to contain his growing grin.

"Penso che mi sto innamorando di te," he says, raising a brow. "Remember?"

I nod with a smile, familiar with the sentence now.

"I fell in love with your drive and your charisma. You know what you want and aren't afraid to show it. You are always confidently optimistic—you always look for a positive outcome, and I believe your strength of will is what brought us back together. And let me tell you, you are everything to me, and I can't get enough of you no matter how hard I try."

I feel a slight tear welling in the corner of my eye, and I sniffle to hold it back. Mason's brows draw together as he notices, but I quickly shake my head and smile, silently motioning with a nod for him to continue.

He swallows hard again, and continues as I listen attentively.

"I know a lot happened at the beginning of our relationship, but love is a choice. It's about choosing who you want to spend your time with, and who you want to cherish. It may have seemed like I had no options at one point, but nothing was going to stop me from making my own choice. I always knew it was you—you were always my choice. You are and always will be the one I choose.

And now, I'm choosing to ask you this, because of all the things that make you uniquely you."

My eyes shift downward and land on the ring box as he slowly opens it. Inside is a sparkling oval-cut diamond, encased in a thin silver halo over a diamond-studded band. *It's perfect.*

A few weeks ago, we had gone ring shopping, and Mason suggested that I pick out a few options for him to select from. I wanted something simple, yet beautiful and fit my style. Although he didn't give me a budget, I tried to keep my options to 3 carats or less, because I knew anything bigger would be too much, and since I've never worn anything that big before, I'd likely knock out a stone that size.

I look down at the ring in the box now and feel my cheeks tighten. Of all the rings we looked at, this was my favorite. It had a center stone that was just over 2 carats, and the small studded band added to the sparkle without it being too obnoxious.

In all honesty, I hadn't expected Mason to choose this ring. It was one of the smallest, and the others were so beautiful. Yet, here it is—*the one I found to be perfect.*

Mason's grin widens as he searches my face and rests on my cheeks, which I imagine are now blushing bright red. I hold my breath as I feel my heart pounding out of my chest with excitement.

This is the man that I couldn't stand in the beginning. The man I despised, and the one I would have never given a chance. But now? I see him so differently.

He's the one that has my heart, the one that I least expected and now, the one who is giving me the over-the-top romance that I didn't know was possible.

As I look at him now, I know his speech will be forever engraved in my heart. His beautiful words, and heartfelt tenderness towards me. A picture-perfect love that I never imagined I'd find with someone—*especially with him.*

Although he hasn't said it yet, I know it's coming. My heart is practically skipping every beat possible, and as soon as he asks me those four simple words, my life will forever be different. *But, nothing would make me happier.*

He licks his lips and his brows come together as he raises the box towards me. I glance down at it momentarily, then our eyes meet again as he takes a deep breath. Then, I finally hear the words I've been waiting so eagerly for.

"Will you marry me?"

Thank you for reading!

I hope that you enjoyed reading *More to Lily* as much as I enjoyed writing it. If you have a moment, please hop online and consider posting a review! As an indie author, I depend heavily on word of mouth and the feedback and support of readers like you.

Thank you!

Glossary

Italian to English translations in order as they appear.

1. **CIAO, BELLO. SONO FELICE DI INIZIARE QUESTO VIAGGIO CON TE:** *Hello, handsome. I am happy to start this journey with you.*
2. **BENVENUTI:** *Welcome!*
3. **SEI QUI A VISITARE UNA VECCHIA FIAMMA:** *Are you here to visit an old flame?*
4. **SIGNORE/SIGNORA:** Sir/Miss
5. **GRAZIE:** *Thank you*
6. **PARLI ITALIANO?:** *You speak Italian?*
7. **POCO:** *Little*
8. **FANTASTICO:** *Fantastic*
9. **PER LA SIGNORA:** *For the lady*
10. **SÌ:** *Yes*
11. **PERFETTO:** *Perfect*
12. **LO ADORERAI:** *You will love it!*
13. **TORNO SUBITO:** *I'll be right back*
14. **SALUTE!:** *Cheers!*
15. **CIAO! BENVENUTO IN ITALIA!:** *Welcome to Italy!*
16. **CHI SEI?:** *Who are you?*
17. **ECCOLO! TUTTI, DATE IL BENVENUTO A MASON!:** *Here he is! Everyone, welcome Mason!*
18. **VIENI QUI:** *Come here!*
19. **CIN CIN, MANGIAMO!:** *Cheers, let's eat!*
20. **DIVERTENTE E BELLO:** *Funny and handsome!*
21. **PER LA BELLA SIGNORA:** *For the beautiful lady*
22. **SCUSA:** *Excuse me*
23. **MIO FIGLIO:** *My son*
24. **LEI NON SA NIENTE:** *She doesn't know anything*
25. **CAPISCO:** *I understand*

26. **PENSO CHE MI STO INNAMORANDO DI TE:** *I think I'm falling in love with you*
27. **PERFETTO**: *Perfect*
28. **TORNO PRESTO:** *I'll be back soon*
29. **VAI A DIVERTIRTI:** *Go have fun!*
30. **MIA MADRE DICEVA CHE ERI BELLO:** *My mother said you were handsome*
31. **AVEVA RAGIONE:** *She was right*
32. **È QUELLO CHE FANNO LE COPPIE:** *That's what couples do*
33. **VOLEVO BACIARE MIO MARITO:** *I wanted to kiss my husband*
34. **SCUSA:** *Excuse me*
35. **FIDANZATO:** *Fiancé*
36. **SCUSA, HO DIMENTICATO:** *Sorry, I forgot*
37. **SEI DIVERTENTE**: *You are funny*
38. **CHE COSA STAI—:** *What are you—*
39. **FIORE NAZIONALE:** *National flower*
40. **MIA FIGLIA:** *My daughter*
41. **MASON SARÀ UN VERO ITALIANO:** *Mason will be a true Italian*
42. **AMERICANO SCIOCCO:** *Foolish American*
43. **AMORE MIO:** *My love*

www.ingramcontent.com/pod-product-compliance
Lightning Source LLC
Chambersburg PA
CBHW020012120726
47903CB00004B/1255